My God, she was beautiful!

He wanted to pull her into his arms to kiss her, but she was not the sort of woman you could do that to—not suddenly and for no reason. What in heaven's name was she doing here, wandering among the buttercups and daisies, miles from home? Who was she?

He felt it too, this strange alchemy, and he supposed it had been there from the start of this strange journey. It was why he was determined to escort her, even when she made it plain she did not want an escort. It wasn't only the mystery surrounding her—perhaps there was no mystery and she was exactly what she said she was—it was something about the girl herself. Her beauty, her courage and independence, all the attributes he had said would make her unfit to be a lady's companion, were the very things which drew him to her.

Dear Reader

In 2008, Mills & Boon® celebrate a hundred years of bringing romance to their readers—no mean achievement—and for twenty-two of those years I have been writing historical romance for them, so you will not be surprised to learn that I love writing for them, and for you, my reader.

The trials and tribulations of each hero and heroine are very different, but the books all have one thing in common—a happy ending. That is what we all wish for, isn't it? I enjoy creating the characters, bringing them to life, watching them work through their problems, and I rejoice with them when everything comes out all right in the end. If, along the way, I make you smile, or even shed a tear on their behalf, then I will have achieved my aim.

I hope you enjoy reading my latest novel, RUNAWAY MISS.

Mary

RUNAWAY MISS

Mary Nichols

MILLS & BOON®
Pure reading pleasure

First published in Great Britain 2007
Harlequin Mills & Boon Limited,
Eton House, 18-24 Paradise Road, Richmond, Surrey TW9 1SR

© Mary Nichols 2007

ISBN: 978 0 263 19782 2

Set in Times Roman 11½ on 14 pt.
08-1207-86955

Printed and bound in Great Britain
by Antony Rowe Ltd, Chippenham, Wiltshire

RUNAWAY MISS

Born in Singapore, **Mary Nichols** came to England when she was three, and has spent most of her life in different parts of East Anglia. She has been a radiographer, school secretary, information officer and industrial editor, as well as a writer. She has three grown-up children, and four grandchildren.

Recent novels by the same author:

THE HONOURABLE EARL
THE INCOMPARABLE COUNTESS
LADY LAVINIA'S MATCH
A LADY OF CONSEQUENCE
THE HEMINGFORD SCANDAL
MARRYING MISS HEMINGFORD
BACHELOR DUKE
AN UNUSUAL BEQUEST
TALK OF THE TON
WORKING MAN, SOCIETY BRIDE
A DESIRABLE HUSBAND

Prologue

1816

It was almost dawn, the eastern sky over the chimney pots of St James's bore a distinct pink tinge, and soon the sun's rays would penetrate to the level of the street and the creatures of the night, human and animal, would disappear and those of the day make an appearance. But the gentlemen sitting at the card table in the gaming room of Brooks's club were unaware of the time. The heavy curtains in the room were drawn against the windows and the only light was from the lamps that had been burning all night, so that now the room was stuffy and malodorous.

The previous evening it had been crowded, all the tables filled, but as midnight approached the first players began to leave, followed by others until, by three in the morning, only one foursome remained intent on their game. Hovering over them, wishing he could go home to his bed, was a liveried, bewigged footman whose task it was to make sure their glasses remained full. Except what was necessary to further the game, no one had spoken for hours.

The four men—Lord Cecil Bentwater, Sir George Tasker, Mr Jeremy Maddox and Viscount Alexander Malvers—were so absorbed that the time of day, even the day of the week, hunger or families and servants patiently waiting for them to come home meant nothing at all. Lord Bentwater, who had the largest pile of coins and vowels beside his elbow, was in his middle to late fifties, dressed entirely in black, unrelieved except for a white neckcloth in which reposed a glittering diamond pin. He had a pasty complexion and dark glittering eyes.

Sir George Tasker was a year or two younger, dressed in a single-breasted green coat, a waistcoat of cream satin embroidered with silver thread and a fine lawn shirt with lace flounces protruding from the sleeves. He wore several rings, a crumpled neckcloth and a quizzing glass dangling from his thick neck. A film of perspiration caked his face. His dark eyes were wary and a twitch in his jaw told of a man reaching the end of his tether.

Mr Jeremy Maddox was just twenty-one, a tulip of the first order. His shirt-collar points stood up against his cheeks and his cravat was tied in a flamboyant bow, the ends of which cascaded over his sky blue waistcoat. Undoubtedly his doting mama would have been horrified if she could see the company he was keeping.

The fourth man at the table, Viscount Alexander Malvers, was very different, both in appearance and demeanour. He eschewed the fanciful garb of the pink of the *ton*, for a well-cut cloth coat of forest green, a white waistcoat and a sensibly tied cravat. At thirty years old, he had come back from service in the Peninsula and Waterloo in one piece and was thankful for it. He was not a habitual gambler, certainly not for higher stakes than he could afford, and had only consented to make up the four when Count Vallon dropped out.

He had been watching them for some time before that and had come to the conclusion that Lord Bentwater was far too clever for Sir George—the latter, if he had had any sense, should have paid up and left long ago. Alex had joined them out of curiosity to see how far Sir George was prepared to go before throwing in the towel. Years in the army when boredom was, more often than not, the order of the day had taught Alex to be a skilled card player and he was prudent in the way he played so that he was a little on the plus side, but not by much. Now he, like the waiter, wished only for his bed.

'Well, George?' Bentwater broke the silence. 'Do you go on?'

'You'll take my voucher?'

'I've a drawer full of your vouchers at home, George. Ain't it time you began honouring them?'

'Drawer full?' Sir George looked decidedly worried. 'I never gave you above three that I can remember.'

'I bought the rest.'

Sir George was startled. 'Why?'

'An investment, my friend. Got them for half their face value, some of the older ones even less than that, since their holders had given up hope of being paid.'

'In that case you don't expect me to honour them for the full amount, do you?'

'Oh, dear me, yes. Plus interest, of course.'

'I can't, you know I can't.'

'Why not? I thought when you married the widow, you were made for life.'

'So did I,' George said despondently. 'I was gulled.'

'You mean she had no money?' Bentwater roared with laughter, though it was not a happy sound. 'Oh, that's a great jest.'

'There was money there, all right, but she didn't have the spending of it. Her baboon of a husband left her a small annuity and tied all the rest up for the daughter.'

'Then you should have married the daughter, George. How old is she?'

'Twenty now, eighteen when I married her mother.'

'Old enough to be married,' Bentwater said, thoughtfully tapping his wine glass against his rotting teeth.

'I didn't know she was the heiress at the time or I might have done. Now it'll all go to whatever cock-brained cabbage marries her.'

'Then, George, you had better make sure she marries where it will do you most good,' Bentwater advised. 'You need her dibs to pay off your debts.'

'Then you had best tell me how that is to be done, Cecil, since the solution eludes me.'

'Is she comely?'

'She is. Fair face. Good teeth. Fine figure. Tall…'

'How tall?'

'Oh, I don't know. I am an inch short of six feet and overtop her by two or three inches or thereabouts. What do you want to know that for?'

'It ain't right for a wife to be taller than her husband.'

'True.'

'And she has a fortune, you say?'

'Will have. Until she marries it is administered by trustees. Thirty thousand a year at least. And I can't lay my hands on any of it.' It was said bitterly.

'Then you have your answer, my friend. I'll take her off your hands for the return of your vouchers…'

'What?'

'You heard me.'

'How many have you got?'

'A drawer full, I told you. Twenty thousand pounds' worth. And there's that diamond pin you gave me which turned out to be paste.' He paused so that the others could digest this news and make what they would of it. 'Have you had all your jewels copied, George?' he added pleasantly, though everyone at the table was aware of the undercurrents of malice. 'That wouldn't sit well with your creditors if they knew of it.'

Sir George gulped, while Jeremy laughed a little crazily and Alex, who had heard some bizarre wagers in his time, was beginning to wish he had never joined in the game and helped to bring about Sir George's humiliation. The whole affair could cut up nasty.

'You want me to give you my stepdaughter?'

'Why not? I need a wife. The others I had were useless, never gave me an heir and a man needs an heir, so the younger and stronger the better. And if she comes from a good family with a generous dowry, that is all to the good…'

'I say, gentlemen,' Alex put in mildly. 'Don't you think that's coming it too brown?'

'None of your business,' Bentwater snapped. 'Unless you fancy buying Sir George's vouchers and taking the chit off his hands yourself.'

'No, I do not. I would never stoop to buying myself a wife. No need to.' He saw the older man's eyes darken with anger, but could not resist adding, 'Supposing she won't have you?'

'In my book daughters do as they're bid.' He turned back to Sir George. 'I'll be fair. Your vouchers and five thousand in cash. With a little luck you could make that grow…'

Sir George's expression betrayed his wildly erratic thinking. His despair was suddenly replaced by hope, as if someone had thrown him a lifeline. He could survive. With five thousand he could make another fortune. All he needed was for the cards to fall right.

'Mind you,' Bentwater went on, 'you don't get the money until after the wedding ceremony.

'Her mother would never agree…'

'Wives, like daughters, should do as they are told.'

'You drive a hard bargain, my lord.'

'So, it is a bargain, then?'

Reluctantly Sir George offered his hand. 'It's a bargain.'

Lord Bentwater shook the hand, gathered up his winnings and rose from the table. 'Gentlemen, I suggest we adjourn. Sir George has some persuading to do.' Then, to George, 'I shall expect to be presented to the lady and her mama at the first available opportunity. Shall we say Almack's on Wednesday?'

'But that's only two days away.'

'One, considering it is now Tuesday. And the sooner the better, don't you think? The interest is accruing every day you delay.'

And with that, he disappeared, leaving Sir George so bemused he didn't seem to know what to do, and Jeremy Maddox laughing fit to burst out of his tight pantaloons. Alex, picking up his winnings from the table, frowned at him. 'Come, Maddox, let's go and find some fresh air. There is a bad smell in here.'

Out in the street it was fully daylight, but blustery. There had been rain overnight and the streets were full of muddy puddles. Alex smiled at the efforts of a tiny crossing sweeper to clear a path for them, and gave him more than the penny he asked for the service. The milkmaids were driving their cows to sell their milk at the kitchen doors of the grand houses, the sweep with his diminutive helper was on his way to his first call, hawkers with their trays were establishing their pitches. A dray rumbled down the middle of the road, but had to give way to a cab rattling towards it at breakneck speed. Another day had begun.

'What an entertaining evening,' Maddox said, picking his way carefully between the puddles. 'I thought Sir George was going to have a seizure.'

'Do you know him well?'

'No, though he has a reputation for playing deep. I had no idea he was so low in the stirrups.'

'You don't think Bentwater will hold him to their arrangement, do you?'

'Oh, no doubt of it, though how long she'll last I have no idea. He's been through three wives already, all of them wealthy. The first died in childbirth and the infant along with her. Rumour at the time had it he was mad as fire because it was a boy. Wife two died in an accident with a coach and wife three was murdered by an unknown assailant who has never been caught. Her brother maintained at the time Bentwater himself was the culprit, but no evidence was found and it was put down to the man's grief. Naturally, his lordship has been finding it hard to persuade a fourth to take the trip to the altar.'

He could not imagine any young lady of twenty years, with an ounce of spirit, agreeing to marry Lord Bentwater. The man was positively repulsive. Nor would any mother worth her salt allow her daughter to be used in that way—Sir George had said as much. 'What do you suppose will happen if she cuts up rough and refuses the old rake? They can hardly drag her to the altar.'

'No idea. Presumably Sir George will have to find another way to redeem his vouchers.'

'If we had not agreed to play, the situation would not have occurred.'

'If we hadn't played, they would have found someone else, if not tonight, then some other time. I'll wager Bentwater didn't just think of that on the spur of the moment, he has been planning it for some time. And I fancy anyone trying to thwart him will find he has made a mortal enemy. If you are thinking of intervening, Malvers…'

'Not I. I do not have twenty thousand pounds to throw away.' Why did everyone assume that, because he had inherited a title, he was a wealthy man? It was far from the case.

'You wouldn't be throwing it away. You would be gaining a wife and, according to Sir George, she has a fortune. I say, you aren't married, are you?'

'No, never had the time. I've been soldiering all my adult life.' The late Viscount had had very little time for his younger son, whom he considered soft and too attached to his mother. He had packed him off into the army to 'harden him up and make a man of him'. The life of a soldier had certainly hardened him, had taught him not to shudder at man's inhumanity to man, to deal with wounds and indiscipline in a measured way, but under that hard shell the core of him remained what it had always been: sympathetic to the plight of others, especially those not able to defend themselves.

He had been known to give up his own billet for a soldier who was ill, but should that same man let him down his wrath could be terrible. Being an officer, it had sometimes been his duty to order punishment for misdemeanours among his men, even when he felt sorry for them, but showing it would have been interpreted as weakness and he would have forfeited their respect. He was not to be duped or crossed, but anyone with a genuine grievance would find in him a ready listener. He could fight ferociously, but at the end of a successful battle could spare the life of an enemy, when others would have slaughtered him with no compunction. The two sides of his nature—the hard, somewhat cynical soldier and the compassionate, caring man—were often in conflict with each other, which made him something of an enigma to those around him.

'So, have you only recently come into your inheritance?'

'Last year. My elder brother died and my father only a week later, of the shock, you know.' Lawrence, seven years older than Alex, had been the apple of his father's eye, a hard-riding, hard-drinking autocrat, and his death in a hunting accident had caused their father to collapse of a heart attack from which he had not recovered.

'My condolences.'

'Thank you.'

'Your brother had no heir?'

'No.' Lawrence had married as society and family convention dictated, money and rank being uppermost in the arrangement, and that had been a disaster. Lawrence had found himself trying to satisfy a wife who would never be satisfied. As far as Constance was concerned, she had married a title and the fact that her husband's pockets were not bottomless carried no weight with her. The more he tried to please her, the more she demanded.

'Why did you marry her?' Alex had asked him after one particularly acrimonious dispute over her extravagance and the disreputable friends she encouraged.

'Because it was expected of me. As the elder son I must have a wife in order to beget a legitimate heir to carry on the line.'

He knew that. 'But why Constance? Why not someone else?'

'She seemed eminently suitable—old established family, good looks—and she set out to charm me. Once the ring was on her finger, I realised how false that charm was. Too late. Just be thankful you are a second son, Alex, and can please yourself.'

Matters went from bad to worse, until the prospect of a career in the army was a welcome escape from the tensions in the house. The men under his command had become his family. They lived, ate, played and fought together and his care of them was repaid with staunch loyalty. He had seen some of them die, seen courage and stoicism and cruelty too. He had watched those women who had been allowed to accompany their men combing the battlefield after every encounter with the enemy, ready to tend their wounds. He admired their devotion, their stoical acceptance of the hard and dangerous life in order to be with their men, to endure heat and drought, rain and snow, to cook for them at the end of a day's march, tend their wounds, even carry their kit if they were too exhausted to do so. He had found himself comparing the steadfastness of these ragged uneducated women with some of the officers' wives who considered it their God-given right to ride in carriages, take the cosiest billets and the best of whatever food was going. And their men, fools that they were, pandered to them, just as Lawrence had done. It hadn't made Constance love him any the more; Alex suspected she despised him. In his opinion, it was the miserable state of Lawrence's marriage and his wife's inability to give him a child that had led to his brother's heavy drinking and ultimate demise. Alex was determined not to let that happen to him.

He had come home after Waterloo to find his mother in mourning, his sister-in-law run off with her latest lover and the estate struggling to pay its way. But he'd be damned if he'd marry for money, which was what the family lawyer had suggested. He had taken over Lawrence's mantle, but he was determined not to fall into the same trap his brother had. If he ever married, and he was certainly in no hurry to do so, he would need to be very, very sure…

'So, what are you doing in London?' Maddox's voice interrupted his reverie.

'I had business to transact.' He had to bring the Buregreen estate back into profit, but, since his father had never allowed him to have anything to do with the business of running it, he knew next to nothing about how it could be done and he needed the help of a good steward. He had come to London with that in mind and had already engaged a man who had been recommended by his lawyer. 'And my mother had an idea a little town bronze…' he added with a wry smile.

'Then why not come to Almack's with me on Wednesday? It's the place to be seen if you're hanging out for a wife. We could take a peep at Sir George's stepdaughter.'

'I am not hanging out for a wife. I would as lief not marry at all.'

'But every man must marry,' Maddox said. 'Any man of substance, that is. It is his duty to find himself a wife to carry on the line, someone from a good family of equal rank and with an impeccable reputation. That is of prime importance. Of course, it helps if she is also decorative…'

'Duty?' Alex queried. 'I did my duty as a soldier.'

'So you may have done, but there are other kinds of duty, don't you know? What would happen to all the great country estates if there were no sons to inherit? They'd go to distant cousins, that's what, and eventually be dispersed. Who would run the country then, eh? Mushrooms, jumped-up cits, men without an ounce of breeding. It wouldn't do, my dear fellow, it simply would not do.'

Alex had heard that argument from both his mother and aunt since he had come back from Waterloo. 'I did not expect to inherit, I wasn't brought up even to think of it. And what I've seen of marriage does not dispose me towards venturing into it.'

'You sound as if you have been bitten, my friend.'

'Not me, but I have seen what can happen. Misery for both.'

'So you won't come to Almack's?'

'The only time I went to Almack's, back in my green days, I hated it. It was too stiff and formal, all that dressing up in breeches and silk stockings and not a decent drink to be had. Besides, I can't. I have a prior engagement. I promised my aunt I would accompany her to Lady Melbourne's soirée.'

Maddox laughed. 'That sounds as exciting as drinking ditchwater.'

'A promise is a promise and it will be preferable to standing in line with a crowd of young hopefuls, dressed like a popinjay, hoping to be noticed. I am too long in the tooth for that. Besides, the chits who are paraded at places like Almack's are too young and silly for my taste. And if you have some crazy notion to throw me in the way of Sir George's stepdaughter, then I advise you to put it from your mind. I have no intention of shackling myself to someone I have never met and do not know just to give you something to dine on for the rest of the Season. It would be the worst possible start to a marriage.'

'I wasn't thinking anything of the sort. It was curiosity, that's all, just to see what she's like. Why, a man would be a fool to jump into matrimony because he felt sorry for the girl. She might turn out to be a real harridan.'

'Quite,' Alex said, thinking of Lawrence. 'Away with you to your bed, young 'un. I am going home to mine.'

They parted on the corner of Mount Street and Alex strode down its length to the house on the corner of Park Lane where he was staying with his aunt, Lady Augusta Banks. He was very fond of his aunt, but he knew she had been asked by his mother to help him find a wife and she was determined to discharge that commission to the best of her ability. Already she was planning to put him in the way of every unmarried young lady in town, but searching for a life partner in that cold-blooded way went so much against the grain he had not been co-operative. It was why he had gone to Brooks's, in order to escape yet another soirée, although he had promised to escort her to Lady Melbourne's. There were often men in government in her ladyship's drawing room and he had a mind to sound some of them out about a pet project of his.

He wanted to do something to help discharged soldiers coming home from the war without employment, which had been on his mind even before he became the new Viscount. It was employment they needed, not charity, and his idea was to set up workshops and small manufactories and provide them with tools so that they could make their own way and provide for their families. He could not do it alone, which was why he wanted to talk to men with influence. If he took his place in the Lords, he might be able to make a noise about the scandalous way the men had been treated. They were in dire need, which was something that could not be said of a chit worth thirty thousand a year.

Nevertheless, it was a long time before he could sleep, though he blamed it on the noises in the street from the increased morning's traffic in the road outside his window as the business of the day progressed.

Chapter One

Lady Emma Lindsay looked at herself in the mirror, not out of vanity but simply to assure herself that the gown she wore would pass muster. It was made in pale blue mousseline de soie, with tiny puffed sleeves, a deep boat-shaped neckline edged with a darker blue satin ribbon, and a high waist marked by the same ribbon. The skirt stopped just short of her feet and revealed satin slippers. Her maid had arranged her dark brown hair *à la Grecque*, held with a coronet of tiny silk flowers.

'There! You look very fine indeed,' Rose said, as she helped Emma on with her velvet cape, handed her a fan decorated with a woodland scene and stood back, smiling at the picture she had helped to create. 'You will have all the eligibles falling at your feet.'

'Too late, Rose, too late. I shall soon be one and twenty, almost at my last prayers.' She was unusually tall, but then all the Lindsays were tall, so it was hardly surprising. What with her height and her age, she despaired of finding a husband, at least not one she could love for himself and who would love her for the woman she was. And that was the problem. It was not finding a husband because her dowry was enough to ensure that, but finding the one to set her heart beating faster. Did such a man exist?

Mama said love did not come into it and she should not consider it, that a fortune and a pleasant temperament were of far more use, which was strange considering Mama had married again less than two years after losing her first husband and Sir George Tasker had neither a fortune nor a pleasant temperament.

Emma had been preparing for her come-out in the spring of 1813, when her father, Earl Lindsay, died suddenly and threw her into deep mourning. Naturally her trip to London had to be cancelled, but in truth Emma, grieving for her dear papa, had been in no mood for frivolity and had been content to spend her time quietly in the country at Pinehill, the family home in Hertfordshire. But one morning a year later, woken by bird song and the sun streaming through her bedroom window, she had suddenly realised that spring had arrived and life was passing her by and she ought to do something about it.

Mama must have had the same thought, because later that day, she had suggested taking Emma to London for her delayed coming out. The Duke of Ranworth, her mother's brother, had offered them the use of Ranworth House in Hanover Square and they had done the rounds, attending balls and tea parties, but in the end it had not been Emma who found a husband but the dowager herself, though calling Mama a dowager was a jest, considering she had not been above forty at the time and still comely.

'Lady Emma, that's just the right age to be,' Rose said, answering her last comment. 'Though you are still young and beautiful, you are past the age of being thought an empty-headed schoolgirl that no one need take seriously. Some gentlemen would value your maturity.'

Emma laughed. 'Thank you, Rose. What would I do without you? It is ridiculous when you think that a lady is not expected to dress herself, to do her own hair, or allowed to go out alone. But it is not only the dressing and looking after my clothes I value you for, it is having someone to talk to. I can say anything I like to you.'

'My lady, I am sure you would manage.' She paused and then took a deep breath before going on. 'My lady, I have to give notice. My mother is having another baby and she needs me to look after the other little ones. There are seven now.'

Emma sank down on to the bed and stared up at her maid, who had been part of her life ever since she could remember. Rose had been a parlour maid at Pinehill, but as soon as Emma had become old enough to have a maid of her own, the girl had been promoted to lady's maid. She was more than a servant, she was a friend. 'Oh, Rose, of course you must go, but I shall miss you terribly. How long do you think you will be away?'

'My lady, my mother is almost past childbearing age and this time she has found it very difficult carrying. I think she will need me to stay. I am sorry, my lady, truly I am. I do not want to leave you, but I must.'

'I understand, Rose, of course I do.' How selfish men were, Emma decided, determined to have their conjugal rights no matter what the consequences to their poor wives, but she did not say it aloud because she knew Rose loved her father—besides, it was not considered a suitable subject for a young unmarried lady to air. 'When will you go?'

'At the end of the week if that is convenient to you, my lady.'

'My convenience is not important, Rose, I would never keep you from your mother. Go and look after her, I shall manage.' She stood up. 'Now, I must be off or we shall be late.'

Hurrying downstairs, Emma found her mother and Sir George waiting for her in the drawing room. Her mother, in a becoming gown of rose-pink taffeta, was looking unhappy, her face pale and eyes bright with unshed tears. Sir George, arrayed in a mulberry evening coat, an embroidered waistcoat, white silk breeches and silk stockings, was standing with his back to the hearth, his mouth set in a thin line of annoyance. There was a tension in the air, which immediately communicated itself to Emma.

'About time too!' Sir George said.

'Goodness, child, whatever do you do up there to take so long to dress?' her mother asked more mildly. She had once been upright and sprightly, but age and being cowed by her demanding second husband seemed to have diminished her.

'I'm sorry, Mama, but I was talking to Rose. She wants to leave.'

'Why? Whatever have you done to her?'

'Nothing, Mama. She has to go and look after her brothers and sisters. Her mother is *enceinte* again.'

'Well, there's nothing to be done about it tonight,' Sir George snapped. 'You can send her packing in the morning.'

'In the morning?' Emma queried. 'She is prepared to stay until the end of the week.'

'No doubt she would like to, but it is my experience that servants under notice are worse than useless; they do no work, undermine the morale of the others and use every opportunity to steal…'

'Rose is not like that,' Emma protested. 'She is honest and loyal.'

'So you may think, but it is my rule that when a servant expresses a wish to leave, they are turned off immediately.' He turned to his wife. 'You will see she goes tomorrow. Now, the carriage is waiting. If we are not careful, we shall be the last to arrive and I particularly wanted to be there on time. There is someone I wish you to meet.'

'Oh?' Had he tired of waiting for her to accept an offer of marriage and found a husband for her? She waited to be enlightened.

'Lord Bentwater.'

'I do not think I know the gentleman.'

'No, of course you do not or I would not be going to the trouble of introducing you.'

'And what am I to make of this gentleman?' She spoke coolly because she would not let him intimidate her as he intimidated her mother; if he expected her to fall into the arms of one of his disreputable friends, then he was going to be disappointed. She was not so desperate to marry that she would accept anyone in breeches. In fact, she was not desperate at all. Her mother's miserable second marriage was enough to put anyone off.

'You may make of him what you will, miss. What is more to the point is what he makes of you. Come, now, the horses will be growing restive.' Followed meekly by his wife and an exasperated Emma, he set off down the hall, where the front door was opened by a liveried footman. A few short steps and he was at the carriage where he stood to one side as one of the grooms opened the door for the ladies to enter. Sir George seated himself opposite them and gave the order to proceed.

Although Almack's was almost certainly the most exclusive club in London, it could hardly be called grand. Lit by gas, the ballroom was enormous, made to look even larger by the huge mirrors and a series of gilt columns. Other smaller rooms were used for supper and cards. The Patronesses who presided over the weekly balls during the Season made sure only the best people attended and that everyone behaved themselves. It was here young ladies were paraded before the eligible bachelors in the hope of finding a husband. Emma thought it unbearably boring and could not understand why her stepfather should suddenly take it into his head to attend. Except for that hint about someone he wanted her to meet. She was curious, but not hopeful.

As soon as they arrived Sir George disappeared in the direction of the card room and Emma and her mother wandered into the ballroom, where the sumptuous gowns of the ladies and the richness of the gentlemen's coats formed a shifting rainbow of colour as they walked and gesticulated and preened themselves between dances. Spotting Lady Standon and her daughter, Harriet, they crossed the room to join them.

Harriet, a year younger than Emma, had recently become engaged to Frederick Graysmith, lawyer and Member of Parliament. He was likeable enough, but there seemed to be no fire in him. He would be safe but dull as a husband. Emma decided she wanted more than that. She wanted excitement and passion and a little something extra, though she could not define it. All she knew was that she would recognise it when it came. *If* it came. And if it did not, would she be able to settle for second best? She had a dreadful feeling that her stepfather was about to try to force a match on her and, if Lord Bentwater was anything like Sir George, she knew she would not like him.

'Emma, I had no idea you would be coming tonight,' Harriet said, her brown eyes bright with excitement. She was dressed in buttercup yellow, which contrasted well with her dark hair.

'It was Sir George's idea,' she said. 'He says there's someone he wants me to meet and it must be important, for he insisted on buying me a new gown for the occasion.' She looked round to see her mother deep in conversation with Lady Standon and lowered her voice. 'We had such a rush to find something in the time available.'

'It is very becoming,' Harriet said, stepping back to appraise her friend. 'You mean he is matchmaking?'

'If he is, I cannot think what is behind it. I'm not sure I shall like it.'

'Being married? Oh, surely you do not mean to be an old maid.'

'It would be better than enduring an unhappy marriage, don't you think? Once the deed is done, there's no going back on it.'

'I know that. But why should your marriage be unhappy? I set my heart on Freddie from the moment I met him and I know we shall deal well together.'

'Then I wish you happy.'

'Oh, I am sure I will be. The wedding is to be in June. I know it is very soon, but we have to be back from our wedding tour by the time Parliament reconvenes after the summer recess. You will be one of my attendants, won't you?'

'I shall be delighted, if Mama says I may.'

'I would be even happier if I thought you were suited too. Do take advantage of the dancing. Almost every eligible in town is here. I am sure if you tried you could find someone.'

Emma laughed. That seemed to be all that mattered: the thrill of the chase, the announcement of the engagement and later the wedding with half the *haut monde* in attendance. But that was only one year— what about all the years afterwards, the children, the problems of motherhood, the steadily growing older? If the man you had married was the wrong one, it would be purgatory. 'Oh, I am sure I could, but how would I know he was not after my fortune?'

'Does that matter, if he is in every other way suitable?'

'Tall, you mean.' It was said with a laugh.

'Yes, but more than that, surely? He must be amiable and considerate and have no bad vices, like womanising and gambling.'

'How right you are, especially about the gambling. I could never marry a man who gambled, however suitable he might otherwise be.' It was Sir George's gambling that was the cause of most of her mother's distress and that had entrenched in her a deep abhorrence of the vice, for vice it was. 'But do you know of such a paragon?'

'No, except Freddie, of course. But no doubt he has a friend…'

'Don't you dare!'

'I was only trying to help.'

'I know you were.' Emma was contrite. 'I did not mean to hurt your feelings, but I am not going to allow myself to be thrown to the wolves without a fight.' She wasn't thinking of Freddie's friend so much as her stepfather. Just what was his game? He had never shown the slightest interest in her before, except to complain to her mother that she was too lenient with her.

'Why must you fight?'

'Because that's my nature. Give me a challenge and I will rise to it. Tell me I must do something and I will refuse, tell me I cannot and I will most decidedly attempt it.'

'Then I pity any husband of yours and perhaps I shan't ask Freddie to introduce you to his friend after all. He would not thank me.' She paused and nodded towards a young man making his way towards them. 'Here comes Freddie, so I'll leave you to enjoy yourself.'

Emma danced with several young gentlemen, none of whom set her heart racing, but she was honest enough to admit she did nothing to encourage them and they must have found her extremely dull. It was not like her to be so ungracious, but she could not concentrate on her partners when her mind was filled with the prospect of meeting Lord Bentwater. Who was he? What was he like? What was to be done if she took him in aversion? Perhaps, after all, he would be young and attractive and she was worrying for nothing. Or perhaps he would not turn up.

Her latest partner took her back to where her mother sat, bowed to them both and disappeared. 'Who was that?' her mother asked. 'It was not Lord Bentwater, was it?'

Emma turned towards her in surprise. 'Have you not met him?'

'No.'

'Then what is your husband about? Surely he has confided in you?'

'He wishes to see you settled. As I do, dearest.' It was said quietly, but Emma knew that her mother was not at all happy about it.

'Am I to have no say in the matter at all?'

'Oh, Emma, please do not be difficult. George tells me the gentleman is in every way suitable…'

'Do you know, Mama, I cannot help wondering what Sir George is expecting to gain by it.'

If her mother intended to enlighten her, she did not do so because Harriet returned on Freddie's arm and after he had bowed and left them, they sat chatting about the young men who were present, none of whom matched up to Freddie in Harriet's eyes. As for Emma, she could not take any of them seriously. They were either dressed in the exaggerated fashion of the tulip, too young, too short or too old. Was Lord Bentwater among them and, if so, which was he?

'Harriet, do you know who that man is, talking to my stepfather?'

'I believe his name is Mr Jeremy Maddox. Don't tell me he has taken your fancy.'

'Goodness, Harriet, you do not think I have developed a *tendre* for someone I have only seen at a distance, do you? And he's a dandy if ever I saw one. I was curious, that's all. I thought he might be Lord Bentwater.'

Harriet laughed. 'Good heavens, no! Why did you think it was him?'

'I didn't, particularly. My stepfather is set upon introducing me to Lord Bentwater and I am expected to be amiable. I am curious to know what he looks like…'

'Bentwater! Oh, Emma, he does not expect you to marry that old roué, does he? He is fifty if he is a day and has gone through three wives already and not one has managed to produce an heir. I hear he is desperate. You cannot possibly consider him.'

'Then I shan't.' She spoke firmly, but they both knew it would not be as easy as that. Perhaps Harriet had been exaggerating or perhaps there was more than one Lord Bentwater.

She realised her friend had not been exaggerating when her stepfather tapped her on the shoulder a little later in the evening. 'Emma, may I present Lord Bentwater. Bentwater, my stepdaughter, Lady Emma Lindsay.'

'My lady, your obedient.' He made a flourishing leg, bowing low over it, giving her time to appraise him. He was taller than she was by an inch, but that was all she could find in his favour. He was thin as a lathe, with sharp features and black brows. His coat and breeches were of black silk, his black waistcoat was embroidered with silver; his calves, in white silk stockings, were plumped out with padding. Emma was reminded of a predatory spider and shivered with a terrible apprehension. Surely her stepfather did not expect her to marry this man?

He was looking her up and down, taking in every detail of her face and figure, and she longed to tell him she was not a brood mare being trotted out for his inspection, but knew that would be unpardonably rude; for her mother's sake, she resisted the impulse and met his gaze unflinchingly. She curtsied. 'My lord.'

He offered his hand. 'Shall we dance, my lady?'

She accompanied him on to the floor where they joined an eight-some. The steps were intricate and they were never close enough to permit a conversation, but she was aware as she moved up and down, across and sideways, that he was looking at her all the time, even when he was executing steps with another of the ladies. How uncomfortable he made her feel! At the end of the dance, she curtsied and he bowed and offered his arm to promenade.

'My lady, you must learn to unbend,' he said in a low voice. 'You are as stiff as a corpse and I would not like to think you are unhappy in my company.'

'My lord, I am neither happy nor unhappy and as the dance has ended, you do not have to endure my company any longer.'

'There, my dear, you are wrong. It is my earnest wish that we shall be often in each other's company in future. Every day. Has your papa not told you of my intent?'

'My father, my lord, is dead. And if you refer to my mother's husband, then, no, he has not.'

'No doubt he left it for me to do so after we had spoken together.' When she did not reply, he went on with an oily smile. 'You are a haughty one, to be sure, but that can be made a virtue, so long as your haughtiness is aimed at those beneath you and not your husband…'

'My lord, I have no husband.'

'Not yet. But the deficiency may soon be rectified. The details have yet to be settled with Sir George, but I think you understand me.'

'You are offering for me?'

'Yes. The offer has been made and accepted.'

'Not by me, it has not.'

'That is by the by. First things first. I have received the proper permission from your guardian to approach you and I shall call on you tomorrow when we will tie the thing up nice and tight.'

She stopped and turned to face him, drawing herself up and taking a deep breath. 'Lord Bentwater, I am aware of the honour you do me, but I must decline. We should not suit.'

He threw back his head and laughed so that one or two people close by stopped their chattering to turn towards them. 'You suit me very well and it suits Sir George to give you to me…'

'Give me?' She was shaking with nerves and seething with anger. How could he assume she would meekly give in? He was a dreadful man. He was older than her stepfather, he had small currant eyes and bad teeth, and his manner was arrogant and self-satisfied. The very idea of being married to him repelled her. 'Why does it suit Sir George?'

He drew his lips back over his yellow teeth in a mockery of a smile. 'Let us say that he has his reasons for wishing to accommodate me.'

Emma realised he had a hold over Sir George and she guessed it was something to do with money. She was being sold! 'My mother will never sanction such a thing.'

'Lady Tasker will obey her husband as every good wife does. Now, my dear…' Again that awful smile. 'Let us not quarrel. I shall not be a bad husband, not if you please me…'

'But *you* do not please *me*, Lord Bentwater. I bid you good evening.' She broke away from him and went to sit beside her mother. 'Mama, you wanted to know which of the gentlemen was Lord Bentwater and now I can point him out. He is that black spider over there, laughing with Sir George, no doubt over me. He tells me he has bought me—'

'Bought you, child?'

'Yes, bought me. I do not know what he has given, or promised to give, your husband for me, but I tell you now, nothing on earth will persuade me to take that rude, arrogant scarecrow for a husband.'

'Oh, Emma,' her mother said with a heavy sigh. 'There will be the most dreadful trouble, if you do not.'

'Why? What has Sir George said to you?'

'He says he cannot afford to cross Lord Bentwater, that the man has it in his power to ruin us, though George will not tell me how or why. All he says—and he says it over and over again—is that without this match we will live in penury, his reputation will be ruined and we won't be able to lift our heads in society again. I think it must be a gambling debt, I can think of nothing else.'

'Mama, surely it cannot be your wish that I marry that man?'

'No, of course not. I have argued until I am spent, but George is adamant.' Lady Tasker sighed heavily. 'If only your papa were alive…'

'You would not be married to Sir George Tasker, would you?' Emma said with unanswerable logic. 'Why did you marry him, Mama?'

'I was lonely and in all my life I have never had to manage alone. My father, the late Duke, looked after me and my affairs until he handed me over to your father when I was seventeen and he carried on as my father had done. I never had to think of anything for myself and, when your papa died, I had no idea how to go on. Sir George was charming and understanding. Even now, when he is in a good mood…' She stopped and gazed across the room where her husband was enjoying a jest with Lord Bentwater. 'I dare not cross him.'

Emma gave up the conversation, knowing she would get nowhere with it. And now she was torn in two because it was obvious that if she was adamant in her refusal to marry Bentwater, her mother would suffer for it. Sir George would not beat his wife, he had too much pride for that, but there were other ways of punishing her: subtle verbal cruelty, forbidding her to receive her friends or call on them, taking away her pin money so that she could go nowhere, buy nothing, without petitioning him first. It had happened before when her mother displeased him and Emma loved her mother dearly and could not bear to think of her suffering in that way. 'Mama, if you say I must, I must, but I shall do it with a heavy heart and I promise you I shall not be an obedient wife.'

'Perhaps it will not come to that,' her mother said hopefully. 'George might relent.'

The music resumed and another partner came to claim Emma and she was not called upon to answer. She went off and danced with the young man, a fixed smile on her face. She even managed to make one or two witty comments about the music and the company, but inside her heart was heavy as lead. If only she could find a way out without hurting her mother. If only she could find her own husband, she could tell the odious Lord Bentwater she was already promised. She smiled a little at her own foolishness. If she hadn't found one in the two years since her come-out, she was unlikely to find one now.

She was about to return to her mother when she saw Sir George returning to her with Lord Bentwater in tow. She turned about and went to the retiring room, where she sat on the stool before the mirror and looked at herself, as if she could find the answer to her problems in her reflection. 'You are on your own,' she told the strained face that stared out at her. 'You cannot depend upon your mama to support you and Sir George is quite capable of dragging you to the altar. And who can you confide in? Not your mother, for she is too afraid of her husband. Not Rose, who is anxious about her own mother and leaving you in any case. There is Harriet, but Harriet is thinking about nothing but her wedding and who can blame her? There is no one.'

Sighing heavily, she returned to the ballroom and put on a brave smile, which she kept in place even when Lord Bentwater came to claim her for a second dance and spoke and behaved as if she had already accepted him. This was reinforced on the journey home, when Sir George told her that he expected her to accept the very next day. 'You are well past marriageable age,' he said. 'It is time you settled down and I can think of no one who will serve you better than Cecil Bentwater. He is wealthy enough, even for you. My God, there must be dozens of young ladies who would jump at the chance...'

'Then let him choose one of those.'

'He has favoured you, though I do wonder if he knows what a hoyden he is taking on.' And he gave a harsh laugh.

'Perhaps you should enlighten him.'

'Oh, I have, but he tells me he enjoys a challenge and there is no gainsaying him.'

'But, sir, I do not, cannot, love him.'

'Love!' He scoffed. 'Love has nothing to do with it. You do not have to live in each other's pockets and, in truth, it would look strange if you did. Husbands and wives lead their own lives, have their own friends and pursuits to keep them occupied and Lord Bentwater would not expect anything else from you, except to do your wifely duty and give him an heir. Once that is done, you may please yourself, so long as you are discreet. Discretion is the name of the game, not love. If you remember that, you will deal very well together.'

The idea revolted her. 'I cannot believe that all marriages are like that. Mama and Papa—'

'Enough!' he said, not wishing to be reminded of his saintly predecessor. 'You will marry Lord Bentwater and that is my last word on the subject.'

Emma felt her mother's hand creep into her own and squeeze it and she fell silent for the rest of the journey.

It was three in the morning before she went to her bed, but even so Rose was waiting to help her to undress. Rose was sturdy, clean and tidy, with light brown hair pulled back into her cap and a neat waist encircled by a snowy apron over a grey cambric dress. 'I shall miss you when you go, Rose,' she said, as the girl helped her out of her ball gown.

'And I shall miss you, my lady.'

'Do you like being a lady's maid?' she asked, watching Rose deftly fold the gown and lay it carefully in the chest at the foot of her bed.

'Oh, yes, my lady, it is cut above other house servants.'

'What is it like?'

'Like, my lady?' Rose queried, puzzled. 'Why, you know my duties as well as I do.'

'I did not mean your duties, I meant the life, how you feel about it. Do you not hate being at someone's beck and call all the time?'

'We all have to work, my lady, unless we're gentlefolk, that is, and I would as lief work as a lady's maid as anything else. You have a certain standing among the others. If you have a good mistress such as you are, my lady, you are treated kindly, fed and clothed and paid well, and there are the perks. You often give me gowns you have tired of and when you are from home and do not need me, I have only light duties such as cleaning and pressing your clothes and tidying your room…'

Emma managed a light laugh, though she felt more like weeping. 'Oh, I know I am not the tidiest person in the world.' She paused. 'But don't you resent being given orders?'

'No, why should I? It is the way of things.'

'But if they go counter to your own inclinations?'

'My inclinations, my lady, do not count. But why are you asking all these questions?'

'Oh, I don't know. It is because you are leaving me, I suppose. And I wonder how I shall manage without you.'

'Your mama will find you someone else.'

'No doubt, but it won't be the same. And what makes it worse is that my stepfather has found a husband for me…' She paused while Rose undid her petticoats, picking them up when she kicked them off. 'He is the most odious man imaginable and how am I to bear it without you?'

'I am sorry, Miss Emma, indeed I am. If I could help you, I would.'

But it was not Rose or her replacement who filled her thoughts when her nightgown was pulled over her head and she settled between the sheets, but the dilemma she faced over Lord Bentwater. She lay wide awake, going over and over in her mind what had happened, wondering what it was that made her stepfather so anxious she should obey him. It had to be money; Lord Bentwater had as good as told her so. Could she buy her way out? But she did not have the spending of her money and her trustees would take the advice of Sir George, especially if her mother agreed with him. Mama would not dare to defy him. Rose's words—*'my inclinations…do not count'*—came back to her. It certainly seemed to be true of the mistress at that moment.

She could run away, but that would break her mother's heart; besides, if she just disappeared, Mama would have half the *ton* out looking for her, not to mention Runners and constables and it would not be fair to worry her so. And it would make no difference in the long run; she would be hauled back in disgrace and she was quite sure it would not put Lord Bentwater off, for hadn't Sir George said the man enjoyed a challenge? It was almost dawn before she fell into a restless sleep and then her dreams were of huge black spiders and struggling in a sticky web from which she could not escape.

It seemed she had barely closed her eyes when a hand shook her awake again. 'Sweetheart, wake up.'

She woke with a half-scream; the nightmare had been very real, but it was her mother standing over her with a lighted candle. She was wearing a dressing gown over her nightgown and her hair hung loosely about her shoulders. 'Shh, not so loud, my love.'

'What's wrong, Mama? What time is it?'

'Just after five o'clock.'

'Five! Couldn't you sleep?'

'No.' She sat down on the side of the bed. 'Emma, I cannot let you go to that dreadful man. You must leave. Now, before George wakes up.'

'But where will we go?'

'We? I cannot go with you, child. My place is with my husband.'

'I cannot leave you. I want to escape that dreadful man, but the thought of leaving you behind is not to be borne.'

'You must. If we both go, we shall attract attention and George will find us and make us come back. It must look as though you have gone alone. I shall deny all knowledge of your intentions.' She opened Emma's wardrobe and began pulling out clothes. 'I've spoken to Rose and she has agreed to go with you. As soon as you are safe arrived, she can go to her mother. If George asks to question her, I shall tell him I obeyed his instructions and turned her off.' She was throwing garments on the bed as she spoke. 'There is nothing suitable here. You cannot go dressed as a lady, that would be asking for someone to become suspicious and if it becomes known Sir George is looking for you, especially if he offers a reward, you will soon be brought back.'

'Mama, do stop throwing my clothes about and come and sit down again. Where am I to go and how will I travel? And how will you know I am safe?'

Lady Tasker sat down and took her daughter's hands. 'You will go by stage to a very old friend of mine who lives in Kendal in Cumbria. Her name is Mrs Amelia Summers. I have had no correspondence with her since I remarried and Sir George knows nothing about her, so he will not think of her. I have no money for a hired chaise and besides, like elegant clothes, it would only cause comment. I will give you all the money I have and the pearls your father left for your twenty-first birthday. George knows nothing about them. I've kept them hidden. You'll have to sell them or perhaps pawn them. You never know, we might have a stroke of luck and be able to redeem them.'

Emma realised that would only come about if Sir George became ill and died, but, as he was disgustingly healthy and never exerted himself, that prospect seemed far distant. 'Mama, I am not at all sure I should agree to this.'

'Do you want to marry that dreadful man?'

'You know I do not. But I am afraid for you.'

'Sir George will not harm me. There is no other way and we are wasting time.' She handed Emma an envelope. 'Here is the letter to Mrs Summers and here, in this purse, is the necklace and twenty guineas. I have no more, but it should be enough for your fares and for Rose's return fare, with some over.'

'Mama, I can't—'

'Please do not argue, Emma. It has taken all my resolve to come to this and I want you to go. When you are safe arrived, write to Lady Standon, not me. You had better have a pseudonym and one Sir George will never guess. Say the first thing that comes into your head…'

She looked about her, noticed the bed curtains and promptly said. 'Draper. Miss Fanny Draper.'

'Good. When you write to Lady Standon, be circumspect.' She stood up, 'Now I am going to send Rose to you. She might have something suitable for you to wear.'

She left the room, leaving Emma shaking with the enormity of the undertaking. She had never travelled anywhere alone before and never on a public coach. But it was not so much that that made her hesitate, it was the thought of leaving her mother. But perhaps it would not be for long. Perhaps Sir George, when he realised how determined she was, would relent and she could come home again. She left her bed and poured cold water from the jug on her washstand into a bowl and washed her face.

She was brushing her hair when Rose crept into the room. 'I've brought a dress of mine for you to wear on the journey,' she whispered. 'But you had better take a few garments of your own for when you arrive. I'll pack them while you dress. We can't take more than a carpet bag, considering we will have to carry it.'

'Rose, am I doing the right thing?'

'Yes. Now do not trouble yourself over the rights and wrongs of it, for the wrong is all with Sir George. We must hurry before the rest of the house stirs.' She finished the packing and turned to look at Emma. A little giggle escaped from her. 'Who is to say who is mistress and who servant now?'

'I cannot get into your shoes.'

'Then you must wear your own. It won't matter.' She picked up a cloak that had seen better days. 'Here, put this on, the morning is chilly.' She draped it over Emma's shoulders and buttoned the neck. 'It's shabby, but that's all to the good, we don't want you recognised, do we? Come on, let's be off.'

'But I must say goodbye to Mama.'

'She is waiting in the kitchen. We will go out of the back door.' She picked up the carpet bag, opened the door and peered up and down the corridor. 'All clear,' she whispered.

The farewell she bade her mother was tearful on both sides, but could not be prolonged in case Sir George woke and came in search of his wife. 'Go now,' her mother said, giving her a little push towards the outside door. 'God keep you and bless you. Rose, look after her, won't you?'

'I'll do my best, my lady.' She turned to Emma. 'Come, my lady… No, that cannot be. What are you to be called?'

'Fanny Draper.'

And so it was Lady Emma Lindsay who stepped out of Lindsay House, but Fanny Draper who linked her arm in Rose's to walk to Lad Lane and the Swan with Two Necks.

'How do you know where to catch the stage?' Emma asked.

'It is how I arrived when I came back after my mother's last lying-in. There is nothing to it. We buy our tickets and climb aboard. I know it is not what you are used to, but think of it as an adventure. As long as no one perceives you for a lady, you should be safe enough. You will not mind if I treat you as an equal? It will look odd if I do not.'

'No, of course I shall not mind. From this minute on, there is no Lady Emma, only a woman called Fanny.'

The Swan with Two Necks was a very busy inn, with coaches coming and going all the time, disgorging and taking on passengers. There was a small ticket office to one side of the building where the two girls were obliged to stand in line for their turn to be served. Waiting was torture and Emma began to worry that there would not be seats for them. And the longer they had to wait, the more likely it was that Sir George would discover her absence and send people out searching for her. The first place he would check would be the coaching inns.

She let Rose do the talking when they reached the little window. 'Two inside seats to Kendal,' she said.

'No inside seats, miss. There's two going on top. Three pounds ten shillings each and that takes you only as far as Manchester. You need another carrier to take you the rest of the way.'

Adventurous as she was, Emma could not view the prospect of travelling outside with equilibrium. 'Oh dear, Rose, what are we to do? Is there another coach?'

'Not to Manchester,' the man said. 'You can go to Chester from the Golden Cross.'

'But we cannot be sure of getting to Kendal from there, can we?' she whispered to Rose.

'No. Perhaps if we take the outside seats, we will be able to change them later when we have gone a little way.'

'Change them now.'

Emma swung round at the sound of the male voice, ready to take to her heels if he should prove to be an emissary of her stepfather's.

The man who faced her was at least a head taller than she was, but the rest of him was in perfect proportion: broad shoulders in a burgundy-coloured coat, slim hips, muscular legs in well-fitting pantaloons tucked into shining Hessians. She looked up into his face. His expression was proud, almost arrogant, and his startlingly blue eyes had a steely depth which indicated he was not used to being crossed. Or perhaps it was sadness; she could not be sure. He smiled and doffed his hat, revealing fair curly hair.

'I beg your pardon.' It was said haughtily. Ladies simply did not speak to men who had not been formally introduced.

'Oh, no need to beg my pardon,' he said cheerfully. 'I can as easily ride outside as in.'

'But, sir, there are two of us and only one of you.'

'My man is travelling with me. We will both climb on top.' He turned to a man who was supervising the stowing of luggage in the boot of the coach which was just then being loaded. 'Joe, what have you done with our tickets?'

The man reached up to his hat where two tickets were stuck in the ribbon around the crown. 'Here, my lord.'

Alex took them and handed them to Emma. 'There, with my compliments. I will take the outside tickets offered to you.'

'I am most grateful, sir.'

'My pleasure. The passengers are being called to their seats. Is this your luggage?' He pointed at Emma's carpet bag and Rosie's bundle.

'Yes.'

'Joe, stow them safely, will you? And then climb aboard. We are going to see the countryside from on high.' He bowed to the girls, settled his hat back on his head and held the door for them to enter. 'Perhaps we shall have an opportunity to speak when the coach stops for refreshments.' He shut the door, took the outside tickets Rose had hurriedly paid for with the money Emma had given her earlier, and hardly had time to climb up beside his man before they were away.

Emma leaned back in her seat and shut her eyes. She had never felt less like sleeping, but she wanted to collect her scattered wits. It was a little over two hours since her mother had woken her and here she was on the greatest adventure of her life. If she had not been so worried about Mama and what might be happening back at Lindsay House, she might have been looking forward to it.

Chapter Two

The other two passengers taking the inside seats were a young man and his wife who sat holding hands and smiling shyly at each other. They posed no threat and Emma allowed herself to relax.

'He is a handsome man, is he not?' Rose commented in a whisper.

'Who?'

'The man who gave us his tickets. Did you hear his servant call him "my lord"?'

'Yes.'

'I wonder who he is. You do not know him, do you?'

'No, thank goodness. The last thing I want is to meet someone known to me.'

'All the same, it was good of him to give up his seats for us.'

'Indeed it was. I am sorry I had no time to thank him properly, nor did I offer to pay the difference in the price.'

'No doubt you will have the opportunity when the coach stops for us to take refreshment.'

'I shall make a point of it.'

They stopped every fourteen miles to have the horses changed, but the passengers remained in their seats for this operation which only took two or three minutes. It was half past ten and they had been on the road just over two hours when the coach pulled in at the Peahen in St Albans and the coachman invited his passengers to partake of breakfast.

Emma and Rose left the coach and stood in the yard, looking at the inn which had a decidedly unpretentious appearance. Emma, who had never been inside an inn before, was reluctant to enter it, but as it was imperative that she find somewhere to relieve herself, she ducked her head under its low lintel, followed by Rose.

Having made themselves more comfortable in a room set aside for ladies, they found their way to the dining room, where the chivalrous lord and his servant were breakfasting together. Normally this would have struck Emma as strange, but as the whole adventure was out of the ordinary and she herself was travelling with her maid on an equal footing, she paid no heed to it, but approached the pair with a confident step.

'My lord, I am in your debt.'

Alex looked up at her as if seeing her for the first time. Here was a very tall young lady, scrupulously clean but dressed in a somewhat shabby cloak, beneath which could be seen a striped cotton skirt in two shades of grey. Her hair was almost concealed by a plain straw bonnet tied on with ribbon. But it was not the clothes that commanded his attention, but the strikingly beautiful face. It was a perfect oval, the skin creamy and unblemished. The strong chin, straight nose, wide violet eyes and arched brows were too refined to belong to a servant and the confident way she spoke seemed to confirm she was other than she looked. The slightly high colour of her cheeks betrayed a certain nervousness. He was intrigued.

'Not at all,' he said, standing out of politeness, something a real servant would have thought strange, but she seemed to accept it as her due. 'My pleasure, ma'am.'

It was not often she had to look up to a man, but she did so now. 'But inside seats cost more than those on the outside, my lord.'

'A mere fribble. Think nothing of it.'

'At least tell me to whom I am indebted.'

Oh, that was not the speech of an ill-educated commoner. He smiled. 'I thought perhaps you knew. You addressed me as "my lord".'

'I heard your servant address you thus.'

She was observant too, and quick. 'So he does, but not always. He has been known to be forgetful and call me Major. I answer as readily to either. Let me introduce myself, seeing there is no one else to do the office. I am Viscount Malvers, one-time Major in the Norfolk Regiment of Foot, at your service.' He bowed as he would to a lady. She did not seem in the least surprised by this, prompting him to add, 'May I know your name?'

Emma felt Rose dig her in the ribs, reminding her of her new identity. 'Oh, I'm no one of any importance at all,' she said, trying to affect a silly giggle which sounded false in her ears. She decided not to try it again. 'I am Fanny Draper.'

'I am pleased to meet you, Miss Draper,' he said, bowing again. 'Have you had breakfast?'

'Not yet.' She looked about her. All the tables seemed to be full and there were only two waiters dashing between them. 'Perhaps we shall not bother.'

'Then please do join me.' And when she appeared to hesitate, added, 'Your companion too. You cannot travel for hours without sustenance and it will be some time before we stop again. You will find I can command a more assiduous service than most.' And with that he clicked his fingers at a passing waiter, who instantly left whatever he had been going to do and approached him. 'Breakfast for the ladies,' Alex told him. 'Coffee, ham, eggs, toasted bread and butter, and be quick about it. Time is pressing.'

Rose laughed and it was Emma's turn to nudge her with her elbow. She stopped instantly and they took the other two seats at the table and were soon enjoying a hearty breakfast. Emma was surprised how hungry she was. Perhaps it was the effect of the high emotion of the past few hours, or perhaps because she had missed supper at Almack's while she had been in the ladies' room contemplating her reflection and had eaten nothing since six o'clock the previous evening.

Alex watched her, a faint smile playing about his lips. 'Do you travel beyond Manchester, Miss Draper?'

The last thing she wanted was to be quizzed on her destination, but she could hardly refuse to answer without appearing uncivil. 'Yes, we are going to the Lake District.'

'What a happy coincidence. So am I. Which lake in particular?'

'I am not sure there is a lake. I am to be met at Kendal to take up a position as companion to a lady.' For a spur-of-the-moment answer she thought it did very well, though she prayed he would not ask any other questions. To prevent that, she asked one of her own. 'Where are you bound, my lord?'

'To Windermere. I have an uncle there. I used to stay with him when I was a boy, but it is many years since I visited him.'

'I expect you were prevented by your being in the army.'

'Yes. I was out of the country from '09 to '14 and I had barely been home six months when I was recalled to go to Waterloo.'

'I believe that was a prodigious gory battle. I heard the Duke of Wellington called it a close-run thing.'

He smiled, knowing perfectly well what she was at and prepared to humour her. If he wanted his curiosity about her satisfied, he would have other opportunities. 'Yes, he did and it was certainly that.'

'Did you sustain any injury yourself?'

'Fortunately, no.'

'And now you are home again and ready to resume your civilian life. No doubt you find it strange.'

'Indeed, I do. I am fortunate in having a home and occupation to return to. Many others are not so lucky.'

'Occupation, my lord?' she queried.

'An estate to run. I have recently come into my inheritance.'

'And is that in the Lakes?'

'No, in Norfolk.'

'You are a long way from home, my lord.'

He laughed. 'Is that meant as a criticism, Miss Draper?'

She blushed furiously. 'Oh, no, I would not dare… I beg your pardon. My mother always used to say I had too much curiosity.'

'I forgive you. And so that you do not run away with the idea that I shirk my duty—'

'Oh, I never would!'

'I will tell you that my uncle is ill and wishes to see me. Once I have satisfied myself as to his return to good health, I shall go home.'

'Not back to the London Season?'

'No, I do not think so, I find it not to my taste.' The evening before he had returned with his aunt from Lady Melbourne's to find a message from his mother telling him his uncle, Admiral Lord Bourne, was very ill and wanted to see him. He had always been close to his Uncle Henry, closer than to his father, and had corresponded with him throughout his years in the army and so he had made preparations to take the early morning coach north. He had sent a message to his new steward to go at once to Buregreen to make a start on the work of the estate and written a letter to his mother telling her he was leaving for the north at once and would write again as soon as he arrived. Joe was told to pack and make sure he was awake in good time to catch the stage.

He did not need his own carriage while he was in London and staying with his aunt, so the family carriage had been left at Buregreen for his mother's use and was not available. Besides, the stage, with its facility for the frequent changing of horses, would have him there all the quicker. He hadn't bargained for riding outside, but he could hardly let two young women sit on the roof while he sat in comfort inside.

Both girls had finished eating, so he beckoned the waiter to pay the bill.

'Oh, my lord, we cannot allow you to buy our breakfast, can we, Rose?'

Rose didn't see why not, but she dutifully answered, 'No, my—' She stopped herself just in time and quickly added, '—Goodness, no.'

'If you think I am such a pinchpenny as to invite two ladies to eat with me and then expect them to pay, you are mistaken, madam.'

'And if you think I am to be bought, then you are the one in error, my lord.'

Instead of being affronted, he laughed. She was no plain everyday companion. She had been brought up a gentlewoman, or something very near it. He was on the point of taxing her with it, but changed his mind. It would provide a little entertainment on a long, tedious journey to watch how she went on and how long she could keep it up. 'I do not want to buy you, Miss Draper. To be sure, I have no use for a lady's companion. Now let us call a truce.' He handed the waiter a handful of coins, telling him to keep the change, which pleased the fellow no end and he went off smiling.

Emma, seeing how much it was, turned pale. If all meals on the way were as expensive as that, her money would never last the distance and her pearls would have to go. It would break her heart to part with them, the last reminder of her father. She had loved him dearly and she knew her mother had too. Oh, why did he have to go and die? And why did her mother have to go and marry that horrible Sir George Tasker? Was that why she was so sharp with Viscount Malvers, when it certainly was not his fault?

'My lord, I beg your pardon. A truce it is and my gratitude with it.'

'Then let us go back to the coach. I heard them calling for passengers two minutes ago.' He stood up and was about to pull out her chair for her and offer his arm, but stopped himself. A lady's companion would not expect such a courtesy and he ought to maintain the pretence until such time as she admitted it *was* a pretence.

They trooped out to the coach, he saw the ladies safely in and then resumed his seat on the roof beside his man. Joe Bland had been his batman almost the whole of his army career and on being discharged was happy to continue to serve him. They had been through so much together, he was more friend than servant. Now he was grinning.

'Pray share the jest,' Alex commanded him.

'The Long Meg,' Joe said. 'If she's a lady's maid, I'll eat my hat.'

'She said companion, not maid.'

'What's the difference?'

'A companion is something above a maid. Not exactly a servant, but not family either. She is what the name implies, a companion. Such a position usually falls to the lot of spinsters who are gentlewomen but have to earn a living, for one reason or another. The death of the family breadwinner, perhaps, and no likelihood of finding a husband. Their duties are to run errands, fetch and carry, and stay meekly in the background. I doubt they are allowed much time to themselves.'

'Hmm. Can't see that one running errands for anyone. I'll wager half a crown she's a runaway and, if she is, you could find yourself in a coil for aiding and abetting, my lord.'

'What you really mean is that you begrudge your inside seat.'

'No, Major. I've travelled in many worse ways, as you very well know. But she's not what she seems, though I think she is in the way of winding you round her thumb.'

'Never! No woman will ever do that to me. But I'll wager you are as curious as I am.'

'Mayhap. I could try and find out from the other one. Now, she is a servant, I'll lay odds.'

'You are probably right, unless the pair of them are putting on a little entertainment for our benefit. I propose to go along with it and see where it leads. We have nothing else to do but enjoy the ride.'

'If it doesn't rain,' Joe muttered gloomily. 'I begin to wonder if we will ever get a summer. It's enough to make you wish yourself back in Spain.'

'I will endeavour to see if we can travel inside when and if the other occupants of the seats leave the coach. To be sure, it will give us time to get to know more of those two.'

Why he was so curious, he did not know. There was something about the tall girl that seized his attention. He had never, to his knowledge, met her before, but he felt as if he knew her, had always known her, and in that knowledge was also mystery, which he found compelling. She was not afraid of him, had met his eyes unashamedly, had conversed intelligently, was self-assured, more than any gentlewoman fallen on hard times ought to be, and yet at the back of those enormous violet eyes was a profound sadness. There was a story there and he was determined to get to the bottom of it.

The coach rattled on through the Hertfordshire countryside, making Emma wish she dare stop and go to Pinehill, but that would be the first place Sir George would look once he had ascertained she was no longer in London. She leaned back and refused to look out of the window at the familiar countryside where her childhood had been so happy, in case the sight should make her weep. How was her mother faring? Would her stepfather be bullying her into revealing where her daughter had gone? Mama was dreadfully afraid of her husband, but she would hold out as long as she could. If she could convince Sir George she was as mystified and concerned as he was, she might not suffer too much at his hands. She could even take to her bed with the worry of it all. Yes, that's what she would do.

'It's raining again,' Rose commented.

Emma opened her eyes and peered through the window. She could see nothing and rubbed the window to clear it of condensation and then all she could see was water beating against the other side and running down the glass in torrents. 'Oh, dear, those poor men. I'll wager they wish they had never given us their seats.'

The horses' swift canter slowed to a trot, as the road became awash and the potholes disappeared, so that the wheels frequently ran into them and everyone on the coach was thrown from side to side. A flash of lightning and a roll of thunder so startled the horses they set off at a mad gallop. Emma reached for the strap and hung on grimly and the young bride opposite her flung herself into her husband's arms and cried out in terror. They could hear the outside passengers shouting, which included some words not fit for ladies' ears and then a thumping on the roof above their heads as if all twelve of them were trying to shift their positions. And still the horses galloped on, dragging their cargo with them.

At last the driver regained control and they resumed their steady pace, but the young lady opposite Emma would not be consoled, even though her husband soothed her over and over again. 'It's all right, dearest, you are quite safe. And I do believe the rain is easing. We shall soon be in Dunstable. There, there, I won't let anything happen to you, I promise.' He smiled nervously at Emma as he spoke.

She leaned forward. 'Pray, do not distress yourself, madam. I admit I was a little nervous myself, but the worst is over. Do dry your eyes and look out of the window. I believe the sun is trying to come out.'

The young lady lifted her head from her husband's shoulder and smiled weakly. 'I am s…sorry to be s…such a watering pot. I have never travelled in a public coach before and never without Mama.'

Emma leaned forward, smiling. 'I'll tell you a secret. Neither have I.'

'Then you are very brave.'

'Not brave, stubborn and too proud to admit to being fearful.' That, she supposed was true, especially with regard to her present situation, otherwise she would never have set out on this adventure.

They stopped for a change of horses, but did not leave the coach, though Alex climbed down and put his head in the door. Water was dripping off his hat and his shoulders were soaked. 'Is anyone hurt?'

'No, we are all in plump currant,' Emma said. 'But you are very wet.'

'Oh, I have been a great deal wetter in my time, ma'am. I shall soon dry when we stop for something to eat.'

'When will that be?'

'At Dunstable. We should have been there by now, but it would have been unwise to hurry the horses when you couldn't see where you were going.'

Emma smiled. 'They certainly hurried themselves when it thundered.'

'Yes, and a devil of a job it was to bring them to order. Horses that shy at a rumble of thunder should not be allowed to draw a public coach. I mean to have a word with the proprietor and hope the next set are more reliable.' With that he disappeared and Emma saw him cross the yard and enter the inn. He came back just as they were ready to set off again.

The remainder of the stretch to Dunstable, through rolling countryside between the Chiltern Hills and Dunstable Downs, was uneventful and they clattered up the High Street and turned under the archway of the White Horse at half past one in the afternoon. Thankfully they stretched their stiff limbs and made a dash for the inn where they were joined by the bedraggled occupants of the outside seats.

The end of May it might have been, but the spring had been so cold and wet, the proprietor had lit a fire in the parlour and soon steaming coats and cloaks were draped around it. Emma looked about for Lord Malvers, but he was nowhere to be seen, though his man, his dark hair plastered to his scalp, had made himself comfortable in the corner nearest the fire and was tucking in to a plate full of chicken, potatoes and gravy. The young man and his bride were in earnest conversation with the innkeeper and were soon conducted upstairs. No doubt they had bespoke themselves a private room.

Emma found a table and they sat down to wait to be served. They had just handed in an order for ham pie and potatoes, the cheapest thing on the menu according to the man who took the order, when the Viscount returned. He had changed his coat and brushed out his hair, though the rain had made it curl even more. He approached Emma. 'May I join you?'

She could hardly refuse. 'Please do. We have already ordered our meal.'

'Ah, I see, that means I am not to be allowed to pay for it.' Nevertheless he seated himself beside them.

'No, my lord, you are not. We are perfectly capable of paying our own way.'

'How independent you are!'

'You are mocking me.'

'Indeed I am not. I admire your spunk.' He turned as the waiter brought the girls' meal and took his order for pork chops, roast chicken, a fruit pie and a quart of ale.

'Spunk, my lord?'

'You do not seem at all distressed by your recent alarming experience.'

She was taken aback for a moment, thinking he must know who she was and had heard about Lord Bentwater's proposal, but then realised he was talking about the runaway horses. 'Oh, that. It did not last above two or three minutes and we did not turn over, did we?'

'No, but it was a near thing.'

She smiled. 'A close-run thing.'

He laughed. 'Yes, if you will.'

'It must have been far worse for those of you travelling on the outside in the rain and wind.'

'A mite uncomfortable,' he said laconically.

The waiter came back with a tray loaded with food and Emma's eyes widened at the sight of it. Her ham pie had barely filled a corner. She watched as he attacked it with gusto.

'And you need not have endured it if you had not given away your inside seats.'

'I hope you are not going to bore me with your gratitude all the way to Kendal, Miss Draper. A good deed once done should be forgotten.'

'By the doer, yes, but the recipient should be thinking of ways to make all right again.'

'Allowing me to bear you company has made it right.' He had noticed her looking longingly at the food on his plate and guessed she had very little money. Putting down his knife and fork, he pushed his plate away. 'Do you know, I am not as hungry as I thought I was. I shall have to send most of the chicken back to the kitchen and I hate waste.'

Rose looked at Emma and Emma looked at Rose, each reading the other's thoughts. 'So do I,' Rose said, knowing Emma would never stoop to admitting such a thing. 'And it is like to be some time before we stop again. If you have truly eaten your fill…'

'Oh, I have. Here, let me help you to a morsel.' And he divided what was left in the dishes between their two plates. 'But do hurry up. We were so late arriving we are not being given the full hour to eat. Apparently, the schedule is more important than our digestions.'

They had eaten half of it when they were recalled to their seats. Almost reluctantly Emma left the cosiness of the warm room and the company of a gentleman she found strangely beguiling and made her way out to the coach, now with a different team of horses. Followed by Rose, she took her place and was taken aback when Lord Malvers's servant climbed in and sat opposite her. Lord Malvers joined them and they were away again.

'You have no objection to my travelling inside with you?' he asked.

'My lord, you must think me very particular and singularly lacking in conduct to object to anyone who has paid for his seat.' She gave a little laugh and added, 'Twice over.'

'Then I shall take it you are content with my company.' He smiled to put her at her ease, but she was wary of him, he could see it in her eyes, such big, expressive eyes. He turned to her companion. 'What about you, Miss… I am sorry, you have the advantage of me.'

'Turner,' she said.

'Well, Miss Turner, do you think you can suffer me to share your carriage?'

'*My* carriage! Goodness, sir, what would I be doin' with a carriage?'

'Quite right. Prodigious expensive things they are to keep.'

'Is that why you travel by public coach, my lord?' Emma asked him, knowing he was throwing darts at her by teasing Rose. It behoved her to come to the maid's rescue.

'You think it miserly of me?'

'I would never accuse you of miserliness, my lord. I was simply curious.'

'Again?'

'*Touché.*' She laughed. 'You do not have to answer me.'

'No, but there is not much else to do is there? The countryside is too wet and bedraggled to be worth our attention, so we must fall back on conversation. Unless, of course, you prefer silence.'

'No, my lord. By all means let us converse.'

'Then I will tell you I did not bother to keep a carriage and horses in town and as my journey was urgent I had no time to go home for it.'

'Home being in Norfolk?'

'Yes. Buregreen. It is on the borders of Norfolk and Suffolk, quite near the sea. There are three farms, mainly arable, but with a fair acreage of grazing. Before the war they were productive, but last year the harvest was not good owing to bad weather and this year the climate has been the worst anyone can remember. I doubt there will be a yield at all.'

'And yet you left it to go to London? Are you not happy at home, my lord?'

'It is the place I most wish to be, but my mother, bless her dear heart, thought I should find me a wife.'

'You are not married, then?'

'No, Miss Draper, I am not. I never had the time or inclination for it.' It was spoken so emphatically she wondered why he was so adamant.

'And the London Season bores you.'

'How do you know that?'

'You said so yourself, earlier today. Not to your taste, you said. Do you think you will find a bride in the Lakes?'

'A mermaid, you mean, half-fish, half-woman.'

It was a moment before his meaning registered and then she laughed. 'Do you always tease, my lord?'

'Only if I think it will make you smile. It is better than being sombre, don't you think? Life is too short to take seriously.'

'We cannot always be laughing. There are times…' She stopped, afraid to go on. He was looking at her with his head on one side, his blue eyes watching her, waiting for her to give herself away. Well, she would not give him the satisfaction.

'Yes,' he said, suddenly serious. 'Times of war, times of bereavement and loss, times when the situation of the poor breaks one's heart and one is left fuming at the callousness of a society that lets them suffer. It is thinking of such things that demand solemnity.'

'You evidently think very strongly on that subject.'

'Yes. Don't you? Or perhaps you have never had to think about it.'

He was fishing, she decided. 'Of course I think about it and I wish I could help them, but it is not in my power.'

'No, you are *only* Miss Fanny Draper, isn't that what you told me?'

'Yes, because that is my name.'

'My dear girl, I am not disputing it.' He waited for her reaction, an angry accusation of impertinence, not only for the way he had addressed her, but for doubting her honesty. For a fleeting second he saw it in her eyes and then it was gone.

She wanted to riposte, but decided against it; any show of hauteur might make him suspicious of the truth. It would be better to remain silent. The coach rattled on through a countryside uniformly wet and uninviting. The trees dripped, the roads were covered in mud, the potholes filled with water. There was nothing worth looking at. The inside of the coach was gloomy and she could not see her fellow travellers clearly. She had had hardly any sleep the night before and the swaying of the vehicle was soporific, making her eyes droop. She allowed herself to doze.

She awoke with a start when they stopped to change the horses again. It was like that all the way to Northampton; wake, nod, sleep, but at least they had left London and her stepfather far behind them. She wondered what Lord Malvers would think of her if he knew the truth. He might be disgusted. On the other hand, he might treat her flight as a missish prank and be ready to turn her in. He might also think that, just because she was travelling incognito on a public coach without an escort, he could take liberties. Not that he had tried; so far he had behaved impeccably, but they had a long way to go and anything could happen. Could she keep up this masquerade right to the end? She had to, so much depended on it.

They arrived at Northampton at six o'clock, an hour and a half behind schedule. Alex opened the door and jumped down, turning to help Emma, who was endeavouring to retie the ribbons of her bonnet. 'There might be time for something to eat and drink, before we go on,' he said. 'Though we must make haste. I'm told we are only to be allowed a quarter of an hour.'

They had barely seen to their comfort and ordered tea and bread and butter, the only thing available in the limited time, when they were recalled to their seats. Alex, who had given in to her insistence that she pay for it, wrapped the uneaten food in a napkin and followed them out to the coach. As soon as they were on the way again, he produced the package and offered it to the girls.

'How clever of you to think of that,' Emma said, helping herself to a slice of bread and butter. 'I never would.'

'I learned in the army never to abandon food,' he said, glad that her wariness of him had dissipated a little. 'We never knew when our next meal would be. We often had to eat on the march.'

'Surely, as an officer, you were not required to march? Were you not mounted?'

'Some of the time, but I liked to march alongside my men. How could I ask them to walk until they were ready to drop if I did not do the same?'

'I am sure they appreciated that.'

'So they did, miss.' This was said by his servant. 'If the Major could keep going, so could we.'

'It must be exciting, going to war,' Emma said.

'Exciting,' Alex mused. 'I suppose it was sometimes. Sometimes it was terrifying and often just plain boring.'

'Boring?'

'Between battles, when we were waiting for something to happen or when we were on a long march from one encounter with the enemy to the next.'

'What did you do then?'

He laughed. 'Dreamed of home, wondering if those we had left behind were well. We planned our next strategy, cleaned our weapons, talked of armaments and supplies. Some of the men had their women and families with them and that made it easier for them. Those without families amused themselves in other ways: boxing matches, running races, hunting and fishing, playing cards.'

'Gambling is an abomination, the ruin of so many lives.'

'Certainly it can be so, but in moderation it can while away the hours.'

'Oh, it can indeed do that, my lord. Hours and hours, whole days sometimes.' She sounded so bitter, he looked sharply at her. Was that the reason she had fallen on hard times? Her own gambling or someone else's?

'You have experience of that?'

'I… Never mind. Tell me about your men. Where are they now?'

'Scattered to the winds. Some are buried where they fell, others are still serving, gone to America to put down the rebellion there, still more have come home to an England they hardly know. It would not be so bad if the country was grateful, if something was being done to alleviate their distress, but I see little evidence of it.'

'What do you think should be done?'

'Employment is what they need, Miss Draper, so they can look after their families and live in dignity.'

'Is there no employment for them?'

He looked sharply at her. She must have been leading a very sheltered life not to know that unemployment was one of the main issues of the day. And wasn't she off to take a job herself? He'd lay odds she had never worked before. 'Not enough,' he said. 'And those whose work is on the land are doubly to be pitied considering it has hardly stopped raining all year. There will be little enough grain this harvest time and a poor harvest means poor wages.'

'Is it the same in the towns?'

'Nearly as bad. The price of bread will soar. If nothing is done, I fear for the working man.' Was she simply making conversation, getting him to talk, or did she really not know how things were? A gentlewoman driven to be a companion almost certainly would. It would have been part of the argument for taking up such a post.

'And woman,' Rose put in.

He turned towards her. 'Yes, indeed, Miss Turner. Do you have employment? Are you to be a companion too?'

'No, my lord. I am going home to help my mother.'

'Is your home in the Lakes?'

'No my lord. It is in Chelmsford.'

'Chelmsford—then what are you doing on a coach going to Manchester?'

'Keeping Miss Draper company.'

'And who will keep you company when you have to leave her?'

'Oh, I shall not need company, my lord. I do not mind travelling alone.'

That gave him food for thought and for a moment he lapsed into silence. If their stations were equal, why did one girl need company and the other not? The answer was, of course, that they were not equal in rank at all. Miss Draper, if that were really her name, was far superior. Was one maid to the other? Then why were they dressed alike? His curiosity deepened.

Emma knew Rose had made a blunder. He was becoming inquisitive and there was a self-satisfied smirk on the face of his man. She did not know what to say to allay his suspicions. She really should not have allowed herself to become involved in conversation with him. What could she say to put him off? Perhaps it would be better not to say anything at all. She had been sitting forward but now, as they stopped for yet another change of horses, she leaned back in her seat and shut her eyes. Perhaps he would take the hint.

Already they had been on the road for twelve hours and there were still many more miles to go before they reached Leicester where, she had been assured, they would be able to put up for the night. Perhaps they would part there; he might go on tonight without stopping or perhaps take a different coach in the morning. But thinking about that made her suddenly aware that she had been glad of his presence, of the way he had gallantly looked after them. He could command instant service at the inns and thought nothing of berating the horse-keeper on the standard of his horses; the very fact that he appeared to be escorting her made her feel more secure.

The latest horses were fresh and the rain had stopped so they made up a little of the lost time. It was ten o'clock and she was dog-tired when the coach pulled into the yard of the Three Crowns in Leicester. Lord Malvers helped her out and took her elbow to guide her into the inn, leaving Joe and Rose to follow. In no time at all his lordship had arranged for a room for her and went with her to inspect it.

'The bed linen is not clean,' he told the innkeeper's wife, who had personally shown them up to the room. 'Change it at once. And replace the water in that ewer. It is covered in scum. We will dine downstairs while you see to it.'

The woman bobbed a curtsy. 'At once, my lord.'

Having laid down his orders, he turned to Emma. 'Come, Miss Draper.'

A little bemused, Emma followed him downstairs, to find Joe and Rose cosily ensconced in the parlour close to the fire where he was regaling her with a gory story of war in Spain.

His lordship ordered a meal, but Emma was almost too tired to eat. Travelling by public coach was very different from going in their own carriage and taking their time about it, very different from going post chaise, though they hadn't done that since her father died. She suspected her stepfather was not nearly as wealthy as he liked people to believe. And he could not touch her inheritance. Of course! That was it, that was why he was insisting on her marrying Lord Bentwater. They had done a deal over her fortune. How hard would they try to find her? If they caught up with her before she reached Mrs Summers, what would her present escort do? Hand her over, or help her? She was too tired to worry about it, too tired to take part in the conversation.

'Miss Draper, I am keeping you from your bed.'

'What? Oh, I am sorry, my lord. What were you saying?'

'It is of no consequence. Come, I'll escort you to your room. You need to sleep and we have an early start in the morning.'

She did not argue, but stood up and followed him from the room, Rose bringing up the rear. At the door of the room she turned to thank him, but he brushed her thanks aside. 'Glad to be of service,' he said. 'I am just along the passage. If you need anything, send Miss Turner to wake me. I'll be with you in an instant.' He bowed and strode away.

The two girls entered the room and shut the door. The bed linen had been changed and there was fresh water in the ewer and the layer of dust she had noticed earlier had gone. Her bag and Rose's bundle were on a chest below the window.

Emma sank on to the bed, while Rose unpacked their night things. 'What do you make of him, Rose?'

'I don't know, my lady. In my book, men don't do favours for nothing and we've landed ourselves very much in his debt. What is he going to ask in return?'

'Perhaps he doesn't want anything. Perhaps he is simply a knight errant.'

Rose's reply was a sniff of disbelief.

'Do you think he believes our story?'

'Does it matter what he believes?' She crossed the room with Emma's nightgown and laid it on the bed.

Emma began unbuttoning her dress. 'I found myself wondering what he would do if Sir George were to catch up with us before we reached our destination. Should I tell him the truth and throw myself on his mercy?'

'No, my lady. You don't know anything about him. He might take advantage. Just think, he is a soldier, used to soldier's ways…'

'But I'm sure he's an officer and a gentleman.'

'You only have his word for that. Does a gentleman travel with his servant and sit at the same table?'

'I am travelling with you in the same manner.'

'That's different.'

'How different?'

'You are not pretending to be a titled lady. Take my word for it, he thinks you are a gentlewoman fallen on hard times and as such ripe for a little sport.'

'Rose, I refuse to believe that.'

Rose shrugged and helped Emma out of her clothes and slipped her nightdress over her head. 'Why did he suggest sending me to fetch him in the middle of the night, then?'

She hadn't thought of that. 'Oh, Rose, I would never have taken that as an invitation. How glad I am that you came with me.'

She went over to the door and turned the key in the lock and then dragged a chair against it for good measure. There was only one bed and they got into it together. Two minutes later they were both asleep.

Alex prepared for bed in a thoughtful mood. The more he saw of Miss Fanny Draper, the more he was convinced she was not what she seemed. She had started out being prickly as a hedgehog, determined to be independent, but that had lasted only until they reached the Peahen in St Albans. Who was she? Was she, as Joe insisted, a runaway? He had no idea how old she was, but she was not a school-girl, so what was she running from? A husband? He hadn't seen a wedding band. The law? If so, what had she done? Was she simply an intrepid traveller, telling the truth, or a clever trickster, manipulating him into feeling sorry for her in order to part him from his money? If that turned out to be the case, she would find he was not such easy game as she imagined. It was a pity because she was too lovely to be a criminal and when she looked at him with those huge violet eyes, he found himself softening. Damn the woman! He thought he knew women in all their changing moods, had met enough of them in his time, but this one had him foxed.

Chapter Three

Emma woke when she heard someone rattling the door knob. She sat up, thankful that she had been warned by Rose and locked the door. She shook her sleeping maid. 'Rose, there's someone outside the door.'

Rose stirred and yawned and then, realising where she was, jumped out of bed, embarrassed to find herself in bed with her mistress, something that had not happened since Emma was small and needed comforting after a nightmare.

'Miss Draper, Miss Turner, it is time to rise. The coach leaves in less than an hour.' It was the innkeeper's wife.

Emma gave a sigh of relief and scrambled from the bed where she had been sitting with her knees up and the covers drawn right up to her chin. 'We will be down directly.'

They washed and dressed, packed their few things and went down to breakfast. Another day of travelling had begun. But before they left they had to pay for a night's board and lodging. It cost them fourteen shillings each and this time there was no Lord Malvers to offer to pay. Not that she would have allowed it if he had. She was already too beholden to him for her own peace of mind, especially after Rose's warning the night before.

'Do you think he has overslept or gone on a different coach?' Emma asked Rose when he did not put in an appearance at the breakfast table.

Rose shrugged. 'Does it matter?'

'Not at all. I am sure we can manage perfectly well without him.'
But she found herself looking for him as they walked out to the coach,
already being loaded. It was not the coach they had arrived in; that
had gone on the night before with those passengers who preferred
reaching their destination to sleeping in a strange bed. This one had
left London the morning before. She saw Viscount Malvers inspecting the horses and harness and talking to the coachman. Was he
always that particular? she wondered.

He doffed his hat when he saw them. 'Good morning, Miss Draper,
Miss Turner. It is a much finer day today and we should make good
time.' He took their baggage from them and handed it to Joe to put in
the boot, then he held the door for them. 'In you go, we'll be off in
two minutes.'

Emma's spirits rose at the sight of him. Rose was adequate as a travelling companion, but it was comforting to know there was a gentleman
in the background ready and willing to smooth their journey. Rose had
advised caution and she would be cautious but that did not mean she
would disdain his assistance. 'Good morning, my lord,' she said, as he
put his hand under her elbow to help her up. It was the second time he
had done that and his grip was firm without being domineering, just the
sort of gesture a gentleman would make to a lady. But she wasn't a lady;
at least, for the purposes of this journey she wasn't. Had he realised the
truth? Was that why he was being so helpful, expecting a reward for his
efforts? But wasn't that just what Rose had warned her about? She was
so concerned with her inner debate, she hardly noticed that everyone else
had taken their seats and they were moving out of the yard.

She had not been able to see anything of Leicester the night before,
but in daylight she noticed that the town was a busy one. Carts and
drays were making their way to market and they made slow progress
through the congestion. The buildings were a mixture of very old and
very new: good brick-built houses interspersed with dilapidated
timbered buildings, whose upper storeys projected into the roadway,
forcing high vehicles like the coach into the middle of the road.

'Leicester is a very old town,' he said as an opening gambit, noticing she was leaning forward to see out of the window. She was near enough for their knees to be almost touching; when he leaned forward too, her bonnet was only inches from his face. It was a huge bonnet, long out of fashion, but then she was not fashionably dressed at all. The cloak, though clean, was worn and she was wearing the same striped dress she had worn the day before. He supposed it was hardly surprising when all the luggage she appeared to have was one quite small carpet bag. He was no expert on the subject, but he would have expected a lady, even lady's companion going to a new position, to take at least one trunk and a hatbox as well as an overnight bag.

'Yes,' she said, leaning back a little. He had been too close for comfort, she could see every line of his face in detail, his healthy complexion, his searching blue eyes that seemed to be taking in everything about her, seeing past the surface to the person she was beneath the skin. 'I believe the Romans were here.'

'Yes. It was central to the Roman network of roads, on the crossroads from north to south and east to west. It still is today. It was invaded by the Danes, and later the Normans came and built the castle. And did you know Richard III's body was buried here after he died at the Battle of Bosworth, though it was removed later and thrown in the river?'

'No, I didn't. How dreadful. But how do you know all this?'

'I like to learn a little of the history of places I visit. It is a subject that has interested me ever since I found myself besieging ancient towns in the Peninsula. I hate to see the destruction of beautiful things.' He paused and added softly, 'Beauty should be preserved, do you not think?'

'Yes, I do.' She had intended to be short with him, to let him know she did not want to converse, but how could she be so uncivil? And he was an interesting man to listen to. 'What else have you discovered?'

'Lady Jane Grey came from here. You remember she was Queen for nine days?'

'Yes, poor thing.'

'Why do you say that?'

'She was manipulated by the men around her.' She sighed. 'But there is nothing new in that. Why do men think they have the God-given right to order the lives of women, my lord?'

It was said with such feeling, he knew something had happened, something to do with a man. Was she fleeing from a man? Father, husband or lover? His curiosity deepened. 'It has always been the way of the world,' he said carefully. 'I suppose it is because they are the weaker sex.'

'And who says that? Men!' The venom was there. 'Oh, I know we are physically weaker, we cannot fight, nor carry heavy weights, but that is not everything. Women can be as learned and determined as men.'

His smile was a little lop-sided. 'Oh, yes, indeed. Are you a determined woman, Miss Draper?'

'I think so.'

'Then I wonder how you will go on as a lady's companion. I cannot see the role suiting you.'

'Why not?' she demanded.

'Determination, independence, more than your share of looks. Do you think your employer will like those traits? The role, I believe, requires you to be self-effacing and to remain in the background.'

How did they get from discussing the history of Leicester to this personal exchange which was making her very uncomfortable? For the first time since her flight she began to wonder about her future, which was in the hands of her mother's friend. If Mrs Summers rejected her, refused to harbour her, what would she do? Rose would leave her soon to go back to her own mother and she would be without any kind of support. What use determination and independence then? 'We shall have to wait and see,' she said.

'And if you do not suit?'

'Then I shall have to find something else.'

'Do you know the Lake District, Miss Draper?'

'No, I have never visited it.'

'If you need assistance, I shall be happy to provide it.'

She laughed, slightly bitterly. 'I thought you said you had no use for a lady's companion.'

'So I did, but perhaps I can help in other ways.'

'And I say again: I cannot be bought.'

It was the most dreadful put-down and she was sorry for it almost immediately, but he had leaned back in his seat and tipped his hat over his eyes, effectively ending the conversation. She looked across at his servant, who was grinning with unconcealed amusement. 'I'd call that a draw,' he murmured.

She gave him one of her Lady Emma looks of disapproval and he hastily turned his attention to the scene outside his side of the coach.

She sat back, turning to look out of the window to hide her tears. She was such a noddicock, quarrelling with his lordship when perhaps he was only trying to be helpful. She could not afford to make enemies. Oh, how she wished she was more conversant with the ways of the world. She wanted to apologise, but his demeanour told her clearly enough he had done with her. And who could blame him?

He was not so much done with her as battling with his inner self. Why was he putting himself out for a chit who seemed to enjoy arguing with him? He was not used to being argued with. Just because he had offered her and her companion their inside seats did not mean he had to look after them thence forward, did it? He was becoming soft. But he had done no more than courtesy demanded, he answered himself, and he would make sure she knew that was all it was. On the other hand, he could see any number of hazardous situations that might befall a couple of unaccompanied women and he did not think they would know how to deal with them. Only a rakeshame would leave them to their own devices.

They were out in the country now and making a good speed between farmland, meadow and the occasional stand of trees. Good hunting country, Emma knew. Her stepfather came up for two weeks every year. Thinking of him inevitably turned her thoughts to her mother. How was she managing? Had Sir George bullied her into revealing where she had gone? If so, how far behind her was he?

They stopped for the first change of horses, but no one left their seats. On they went and without conversation she was left to meditate and that did not help her at all. She worried about her mother, she worried that her stepfather and that odious Lord Bentwater were hot on their heels, she worried about her reception when they reached Mrs Summers, she worried about Rose making the return journey all on her own. Had she done the right thing? If she had stayed in London, could she have found another way out of her predicament? Had she jumped from the frying pan into the fire? Her thoughts went round and round and led her nowhere. They were pulling into the inn at Loughborough before she realised how far they had come.

Pulling herself together with an effort, she allowed Lord Malvers to hand her down and then went ahead of him into the inn, where she escaped to the ladies' room until it was time to return to the coach.

Kegworth, Derby, Ashbourne and Macclesfield went past in a similar manner and because he was not going to risk another put-down, she learned nothing of the history of these places. The silence would have been unbearable if his lordship's servant and Rose had not been carrying on a lively conversation to which Lord Malvers contributed now and again. He was not angry with Rose, and yet it was Rose's advice which had prompted her to speak so sharply. She was beginning to question the maid's wisdom. Perhaps the servant classes expected men to behave badly, but that did not mean they were all like that, and Rose evidently did not include Joe Bland in her assessment.

'What time are we expected in Manchester, my lord?' she ventured at last.

He smiled. He had guessed she was stubborn, but he had not expected her silence to last so long. What had made her like that? What was there in her past that made her so wary of him? He had done her no harm, meant no harm, certainly had no designs on her and was only trying to be helpful in the way he would help a motherless kitten. Except she was no kitten, she had sharp claws. 'If we make good time, it will be just after one, ma'am,' he answered. 'We will have a little wait there, I think, time for a proper meal and a rest before we have to go on.'

'Thank you, my lord.'

'I shall be glad to take a walk,' Rose said. 'I am stiff as a board with sitting so long.'

'Do not go without an escort, Miss Turner,' Alex advised. 'There is a great deal of unrest in the town due to men being out of work and their demand for enfranchisement. The spinners and weavers are particularly up in arms.'

'Why should they bother us?' Emma asked. 'We are not in dispute with them and have nothing they might want.'

'Perhaps not,' he said, smiling at her naïveté. Her straight back and top-lofty manner was enough to brand her one of the oppressors. 'But there is no reason to take risks, is there? If you wish to take a walk, please allow me to accompany you.' He held up his hand as if to ward off a blow. 'And do not take offence at that, madam. If you do not care for my company, I will walk along behind.'

'Do not be so touchy, my lord.' She paused to smile at him and he was taken aback by its radiance. It was like the sun coming out after a storm. 'How am I to learn anything of the place if my history teacher is not by my side to inform me?'

They stopped frequently to change the horses and once they left the coach for refreshment, which Emma would not allow his lordship to pay for, though she feared she might have affronted him by doing so. He sat silently contemplating the scenery the rest of the way to Manchester.

From a distance, all Emma could make of it were chimneys belching smoke, which seemed to hang over the whole place. And when they entered the town, they found themselves enveloped in it. The rain may have made the countryside fresher and greener, but all it had done in the town was deposit a muddy layer of soot everywhere. The roads were narrow and the buildings a mixture of enormous mills with rows and rows of dirty windows, manufactories and warehouses that dwarfed the lodging houses and tiny hovels, which seemed to have been put in haphazardly wherever there was space among them. It was the most dismal place she had ever been in. No wonder the people were discontented.

'A true industrial town,' he said, noticing her expression of distaste. 'An overgrown village, put together at the dictates of commerce.'

'How can they endure it?'

'For money, Miss Draper. The cotton industry generates great wealth for some and the workers must go where the work is.'

She fell silent as the coach took them into the heart of the town, through a very narrow lane lined with shops and tenements, and deposited them in the yard of a busy inn. This was the end of the line as far as that particular coach company was concerned and passengers were obliged to make new arrangements to convey them further north. While Joe Bland fetched their luggage, Alex escorted them into the inn and ordered a meal for all four.

'My lord,' she protested, 'you must not feel you are responsible for us, you know.'

'Someone has to be.'

'On the contrary, we set out alone and expected to make our own way. We are not helpless.'

'No?' he queried. 'Two ladies venturing on such a long journey without an escort must either be very reckless or very desperate.'

'Why do you say that?' she demanded, suddenly afraid that he had somehow divined the truth about her situation. 'We are not ladies, certainly not the helpless sort that cannot stir a finger without a man in attendance. And what makes you think we are desperate, I cannot think.'

'You wish me to withdraw?' It was said mildly, but she detected the annoyance behind the question. If she said yes, he would go and she did not want him to go. But she did wonder if she dare risk remaining under his protection, because that was what it amounted to.

'Oh, Fanny, do not be so fussy,' Rose said suddenly. 'If the gentleman wishes to order for us, why not let him?'

Emma looked sharply at her maid, who would never have dared speak to her like that while they were in London, but circumstances were very different now. Besides, Rose was right. 'I am not disdaining his offer,' she said. 'I was simply pointing out we should not take it for granted.' She turned to Alex. 'My lord, we will sit with you, but we pay our own way, if you please.'

He shrugged. 'As you wish. What would you like me to order for you?'

'I am not very hungry. The swaying of the coach has made me feel a little sick.'

'I am sorry to hear that,' he said, not believing a word of it. 'Would you like me to ask the landlord to find you a room so that you may lie down and recover?'

'No, no. I am only a little queasy in the stomach.' She spoke sharply, knowing that a room would be more than she could afford and she certainly would not let him pay for a room. It would be the height of folly. 'I will have a cup of tea and some bread and butter.'

She sat over her meagre repast, looking with envy at the pork chops, the chicken legs and ham the others were consuming. When they had finished, Alex said, 'The coach for Kendal leaves at half past four, so we have two hours to while away.'

'Are there any parks, my lord? I do not think walking these filthy streets will be at all pleasant.'

He went off to consult the innkeeper. 'There are no parks,' he said when he returned. 'You need to go into the countryside to find anything green. However, I have bespoken a light carriage to convey us there. It will only take us a few minutes and we will be able to walk in clean air and refresh ourselves for the next part of our journey.'

Emma was about to refuse, but the offer was too tempting. She was used to the dirt and fog of London, but this was a hundred times worse. Already the smoky, malodorous atmosphere was clogging her lungs. She smiled. 'Thank you, my lord.'

Alex drove the carriage himself and steered it expertly through the narrow streets, while Emma looked about her. The whole place seemed to consist of huge mills, pouring more smoke into an atmosphere already laden with it, and great warehouses with their porticoed fronts. There were some shops and dozens of hotels and inns. How could people bear to live here? she thought, watching a band of fustian-clad workmen and factory girls in dingy dresses and dark shawls, all speckled with flakes of cotton. Those flakes seemed to hang in the air, which was too heavy to carry them away. The smells that assailed her nostrils made her choke and put her handkerchief to her face.

'It is bad,' he said. 'But we shall soon be out of it.'

'How can people bear to live like this?'

'They have no choice when cotton is king,' he said. 'The mills produce the wealth and for that they need workers, thousands of them. And they must live near their work. The trouble is that the mill masters as a general rule do not think it is incumbent on them to do anything about how their workers live beyond putting up rows and rows of back-to-back hovels.'

'And not a blade of grass to be seen. No wonder there is unrest.'

'My sentiments exactly, Miss Draper.'

They left the mean streets behind and were travelling along an avenue of grand houses, each with its own garden. Here the mill owners had decamped to get away from the misery they had helped to create. And a few minutes later they crossed the river and were in the open country. Here were fields and meadows and copses of trees. They hitched the horse to a tree branch and set out on a well-worn path.

Emma's spirits lifted almost immediately. She and Alex walked side by side, leaving Rose and Joe to follow. 'This is heaven,' she said, throwing back her cloak and turning her face up to the sun. 'We have seen nothing but rain since leaving London, I had forgot it is meant to be nearly summer time.'

He turned to look at her as she arched her neck upwards. It was a long smooth neck, rising from the collar of the striped dress. He felt an almost irresistible urge to lower his head to kiss her throat and was shocked by the sensations that aroused in him. He raised his eyes to her face. It was as smooth and unblemished as her throat. Her cheeks, which had been pale, were rosier now, her lips, slightly parted, revealed perfect teeth. Her eyes were shut against the bright light and her long lashes lay on her cheeks. My God, she was beautiful! He wanted to pull her into his arms to kiss her, but she was not the sort of woman you could do that to, not suddenly and for no reason. What in heaven's name was she doing here, wandering among the buttercups and daisies, miles from home? Who was she?

Tilting her head upwards, Emma had not been looking where she was going and her foot stumbled into a hole. She cried out as she began to fall, putting out her hands to save herself, only to find herself clasped in his arms. It had the most extraordinary effect on her. She could feel the warmth of his body spread from him to her and course down through her body until it reached her groin and there it was held in a pool of what could only be desire. It was an entirely new sensation for her and her heart began to pound and she found herself leaning into him, as if she had no will of her own to break away or even stand unaided. And it had nothing to do with the stumble.

He felt it too, this strange alchemy, and he supposed it had been there from the start of this strange journey. It was why he was determined to escort her, even when she made it plain she did not want an escort. It wasn't only the mystery surrounding her—perhaps there was no mystery and she was exactly what she said she was—it was something about the girl herself. Her beauty, her courage and independence, all the attributes he had said would make her unfit to be a lady's companion, were the very things that drew him to her.

He leaned back, but did not release her. 'Are you hurt?' His eyes searched hers, looking for answers.

'No, I do not think so. It was the suddenness of it, that's all.' She made to step away from him, but he still held her.

Suddenness, his head echoed. Oh, it had been sudden, no doubt of it, but not in the way she meant. Surely he had not been such a fool as to be taken in by a beautiful stranger, someone he knew nothing about? For all he knew she might be a criminal, a thieving maid running away with her mistress's jewels, a confidence trickster, out to trap him. She could be another Constance. He looked behind him; Joe and Miss Turner were nowhere in sight. They were alone. 'Are you sure you are not hurt? Shall you try and test that foot?'

He held her while she put the foot to the ground and winced. 'I must have twisted it.'

He put her arm about his shoulder so that he could span her waist and help her hop along to a boulder beside the path. He lowered her on to it. 'Let me see. I am used to looking after injuries.'

'Soldiers' injuries, my lord,' she said, watching him kneel at her feet and pick up her foot. 'I am not hurt, truly I am not. I shall be able to walk by and by.'

He took her ankle in his hand and she felt again that strange trickling of desire. His gentle probing produced, not pain, but the most unutterable pleasure. She had an urge to remove his hat and pull her fingers through his hair, throw herself back into his arms where she felt warm and protected. None of the beaux who had courted her in her society days had made her feel anything like this. It was shocking and she ought to be ashamed of herself. But shame was not what she felt at all. Oh, if only they had met in London before Sir George tried to force her to marry Lord Bentwater, things might have been very different. But would they? He did not find the London scene to his taste and had decried marriage, and added to that he was a gambler. She must remember that and harden her heart.

'My lord,' she protested.

'I don't think there is any serious damage,' he said, putting her foot back on the ground beside the other. 'Shall I carry you back to the carriage?'

'Certainly not!' She had recovered her wits. 'I am perfectly able to walk.' To prove it she stood up and limped away from him, away from the terrible temptation to pour all her troubles into his receptive ear and fling herself on his mercy, not to mention have his arms about her again.

He smiled ruefully and got to his feet to follow her; the toplofty lady was once more to the fore. And now he was sure she was a lady. Her shoes had been made of the finest leather and her stockings were of silk and the glimpse he had had of the hem of a fine lawn petticoat trimmed with lace proclaimed wealth that did not accord with the cotton dress and the shabby cloak and bonnet. He would stick to her like glue until he solved the mystery.

He put his hand under her elbow. 'Lean on me, it will help you along.'

She complied because it made walking easier. It was only then as they faced about to go back the way they had come that she realised her chaperon had disappeared. 'Where is Rose?'

'Wherever she is, I'll wager Joe Bland is not far away,' he said.

'Oh, but we cannot go back without them.'

'Joe knows the time. They will join us directly.'

'Are you not concerned?'

'Why should I be?'

'They are unchaperoned.'

He laughed. 'My dear Miss Draper, so are we.'

'Yes, but…'

'It is their business, Miss Draper. I would not dream of interfering.'

'A fine employer *you* are.'

'No more than you.'

She remembered her circumstances just in time. 'I am not Rose's employer, my lord. We are friends, and it is as a friend I am concerned.'

'Because if Joe Bland is anything like his master…'

'I never said that.'

'No, but you were thinking it.'

'I was not! I would have fallen if you had not caught me.'

So, she knew what he meant. He smiled. 'No need to worry. Here they are.'

Joe and Rose were strolling back in animated conversation. It did not look as though they talked to each other in riddles, as she and Viscount Malvers seemed to do all the time. Things half-said, things implied, touches disguised as accidents, all contributing to a feeling of frustration, fear and annoyance.

'Come, we must be going back or we shall miss the coach,' Alex said, as they drew near.

They climbed in and this time Alex let Joe drive and he sat with the ladies. It was not a very large conveyance and they were obliged to sit very close together. Emma could feel Alex's breeches-clad thigh against her skirt, which was too thin to resist the pressure. If she was not careful, she would explode, she thought, and could only control her shaking by hanging on to the side and looking out at the countryside, which soon changed to the townscape of squalid houses and mills belching smoke and terrible smells she was in no hurry to define.

The carriage was being loaded as they arrived and in no time at all the short interlude was over and they were once more on the open road, travelling northwards. But the relationship between the four of them had subtly changed. They were no longer strangers and that would probably make his lordship more likely to quiz her. She must be very careful. He might very well be a friend of Sir George Tasker; he would certainly know him by name and her masquerade must be maintained.

Chapter Four

The journey from Manchester to Kendal would have been far more enjoyable, passing as it did through pleasant hilly country dotted with grazing sheep on hills alive with purple heather, if Emma had not been so busy worrying about her finances. When she had paid their dues at the inn and bought two inside tickets to Kendal she was left with less than eight guineas of the twenty her mother had given her, and she would have to give seven to Rose for her return journey. It brought home to her the precariousness of her position. Everything depended on Mrs Summers, a lady she did not remember ever having met. She could not arrive on her doorstep penniless and would have to find a jeweller in Kendal and pawn her pearls before she ventured a step further.

'You are quiet, Miss Draper,' Alex murmured. 'Do you perhaps have something weighing on your mind?'

Startled out of her reverie, she looked across at him, wondering what lay behind the question. 'Nothing of any significance, my lord. I was just wondering what my new employment might be like.'

'Is it a situation you have not experienced before?'

She paused and decided it would do no harm for him to think she was a gentlewoman fallen on hard times. She would test him with half a secret. 'No. And your comments about my unsuitability have set me thinking.'

'Oh, dear, I wish I had never spoken. I did not mean to undermine your confidence. Of course, you will do the job admirably and your new mistress will soon not be able to part with you. But why do you have to do it at all?'

'I have to earn my bread, my lord. Everyone does, surely? Even you must work to make your estate profitable in order to maintain your family and those who work for you. And your man must work and Rose must work. Where's the difference?'

'You are right of course. But for you…' No, he would not suggest she was a lady who should never be required to be anything other than decorative. 'Is there no other way? Surely there must be a young man in the background, one able to look after you?'

'You mean someone to take pity on me and marry me? How condescending! Do you think I would agree to marry someone simply because he feels sorry for me? I have my pride, Lord Malvers.'

'No doubt of that,' he agreed wryly. 'But what I meant was that you are beautiful enough to take your pick.'

'I am flattered you think that, my lord, but a man who married simply because his bride was beautiful would probably live to regret it. *You* would surely not be so foolish?'

He laughed. 'No, my dear, I would *not* be so foolish.'

'There you are, then! For once we are in agreement.'

There seemed to be no answer to that and he realised she was not going to tell him the whole truth, though he was beginning to believe she was being forced into taking employment. But why so far from London? Was that her home, or had she been simply passing through when he saw her at the Swan with Two Necks? What was driving her? He mused on the pros and cons of that as the horses cantered on.

When they stopped for supper at Preston, he settled the ladies at a table in the dining room and then took Joe on one side, ostensibly to discuss with him what to order. 'Have you learned anything from Miss Turner?'

'Not a thing. She's loyal, I'll give her that. I do know she's anxious to see Miss Draper safely at her destination so that she can return to her mother. Apparently Mrs Turner is expecting her eighth any day now, and Rose has to go home to take over the household while she is laid up.'

'And yet she consents to come all this way with Miss Draper. Is she being well paid for her trouble?'

'Don't think so. From what I gather, Miss Draper don't have a feather to fly with.'

'I want you to do something for me, Joe. When we reach Kendal, I want you to see Miss Turner safely home. I fancy it will set Miss Draper's mind at rest to know her friend has an escort. And while you are down south, go back to London and put your ear to the ground…'

'What am I to be listening for?'

'Rumours of runaways, absconding wives or missing heiresses, servants running off with the family silver…'

'I don't reckon they've done that. They ain't got two groats to rub together atween the pair on 'em.'

'No,' he said, remembering that glimpse of petticoats. If a servant stole her mistress's clothes, she would hardly don the underwear and continue to wear her own shabby gown over them. 'But you know what I mean.'

'And what will you be a-doin', while I'm doin' that, Major, if I may make so bold as to ask?'

'Working on Miss Fanny Draper. If that is her name, which I doubt. Between us we'll crack this mystery.'

Joe laughed and tapped his nose.

'And don't you be so insolent, man. Remember who pays your wages.' If he meant to sound severe, he did not succeed and, laughing, Joe went back to the ladies, who were whispering together, as he and his master had been. Alex, following him, noticed it too and wondered what they were saying that needed such intense concentration.

'Ladies,' he said, affecting joviality. 'Do you wish to rack up here for the night or go on? I only ask because it will be necessary to arrange for a room if you decide to stay.'

'No, we go on,' Emma said without hesitation. 'The sooner we reach our destination, the better. Do you stay?'

He wondered whether that would please or disappoint her. 'I am no less anxious than you to reach my destination.'

He stopped speaking as a waiter brought them food and set it on the table.

'There is so much of it,' Emma said, eyeing the dishes with a mixture of dismay and longing.

'There are four of us, Miss Draper, and Joe always has a prodigious appetite and I must confess to being peckish. Surely you are not going to say you are not hungry? It is some time since we ate last and since then we have had a walk in the fresh air and a long journey.' He paused and smiled at her, a gentle smile of understanding. 'Go on, Miss Draper, eat something. It will only be wasted if you do not.'

All Emma could think was that her mother, sheltered as she always had been, could have had no idea of the cost of fares and food in coaching inns when she sent her off on this adventure. 'To please you and stop you nagging, I will take a little,' she said, helping herself to a small pork chop, a few slices of roast chicken and some vegetables from some of the dishes. He poured everyone a glass of wine and, lifting his glass, proposed a toast. 'To life's little journeys,' he said. 'And may they all end happily.'

'Amen,' she said, with feeling, as she raised her glass.

It was growing dusk as they returned to the coach and fully dark before they had been on the road more than half an hour. The food and the wine must have eased her mind as well as her hunger, for Emma found her whole body giving way to weariness and could not keep her eyes open. She put her head back and allowed herself to doze.

He sat and watched her in the gathering gloom relieved only by the light from the lantern attached to the outside of the coach. She looked vulnerable like that, her head lolling, her bonnet awry and her hair coming down from its pins. It occurred to him he had never seen her without that monstrous bonnet and had no idea what her hair was like. What little of it that peeped from beneath the hat seemed to be dark; certainly her eyebrows were. Unaccountably he was filled with tenderness for her, a devout wish to protect her from harm, which did battle with his determination to steer clear of allowing any woman into his heart. Could he turn his back on her when they reached Kendal and forget he had ever met her?

What else could he do? She would never take money from him and he would not insult her by offering it. It was strange that he should think that now, whatever he had suspected at the beginning of this journey. What had made him change his mind? Her frailty? No, never that. He laughed inwardly at his own folly. He was anxious to see his ill uncle and he ought to remember that and not worry himself over a woman he had met less than three days before.

Would his aunt know what to do about her? That would mean persuading Miss Draper to go with him. On what pretext? She was so wary of him, so ready to curl herself into a ball and display her prickles like a threatened hedgehog—he would have to be very convincing. And what would his aunt and uncle make of him arriving at a sick bed, with a waif in tow?

He gave a grunt of annoyance at himself. He was turning soft. He was never like that in his soldiering days. Then he knew what he wanted, knew how to get it too, would never have dreamed of listening to a counter-argument when convinced he was in the right. Since he had set off on this journey he had done nothing but argue and try to placate. She was either very naïve or very clever.

She stirred when they pulled into the King's Arms in Lancaster, mainly because it was such a busy place, all hustle and bustle as people went in and out and horses were led out from the stables and hitched to waiting coaches. The lanterns the ostlers and grooms were carrying cast moving shadows across the interior of the coach, waking her. 'Where are we?' she murmured.

'Lancaster,' he answered as Joe and Rose disappeared in the direction of the inn looking for refreshment. 'We are here for fifteen minutes. Do you wish to go inside?'

'No, I don't think I'll bother.'

He moved to sit beside her. 'I'll fetch you something, if you like, a drink or something to eat.'

'No, thank you. What time is it?'

He took his watch from his pocket and leaned across her to consult it by the light of the coach's lantern. 'Eleven o'clock.'

'Have I been asleep all that time?'

'I think so, it's difficult to tell in the dark. You must have been very fatigued to manage it in that uncomfortable position.'

'It has been a very long day.'

'Yes. I have to admire your fortitude, Miss Draper.' And then, apropos of nothing at all, added, 'How is your foot?'

'My foot?' She hoped he had forgotten that stumble and the intimacy of their embrace. 'It was nothing. I have made a full recovery and no damage done.'

'Good. You know, I meant what I said. If your position as a lady's companion does not suit, I will do what I can to help you.'

'Why should you do that, my lord? I am nothing to you. A travelling companion and one that has caused you no end of inconvenience.'

'Inconvenience, certainly not!'

She chuckled. 'Not inconvenient to be soaked to the skin on top of a coach when you could have travelled inside in comfort; not inconvenient to find yourself shepherding a couple of silly women into inns and hotels and making them eat because they are too foolish to think of it themselves; not inconvenient to have to go to the trouble of hiring a carriage because those two same silly women took it into their heads to want to walk in the fresh air. And then to have one of them stumble…'

'Not inconvenient,' he repeated, taking hold of her hand. She did not withdraw it and he was encouraged to go on. 'A privilege and a pleasure. But forgive me, I am curious about the reason for your journey. You have never travelled by public coach before, I'll take an oath on it. That is why I admire your fortitude.'

'I told you: I am going to take up a position as a companion.'

'Hmm,' he murmured. 'As far away from London as possible.'

She was startled. 'What do you mean by that, my lord?'

'I mean I am on to you, my dear.' She shrank from him, but he still had hold of her hand. He lifted it to his lips, looking at her over the top of it, testing her reaction. He could not see clearly, but he could tell by the widening of her eyes and her little gasp of shock that he had hit a nerve. 'What are you afraid of? Are you afraid I will take you back to face your demons? Or that I will ravish you, here in this coach, with everyone coming and going around us?'

'Don't be silly.'

'You were the silly one a moment ago. Now I am to join you. Two silly people holding hands in the dark.' He opened her hand and put his lips to the palm and then brushed them up to her wrist, sending shock waves all up and down her spine and into her belly.

She had to stop this right now. He must think she was either a little innocent whom he could manipulate or a demi-rep of the kind who would pick up a perfect stranger in a coach and go with him for whatever she could get out of him. Before she could stop herself, she had said it aloud.

He laughed. 'Which is it, Miss Draper, the innocent or the demi-rep?'

'I will not dignify that question with an answer.'

'Let us try something else then, something which will undoubtedly tell me the truth.'

His arm was about her and his lips on hers before she had any idea of what he intended. She struggled, but he held her firmly and then she realised she had no more fight left in her. She was tired of struggling, tired of pretending. Her mouth softened and she let the sensations that coursed through her have their way. His kiss, featherlight at first, deepened and she surrendered to a soaring giddiness that made her cling to him and took no heed of time and place, or the possibility that Joe Bland and Rose might return at any moment.

He found himself wanting her, wanting her so badly he could hardly contain himself. And even when he finally lifted his mouth from hers, breathless and unsatisfied, he still did not know the answer to his original question: innocent or demi-rep? Was her response instinctive or the clever strategy of one experienced in the art of dalliance? And her quiet hiss of 'How dare you, sir?' told him no more.

Nor was he to learn any more because Rose and Joe returned and, seeing them sitting side by side, drew their own conclusions and sat opposite them. They were obliged to remain side by side all the way to Kendal, being thrown against each other with every bump in the road, each smouldering with anger and resentment, mixed with a fierce longing for more time. Time they did not have.

It was half past one in the morning when the coach slowed to enter Kendal and turned in under the arch of the Woolpack where it stopped. Alex opened the door, jumped down and turned to hand Emma down. As soon as she was in the yard she marched ahead of him into the inn. After two days she had lost her nervousness about entering such places and seemed able to find her way about them like a seasoned traveller, which was as well, she told herself, because she meant to disdain all attempts to help her. His assistance came at too great a price: the loss of her pride and her dignity, not to mention the surrender of her secret. His quizzing her about the reason for her journey worried her. He had never mentioned Lord Bentwater to her, but she dare not risk him not knowing the gentleman.

If she could have found her way to Mrs Summers there and then, she would have done so, but she could hardly arrive on her doorstep in the early hours of the morning, dishevelled and penniless. She did not fancy sitting in the parlour all night, even if such a thing were allowed, so a bed for the remainder of the night was called for. She went into the parlour and marched purposefully up to the counter and gave the bell on its top a good shake.

'I need a room for the night,' she told the woman who answered its summons. 'For me and my friend.' She nodded at Rose, who had just entered the room behind her.

'Sorry, can't help,' the woman said.

'Then what am I to do? I cannot go on tonight.'

'I can give you a blanket for the settle in here.' The woman pointed to a padded bench against one wall.

'Oh.' She had not been prepared for that; Lord Malvers seemed only to click his fingers and they were given everything they needed. 'I suppose that will have to do.'

'It'll cost you three shillings, three more for breakfast.'

Emma did not dare question what she thought was an exorbitant price for the use of a blanket. 'I shall not require breakfast, thank you.'

She and Rose went to sit down while the woman went to fetch the blanket. There was no sign of Lord Malvers or his man and she wondered if they had continued on with the coach, which might take them nearer Lake Windermere. It had left, together with its new passengers, as soon as the horses had been changed. The feeling that, for the first time since leaving London, she and Rose were entirely alone and dependent on each other was a dismal one.

'Miss Emma,' Rose whispered, forgetting, in her concern, to address her as Fanny. 'The southbound coach is due in at any time and there is room on it for me. If I do not take it, I must wait another twenty-four hours. We have been longer on the road than I thought and I am worried about my mother. I promised her…'

'Oh, Rose!' Could things get any worse? Emma wondered. This was no longer an adventure, it was a nightmare.

'Please, my lady. You knew I wanted to leave at the end of the week and today is Saturday.'

'Is it?' Emma had lost all track of time. She seemed to have been travelling forever. Rose was looking at her expectantly. 'Of course you must go, Rose. After all, you only undertook to bear me company to my destination and here we are. First thing in the morning I will enquire my way to Mrs Summers. Her direction is written on Mama's letter, so she won't be hard to find.' It was said with a cheerfulness that did not deceive Rose.

'Come back with me,' Rose suggested. 'I am sure we can find a corner for you at home until your stepfather relents.'

Emma realised immediately that it would not do. A labourer, a woman big with child, not to mention an army of small children, all sharing a tiny cottage—she could just imagine the confusion her arrival would cause. 'Bless you, Rose, but I shall manage. You have done your duty admirably. And if you ever want a character…'

'Your mother gave me one, my lady.'

The sound of another coach drawing into the yard brought both girls to their feet. Emma took seven guineas from her purse and pressed them into Rose's hand. 'You will need this.'

'It is too much, my lady. I can travel outside.'

'Certainly not. I would give you more, if I could.'

They went out to the yard where Rose paid the coachman for her ticket to Manchester and turned to say goodbye. The two women hugged in tears and then Rose climbed in and was borne away. Emma stumbled back into the inn to find the innkeeper's wife standing looking about her with a blanket and pillow in her hand. 'Thought you'd changed your mind, miss.'

'No, I will spend what remains of the night on your settle. I need to be up betimes anyway.' She took the blanket and pillow and retired to the farthest corner of the settle. Now the coach had gone and no more were expected, the room was quiet. Even the noises in the yard outside ceased as the horses, fed and watered, settled down in their stalls. The landlady turned down the wicks in the oil lamps, leaving the room in semi-darkness.

Emma put the pillow into the wing of the settle, laid her head upon it and shut her eyes. She did not expect to sleep, there was too much on her mind. She would not allow herself to dwell on the fact that she was quite alone in a strange place with only a few shillings in her purse; better to concentrate on something positive, like planning what she would do when daylight came. First, find a pawnbroker and get what she could for her necklace, then enquire the way to the Windermere Road and find Larkrise House. By then it should not be too early for callers. If Mrs Summers refused to see her, or, seeing her, refused to help... No, she must not even contemplate that.

Alex, having seen Joe into the coach ahead of Rose, had done what he had done many times before when on the march; he had bedded down in the straw of the stables. Miss Draper was safe in the inn's parlour, not very comfortable, it was true, but even he could not rustle up a bed when every one in the inn was already occupied. The poor girl was exhausted and would probably doze. He would wait around in the morning to see if she was fetched as she said she would be and, if she was, all well and good; he would go on his way. If not, he would make her tell him the truth, even if he had to shake it out of her. He smiled to himself, remembering that outing at Manchester—had she really twisted her foot, or was that a ruse to have his arms about her? Ruse or not, he had enjoyed it, had felt the slight shudder that had passed through her and knew she had not been indifferent to him. And later, in the coach, when he kissed her... He hadn't meant to, not at first; all he had intended was to offer to help her find employment. Should you kiss somebody simply because they exasperated you? Or was it himself he was exasperated with? Whatever the cause, it had been a heart-stopping experience.

He had kissed a great many women in his time, mostly Spanish beauties who were paid with food or a ride in one of the carts that followed the march. None had touched his heart, he supposed, because he was still thinking of his brother; if Lawrence had ever loved his wife, he had soon become disillusioned. Alex had no illusions to start with. Having survived heartwhole, he had suddenly had his peace of mind shattered. Miss Fanny Draper had breached all his defences with a kiss that was like nothing else that had gone before. He could not explain it. That was what exasperated him.

He lay in the straw, listening to the snuffling of the horses, and tried to analyse it, but was unable to come to any conclusion except he must have fallen head over heels in love for the first and last time in his life and that was something he would not admit, even to himself.

He slept at last and it was the stable lads coming to feed, water and groom the horses who woke him. If they were surprised to see a man with his hair full of wisps of straw and his coat hanging over a post, they did not say so. When he asked, they pointed out a trough where he could wash his face and continued with their work.

Half an hour later, having shaved without a mirror, put a comb through his hair and crammed his hat on top, he was once more reasonably presentable. Taking a deep breath as if he were going into battle, he picked up his portmanteau and made his way through the yard and into the inn. But there was no battle because there was no sign of Miss Draper.

'Oh, she left an hour ago,' he was told by the innkeeper's wife.

He had not expected that and his heart plummeted with disappointment. Had he been weaving fantasies about her when, after all, she had told him nothing but the truth? He smiled wryly at his own folly. 'Did someone meet her?'

The woman shrugged. 'Don't know. There's a deal of coming and going in the yard at any time of day, but always more of a mornin'. People going about their business, don't ye know. She could ha' bin met for all I know.'

Now what should he do? Wash his hands of her and set off for Windermere? He ought not to delay going to his uncle. After all, it must have been a week since the message was first sent to his mother, and though he could not have done anything to hasten his journey on the road, except perhaps travel post chaise, there was no excuse to dawdle now. He was torn between duty and desire and duty won. 'I need to hire a gig,' he said. 'I will return it tomorrow or the next day.'

When he returned the equipage, he would look for her. The town was not large and someone, somewhere, must know where she had gone. Ladies usually knew when other ladies were looking out for a companion. Come to that, his aunt might know.

'I'll ask my husband. I think he will be able to accommodate you.'

'Thank you. I will have breakfast while I wait.'

His mind made up, he ate a hearty breakfast, then, having paid for it, went out to the yard where a small pony and trap awaited him.

Emma stood outside Larkrise House and looked up at its façade. It was a substantial villa set in a small garden on the outskirts of the town. But the garden looked overgrown, with leaves and bushes dripping moisture, the rows of windows looked dusty, the curtains were drawn across and the paint on the front door was peeling. No smoke rose from its chimneys. It had once been a fine solid house, but its neglected air filled her with apprehension. She took a firm hold of her carpet bag and climbed the dirty front steps and used the tarnished brass doorknocker. The sound echoed forlornly.

After several more abortive knocks, she went down the steps and walked round to the back. No one came in answer to her knock there either. The house was uninhabited and had been for some time. Neither she nor her mother had envisaged that possibility—nor that her pearls would be next to worthless.

After persuading a reluctant pawnbroker she had not stolen them and had every right to dispose of them, he had offered her five guineas and a ticket that would allow her to redeem them, provided she brought seven guineas to him within a month. She had pointed out they were worth more than that, but his answer had been unequivocal. 'Paste,' he said. 'Not worth five guineas, not even that if truth be known.'

'But my father bequeathed them to me. He would never…' She

stopped, remembering Sir George's penchant for falling into debt, which had led to him purloining most of her mother's jewellery. Mama had said he knew nothing of the pearls, but supposing he had found them and had them copied? She looked at the man, who stood holding the string up to the light. Then he bit hard on one of them.

'No doubt of it,' he said. 'Do you want to leave them here or not?'

'I will leave them.'

He counted out five guineas into her hand and wrote out a ticket, which she put in her purse with the money. Her last asset was gone and that had proved not so much of an asset as she had hoped. And now here was a further disappointment—more than that, a catastrophe.

Fighting tears, she returned to the road, looking back at the house, wondering if Mrs Summers had died or simply moved house. She wished she had not let Rose go. She wished she had not quarrelled with Viscount Malvers. He was the most annoying, conceited, top-lofty man she had ever met, but he had offered to help her. It was too late now. She would have to go back to the town and take lodgings, while she made up her mind whether there was any alternative to going back to London and throwing herself on the mercy of Sir George. Except, of course, she did not expect him to show any mercy.

'You looking for Mrs Summers, my dear?' The voice, coming as it did from the other side of a hedge, startled her. Then a head popped up. It belonged to a white-haired lady with rosy cheeks and friendly blue eyes.

'Yes, I am.'

'She moved. Two year ago, it would be now, when her brother started ailing. Went to housekeep for him.'

'Oh, I had no idea. Do you know where she lives now?'

'At Waterhead on the road to Ambleside. I think it's called Highhead Hall.'

'How far is it?'

'Eight mile or so that way.' She pointed along the road leading out of the town. 'There's a carrier goes every morning, but not on a Sunday.'

Emma contemplated going back into town and putting up another night in a hotel, but she was already on the road and anxious to reach the end of her journey. Not until then could she make any decisions about what she ought to do. 'Then I must walk. How do I get there?'

'Do you reckon you are up to it? It's a fair step.'

'I think so.' She smiled to show a confidence she did not feel. 'I'm as strong as an ox.'

'Then take this road to Bowness on Lake Windermere. Go through the town and when you come to the lake, turn right and follow the road northwards, keeping the lake on your left. Waterhead is naught but a small village, you will find it easy enough.'

'Thank you, ma'am.'

'Good luck to ye.' The head disappeared.

Emma took a deep breath and picked up her bag, which she had put down while talking, and set her feet firmly upon the road.

It was pleasant walking at first. Although still cloudy, the weather was fine for a change and the countryside verdant; all she had to do was avoid the water-filled potholes. After trudging up one hill and down another, only to have to do it again, her bag began to grow heavy and the pleasure palled. There was little traffic, and most of it seemed to be going in the opposite direction. In any case, she was not sure she dared accept a lift.

She heard the smart trot of a pony behind her, but, almost too weary to turn, trudged on. It slowed down to her walking pace, which made her look up and then she found herself looking into the smiling face of Viscount Malvers.

'Oh, you don't know how pleased I am to see you,' she blurted out, as he stopped and leaned down to offer her his hand.

She put her bag behind the seat, took the hand and climbed up beside him. He flicked the reins and they trotted forward.

'What happened to you?' he asked, when, after several moments' silence, it became apparent she was not going to volunteer the information. 'I thought you were safely with your employer. Did you find you did not suit, after all?'

'Nothing like that. Did you think I was going to take you at your word and ask for your help?'

Seeing her trudging along the road, weariness in every contour of her body, had filled him with pity. He had to remind himself that pity was no basis for marriage and falling in love with a mysterious stranger the height of folly. Nevertheless his heart had jumped at the sight of her. 'It crossed my mind.'

She was beginning to regret greeting him so thankfully, as if he were her saviour. She must remember he had taken advantage of her half-asleep state in the coach and… No, better not remember that; it was too disturbing. She would give him no opportunity to repeat it. 'Then let me relieve your mind. It appears my employer has moved house. I am on my way there.'

'Why did she not meet you as you expected?'

'She was detained, but sent a message where she was to be found.' She was surprised at how easily the lie slipped off her tongue. And none of it would have been necessary if her mother's husband had had an ounce of humanity. She hated him, not only for what he expected of her, but for disposing of her pearls and leaving her with worthless copies. Her hate was so raw, and the business of the pearls so new to her, she was ready to take her fury out on any man who crossed her path, however well intentioned.

'And where is that?'

'Why are you quizzing me?'

'My dear Miss Draper, I am not quizzing you, simply wishing to know whither we are bound.'

'You, I collect, are going to Lake Windermere. I do not remember demanding to know exactly where, as if it was of any business of mine.'

'I merely wanted to know where you wish to be delivered.'

'Like a parcel.'

'No,' he murmured in an undertone. 'Baggage.'

He did not realise she had heard him until she said sharply. 'Well, you may set this baggage down anywhere in Bowness, my lord, preferably near the shores of the lake. I can find my own way from there.'

'As you wish.' So much for his pity. He ought to know better; wounded soldiers, unemployed ex-soldiers, men whose wives had given up the struggle to wait for their return and gone off with someone else, did not want pity. You could not eat pity, you could not sleep on a bed of pity, or warm yourself by pity's fire. It was a lesson he had learned very early on in his career and it had been reinforced since his return. This proud, independent woman was no different from his men. Except she was beautiful and she intrigued him.

He flicked the reins at the mare and clicked his tongue to make her go faster, but was obliged to slow her again while they were passing through a small hamlet, where women and children were out on the streets. Then on they went. Neither spoke. Both looked grimly ahead.

As they approached the little town of Bowness, water could be glimpsed in the distance and some white sails. 'Anywhere in Bowness?' he queried mildly.

'Yes.'

He took her almost to the lakeside and drew the little horse to a halt. She did not wait for him to jump down and come round to help her, but scrambled down and retrieved her bag. 'Thank you, my lord.'

He came swiftly to her side, putting a hand on her arm to detain her. 'Are you sure you know where you are going?'

'Yes.' She tried to sound positive. 'Thank you, my lord, for your help.'

'No doubt we will meet again.'

'Do you think so?' For a moment, her eyes brightened and then the veil dropped over them again and shut him out.

'Yes, I am sure of it. This might be the largest lake in England, but the villages and hamlets around it are not so big one can lose oneself in them.'

'But you, my lord, are expected to go home to Norfolk, are you not?'

'Yes, when I have seen my uncle and aunt.'

'Then goodbye, my lord.'

He watched as she set off down the road. *'Au revoir,'* he murmured to her back. She had disappeared from sight before he remembered he should have apologised for his behaviour in the coach. No wonder she had been so uncommunicative. If he had said he was sorry and asked her forgiveness, she might have told him where she was going; they might have parted as friends. He climbed back into the gig with a heavy sigh, wondering why that was so important.

Emma waited out of sight until she was sure he had gone, then emerged and retraced her steps to the edge of the lake and then turned north. Low in spirits as she was, not only because of her situation, but also at having to say goodbye to Lord Malvers, the pretty scenery made her feel more cheerful. As the road wound round the lake, she glimpsed boats: sailing boats, some with white sails, some with brown, some flying coloured pennants, rowing boats and a ferry taking people across to the other side, where woodland and hills and fleecy clouds were reflected in the water. At the water's edge fishermen sat over their rods. Ducks and diving birds busied themselves searching for food. To her right as she walked, the hills rose above her, where sheep and goats grazed in fields criss-crossed by stone walls. Here and there were magnificent mansions, which commanded views across the lake and were reached by winding paths. She wondered if Mrs Summers lived in such a one.

She came to the head of the lake at last and asked her way to the Ambleside Road. Ten minutes later she was standing outside a large villa built of the local grey stone. A path led from the gate on the road to a central front door, flanked by evenly spaced windows. Her heart sank when she realised the curtains of these windows were drawn, just as those in Kendal had been. The difference, she realised when she had recovered from the shock, was that these windows were clean and the paintwork fresh. But there was a huge black crepe bow tied to the door knocker. It was a house in mourning.

She stood undecided, not wishing to intrude on anyone's grief, not sure of her welcome at such a time. She was exhausted, her feet hurt and her arm ached with carrying her bag and there was no Viscount Malvers to come to her rescue this time. Reluctant to take that knocker in her hand and remembering her poor appearance, she took a deep breath and made her way round to the back of the house and knocked on the kitchen door.

Chapter Five

The woman who came to the door was wearing a black dress and a spotless white apron. Her hair was invisible beneath a starched white cap and her cheeks were rosy from the fire; the cook, Emma guessed. Her blue eyes looked Emma up and down. 'Have you come to help with the funeral tea?'

Emma was about to say no, but changed her mind. 'Yes. What needs to be done?'

The cook held the door open wider. 'Come on in, then. You took your time about getting here.'

'I'm sorry. I only just heard.'

'Only just heard? Where have you been this past week? His lordship's known to everyone hereabouts. Great loss to the community, he is. We'll miss him. Goodness knows what we will do now he's gone.' She stopped talking because Emma had put her bag down and was standing looking about her in a kind of trance. The kitchen was large and old-fashioned. There was a dresser all along one wall full of pots and pans, dishes and plates. A huge fire burned in a wide chimney opposite the dresser, where chains and a spit, a huge kettle, a large iron pot and several trivets bore evidence to its use for cooking. On a table in the centre of the room were dishes of food being prepared by three servants for the funeral feast. And judging by the amount, a great many were expected to partake.

'Well, girl, where's your apron? They'll be back from the funeral any minute now.'

'I don't have one.'

'Don't have one! What was the agency thinking about sending you out without an apron? What have you got in that bag, then?' And before Emma could stop her, she had picked it up, dumped it on a chair and opened it. 'What's this?' Her delving hand produced a jaconet gown the blue of a hazy summer sky, a satin nightgown and a long blue pelisse.

'I'm sorry, I'm not from the agency,' Emma said, and then, suddenly overcome by everything that had happened in the last three days—the horror of her stepfather's demands, the long worrying journey and her confused emotions over Lord Malvers—she sank into a chair near the fire and sobbed.

The cook stood and looked at her in bewilderment, but, realising something had to be done if this weeping girl was not to disrupt the whole business of sending the Admiral off in style, she patted her on the shoulder. 'There, there, don't take on so. We are all very sad today, but we have to bear up, don't we?'

'Yes,' Emma sniffed. 'I'm sorry.'

'So if you're not from the agency where are you from?'

'London.'

'Lunnon! Good heavens! More kin of his lordship, are you?'

'No. I came to see Mrs Summers. I went to her house in Kendal and the neighbour said I should find her here. I had no idea…'

'Wait here, I'll go and find her.' She disappeared through a door on the other side of the kitchen. Emma found a handkerchief in her pocket and mopped her eyes, then went to her bag and extracted her mother's letter, which she hoped would explain everything, and sat down to wait.

After a few minutes Mrs Summers bustled into the kitchen ahead of her cook. She was a short dumpy woman, her ample frame encased in a stiff black taffeta gown, her grey hair pulled tightly back under a black lace cap. Her complexion was good and her eyes a warm brown. 'Do I know you, young woman?' she asked.

'No, but you know my mother. She sent you this.' Emma offered the letter.

Mrs Summers took it, put on a pair of spectacles that dangled from a ribbon round her neck, and began to read, while Emma watched with her heart in her mouth and the cook watched with open curiosity.

'Oh, dear.' The words were murmured. And then a little later, 'Shocking. Unbelievable. Oh dear, oh dear.' Coming to the end of it, she looked Emma up and down over the spectacles. 'Well, there's nothing to be done about anything now. As you see, this is a house in mourning for my brother, Lord Bourne. The ladies are in the drawing room and the gentlemen will be back from the funeral at any moment and I must look after them. I do not think now is a good time to introduce you to them, do you?'

'No, ma'am, I do not.'

Mrs Summers turned to the cook. 'Mrs Granger, can you find a little food for—'

'Fanny Draper, ma'am,' Emma put in before the lady could use her real name. She did not know why she did it except that she could not rid herself of the idea her stepfather would not give up and might even now be hot on her heels.

'Fanny.' Emma saw the smile that briefly lit the old lady's face and was heartened by it. 'Mrs Granger, Miss Draper will be staying with us for a little while. Please make up a tray for her while I take her up to her room.'

'Yes, madam. The agency didn't send that girl.'

'No? I'm sorry, we shall just have to manage between us.'

'Can I help?' Emma asked, though she was still feeling a little tearful.

'No, my dear,' Mrs Summers said firmly. 'You are done in and must rest. And after that, when all the mourners have gone and the will's been read, we will have a good long coze and you can tell me all your adventures.' She picked up Emma's bag as she spoke. 'Is this all the luggage you have?'

'Yes, ma'am. I couldn't carry any more.'

'Never mind. Come along.' She ushered Emma from the room and into a wide hall from which a cast-iron staircase rose to the next floor. In a room nearby Emma could hear the low murmur of ladies' voices, but Mrs Summers ignored them and led the way up the stairs. 'I wasn't sure how many people would be coming to the funeral and who would need to stay over, so there are beds made up. Here we are.' She opened a door and ushered Emma inside.

'I do not want to take someone's room,' Emma said, looking round her. The bed was a sturdy four-poster and the rest of the furniture heavy and old fashioned, though an attempt had been made to lighten it with pretty curtains and a colourful bedside rug.

'You aren't. It is only my nephew staying after all. Everyone else has elected to go home or has booked into the Lakeside Hotel.'

'I am more grateful than I know how to tell you.'

'Tush, it's the least I can do for an old friend. I am agog to hear the whole story from your own lips, but it will have to wait until you have rested and I have got over this dreadful day. I can hear carriages, so I must leave you. Sleep if you can.'

And with that, she kissed Emma's cheek and left the room.

Emma collapsed on to the bed and wept forlornly, which was perfectly silly of her, considering what she had been through. To cry when it was all over was the height of absurdity.

When Mrs Granger came up with tray on which was a plate of cold chicken and ham, a few boiled potatoes, some bread and butter, beside a glass of cordial, taken from what had been prepared for the funeral guests, for there was no time to do anything else, she found Miss Fanny Draper fully clothed and fast asleep. She put the tray down and crept away.

Emma woke to see Mrs Summers sitting by the bed, her face lit by a lamp on a table beside her, which must surely mean it was dark outside. She sat up, noting her crumpled dress. She tried to smooth it down. 'I'm sorry, I must have dropped off.'

'That is hardly surprising, my dear. Now, the funeral is over, the mourners, apart from my nephew, have departed and I am at your disposal at last. But tell me, child, why did your mother think of me? I have not corresponded with her since your dear papa died and I sent my condolences. I did not even know she had married again.'

'That was one of her reasons. She said my stepfather knew nothing of you and would never think of looking for me here. She gave me your address in Kendal. When I found it unoccupied, I was at a loss to know what to do.'

'I left there two years ago to keep house for my brother. It seemed silly to keep it on, so I sold it. I am surprised the new owners have not yet taken up residence. But enough of my affairs. I think you had better tell me the whole story from the beginning. Why are you alone? How did you get here? And why did your mother not come too?'

When the tale was finished, Mrs Summers remained silent and thoughtful. Emma was afraid she would not be able to stay. It was one thing to be sympathetic, another to provide a strange young lady with a home. It was a great deal to ask, especially as Mrs Summers had just lost a beloved brother, for whom she must be grieving, and having to arrange the funeral and everything else.

'I'm sorry, I should not burden you with all this,' Emma said. 'If I could stay just a day or two, until I can think what to do.' She fished in her pocket for the five guineas and offered it. 'Mama gave me a pearl necklace, but when I tried to pawn it I found it was only worth five guineas. You can have it for my keep until I find a position: companion, teacher, or even housemaid if it comes to that. I will not return to London, not while that man—'

'Of course you will not. It is not to be thought of.' Mrs Summers reached out and closed Emma's hand over the money. 'I do not need that. I was just considering what could be done. I wish now I had not sold my house. I have the money carefully invested and my brother left me a small annuity, but where I am to live, I do not know.'

'But this house…'

'Gone to my nephew and I cannot see him wanting to keep it on. He has his own estate.'

'Do you mean you are to be homeless too?'

'Not immediately. My nephew is a darling boy and he will not turn me out or see me in want, but you see how I am placed?'

'Oh, yes, indeed. I will look for employment first thing tomorrow. I may stay here tonight, mayn't I?'

'Of course. I am not thinking very clearly at the moment. Tomorrow, I am sure, we shall think of something between us. Are you hungry?'

She was ravenous. 'A little.'

'Then I will take this away and have something fresh sent up.' She indicated the tray on the table. 'You were asleep when Mrs Granger brought it up. Poor thing, you must have been exhausted.'

'I did not realise how tired I was, ma'am. But don't take it away. I'm sure it is still perfectly edible.'

'If you are sure.' She reached over to the table and lifted the tray on to Emma's lap. 'While you are eating it, I'll have some hot water sent up so that you may refresh yourself. Then I suggest you undress and get into bed. Time enough for introductions tomorrow morning, when you will feel more the thing. We will have a conference and something will come of it, I am sure.' She patted Emma's hand. 'Do not worry. You are safe here.' She left Emma to her meal. A kitchen maid brought hot water just as she finished it and took away the tray.

Half an hour later, nightgowned and feeling properly clean for the first time since leaving London, Emma curled herself up in the bed; it was bliss after sleeping fully clothed in coaches and on settles. Was she really safe? Dare she believe it?

Her thoughts went to her mother. As soon as she could, she must send the message they had spoken of to tell her she had arrived safely, though what would become of her now she was here, she had no idea. But whatever it was, it could not be worse than marrying Lord Bentwater. If only her pearls had not been made of paste, it would have been so much easier. But she would not worry her mother with that. What had happened to Viscount Malvers? she wondered dreamily. How far away was he? Wouldn't it be strange if, going about the village, she should come across him? If everyone in the vicinity knew Lord Bourne, he might even call to pay his respects. Oh, dear, in that case, she must remain Fanny Draper, companion. She must be sure to tell Mrs Summers that in the morning…

Alex, ensconced in a wing chair in his Uncle Henry's drawing room, stretched out his long legs and sipped the glass of cognac that his Aunt Amelia had put at his elbow. It had been an extraordinary day, extraordinary week, really, and though he had known his uncle was ill and would not have sent for him if it had not been important, he had not been prepared for his death. 'If only I had travelled post as soon as I heard, I would have been here at least a day sooner,' he had told his aunt when he arrived. 'I have become so accustomed to considering the expense of things and not being extravagant—'

'It would not have made any difference,' she said, perfectly aware that her brother-in-law had always kept his younger son on short commons, saying he had to learn to fend for himself, since he was not the heir. It had incensed Henry, who had loved the boy like a son. 'He died over a week ago.'

'At least I am here in time to attend the funeral.'

'Yes, and right glad I am of it, otherwise the only support I would have in the family is that widgeon, Francis, his even more foolish mother, and Bertie who is only here because he expects to be the richer for it. A greedier man I have yet to meet.'

He had smiled at that. Francis Waldover was the son of Lord Bourne's cousin, which made him Alex's second cousin. They had known each other as boys, but were never close; Frankie was several years younger than Alex. He and his widowed mother lived in Lancaster. Sir Bertram Hudson was another distant cousin, but if he had met him before, he could not remember him.

The ladies, of course, had not attended the funeral, but had waited at the house until the men returned; then everyone stood about talking and drinking sherry or ratafia or tea and eating the refreshments Mrs Granger had prepared. The large drawing room had been crowded with friends of the deceased from the town and his time in the navy, together with the Reverend Andrew Griggs, Dr Hurley, who had looked after his lordship ever since he left the navy many years before, and Mr Dewhurst, the family lawyer. Some Alex already knew; his aunt had introduced him to others.

She was a marvel, the way she coped. She had told him Uncle Henry had been ailing for some time, but had gone downhill swiftly in the last three weeks of his life, and in the end, because of the pain he suffered, it had been a release.

One by one they had begun to drift away, until only the family and the lawyer were left to hear the reading of the will. Its contents had shocked Alex. After gifts to the servants, and an annuity to his sister, 'for her devoted care', the bulk of Lord Bourne's estate, including the house, its lands and his small yacht moored at Waterhead, had been left to 'my nephew, Major Alexander Malvers, knowing he will, among my various kin, make the best use of it'.

There had been a gasp among those present, particularly from Mrs Waldover and Sir Bertram Hudson. Mrs Waldover had, according to his aunt, been toadying to his lordship for months in the hope of seeing her son inherit Highhead Hall. Sir Bertram being thirty-five years old, and in the import and export business at Liverpool, had assumed that, because he was the elder, he would inherit. Neither had even thought about Alex, who had been away fighting Napoleon. Alex had been as dumbfounded as they were.

'When did he make that will?' Bertram demanded, while Alex sat silently trying to absorb the implications. Besides this solid granite house and the grounds that surrounded it, there were several hundred acres that were let out to a sheep farmer, interests in the woollen industry and a substantial sum in cash and stocks, as well as the *Lady Jane*, moored on Lake Windermere.

The lawyer consulted its date. 'Five years ago.'

'I thought so. He'd never have called Alex a major if he had known he was already a viscount.'

'What is that to the purpose?' Aunt Amelia had asked.

'He would not have named Malvers if he had known he'd already got his inheritance. I'll wager there's a more recent will somewhere.'

'There is not.' The lawyer was adamant. 'Do you think I would not have known if he had wanted it changed?'

'You are not the only lawyer in the county.' This from Mrs Waldover.

'No. If it pleases you to do so, then I have no objection to your consulting any one or all of them.'

'What have you got to say for yourself?' Bertram demanded of Alex.

'Me? Nothing. I am as astonished as you are.' He turned to Mr Dewhurst. 'Are you sure there is no more recent will?'

'I am positive, my lord. This house is yours, the land attached to it is yours, and the business interests are yours. I will go over it in more detail at your convenience.'

'What did my uncle mean by "make the best use of it"?'

'I think, my lord, he was referring to something you conveyed to him in letters written from Spain, concerns you had for the men under your command.'

It was true that in his frequent letters to his uncle he had written of his strong feelings on the subject of gratitude, or lack of it, from a country towards the men who fought so bravely for so little reward. Why, even Wellington had called them the 'scum of the earth', though he had praised them too. But praise was not work, nor did it feed the bellies of starving children. Was that what his uncle had meant? Sad as he was at his uncle's demise, he could not help feeling a quiver of anticipation at the prospect of being able to do something, even if it was only a little.

They had all gone now, scorning Aunt Amelia's offer of accommodation, and he was here alone, enjoying a quiet cognac and dreaming of what he might do. And then his thoughts turned to Miss Fanny Draper. She had been in the back of his mind all through that long day, pushed to the back out of necessity, but certainly not forgotten. He could not forget her: her courage, her quiet humour and her determination not to let her circumstances get her down, a resoluteness in the face of adversity that amounted to exasperating stubbornness, and her clear-eyed, clear-skinned beauty. It was not just the perfect oval of her face and trim figure which made her stand out, but the woman beneath.

That she was in some kind of scrape he did not for a minute doubt and it worried him. He wanted to find her, enfold her in his arms, kiss her troubles away and promise to look after her for the rest of their lives. If she was in trouble of some sort, then he must do something quickly. If she would let him. That was his dilemma; she was more independent than any woman ought to be and he had to respect that. She would not allow him to ride roughshod over whatever plans she had made for herself. Tomorrow he would take the gig into Bowness and look for her. He prayed she had not taken it into her lovely, foolish head to board another coach and go heaven knows where.

He looked up as his aunt came into the room. She looked tired, but there was a kind of glow about her, as if something had happened to bring her out of the dejection she had been experiencing all day. Her old eyes sparkled. 'There, everything is all right and tight, shipshape and Bristol fashion, as Henry always put it. Now we can sit quietly and have a comfortable coze.'

He smiled at her. 'Aunt Amelia, I am so glad Uncle had you in his last days. You must have been a great comfort to him.'

She sat opposite him. 'I did my best. I loved the silly old man, you see. And he never married. He always used to say his many years at sea had made him unfit for it.'

'He wasn't silly, Aunt.'

'No, of course he wasn't. He was the kindest, wisest man I ever knew, barring Mr Summers, of course. But I used to call him that, just to see him rise to the bait. And he would call me an interfering harridan. It was only our fun, you understand.'

'Yes, of course I do. Have you made any plans?'

'No, but do not worry about me. Henry left me provided for and I have invested the proceeds from my old house and what my husband left me. I have enough. A small cottage somewhere, perhaps…'

'You can stay here as long as you want to. It is your home.'

'Thank you, my dear. But are you not going to sell up? After all, you are a long way from your own home here.'

'I know, but this has always been a second home to me. I need to give it some thought, but there is no hurry, no hurry at all. You stay here. We will both stay. There is something I must do and I do not know how long it will take.' He smiled suddenly. 'I shall need a housekeeper, shan't I?'

She laughed, feeling a weight lifting from her shoulders. 'Oh, I hoped you would say that. Now I think I am ready for my bed.' She stood up and moved towards the door. 'I shall see you tomorrow and we will talk some more. There is a favour I want to ask you.'

'Anything, Aunt, anything in my power,' he said, standing and following her from the room.

It was mid-day when Emma, having slept soundly and late, went downstairs the next morning to find Mrs Summers in the morning room, reading the newspaper with her glasses perched on the end of her nose. 'Good morning, ma'am,' she said.

'Oh, Emma, there you are. Did you sleep well?'

Emma sat down opposite her and folded her hands in her lap. 'Wonderfully well, and the breakfast you sent up was delicious after the food we had on the journey coming up.'

'Yes, I should like to hear more about that journey. I cannot imagine how you managed that all alone. It must have taken a great deal of courage.'

'I was not alone, I had my maid with me, but she had to return home to her mother, and there was a kind gentleman…' She stopped, reminded of the reason for her flight and her determination to remain incognito. 'Mrs Summers, do you think you could call me Fanny? You see, I am not at all sure that I might not have been followed.'

'Surely not?'

'It is possible. My stepfather is not one to give up and neither, I believe, is Lord Bentwater. And there is the question of who I am for the benefit of your relations and friends. Should any of them have contacts in London and casually mention in a letter that Lady Emma Lindsay was staying with you, Sir George would be here post haste. And, as for my poor mama…'

'I see. Yes, you are right. Fanny Draper is your name. But who and what are you?'

'Could I be your companion? You see, there was a gentleman on the coach who asked me who I was and I told him I was coming north to be a lady's companion and if he should be about…'

'He came here, to Waterhead?'

'He said Lake Windermere, Mrs Summers.'

'Near enough,' the old lady murmured, looking thoughtful.

'Of course I shall have to look about in earnest for such a post, for I cannot impose on your generosity any longer than I need to.'

'But that is perfect,' Amelia cried. 'You can be my companion. After all, now poor dear Henry is gone, I shall need one, shan't I?'

'Oh, thank you. That would be wonderful.' Emma's eyes lit up and Amelia realised that this young lady had the most luminous eyes she had ever seen, and when she smiled, she was likely to devastate any young man's heart. 'I will try to learn my duties conscientiously. It should surely not be difficult. My mother has a friend in London who has a paid companion, though I must confess I never noticed her particularly.'

Amelia burst out laughing.

'Have I said something amusing?'

'Oh, Fanny, Fanny, that's just what paid companions are supposed to be: invisible. At least until something wants fetching.'

Emma joined in the laughter and that was how Alex found them.

He had gone out very early in the hired gig and spent at least three hours in Bowness looking for Miss Draper, going to inns, hotels, an employment agency for female servants, the local vicar, the doctor, all to no avail. No one had seen her. Thoroughly dejected, he had returned to Waterhead, keeping a sharp look out for a glimpse of that awful bonnet and the shabby cloak, all along the way, but Fanny Draper had disappeared. Determined not to give in, he decided he must go back to Highhead Hall because his aunt would wonder what had become of him and then continue his search in Ambleside after nuncheon.

And she was here! He stood and stared, wondering for a moment if his eyes deceived him. The dejected, prickly girl in the unbecoming bonnet was gone and in her place was a lively young lady, with rosy cheeks and sparkling eyes, dressed in a blue gown, which, though plain, was superbly cut. It was the kind of garment to go with that lacy petticoat he had glimpsed and could not get out of his head. And her hair, another thing he had only glimpsed, was the colour of a ripe chestnut, glossy and brown, and it was drawn up on to the crown of her head, tied by a ribbon bow and then left to cascade in ringlets about her ears. A tendril curled over her forehead. He had known she was beautiful, but the vision before him was breathtaking.

When they heard the door open, they stopped laughing and turned towards him and then Miss Fanny Draper's mouth fell open, making him smile. 'You!' she said, which was all she had breath for.

'So this is where you are!' he said heartily—too heartily, because he had been taken by surprise and could not seem to moderate his voice. 'There I was, searching the whole of Bowness for you, and you are hiding in the one place I would never have thought to look.'

'Searching for me, my lord?' she queried, while Amelia looked from one to the other, saw the expression in his eyes and the wariness in her new companion and drew her own conclusions. 'Why were you doing that?'

'Because, you foolish woman, you would have got yourself into more scrapes if left on your own.'

'I am not in a scrape. And I was certainly not hiding.'

'Am I to suppose you are known to each other?' Mrs Summers asked mildly.

'Yes,' she said.

'No,' he said.

'Oh, dear, which am I to believe?'

Alex turned to his aunt. 'Present me to the young lady, if you please, ma'am.'

Amelia glanced swiftly at Emma, who nodded imperceptibly. 'Miss Draper, I have the honour to present my nephew, Viscount Malvers,' she said formally. 'Alex, this is Miss Fanny Draper. She is to be my companion.'

'Your companion!' He almost choked on the words. What a fool he was, weaving fantasies about her, when she had been telling him the truth all along.

'Yes, you surely do not object? Now Henry is gone…'

He pulled himself together. 'Of course I do not object, Aunt, but when did you send for her? She has come all the way from London.'

'At the same time as I sent for you, dear boy. I knew, or thought I knew, I would soon be on my own and I had a friend, fallen on hard times, who needed to get her daughter off her hands.'

'Isn't that a trifle drastic? She is marriageable, after all.'

'Do you think getting married is all we women think of?' Emma demanded, realising he was clever enough to trip Mrs Summers up. 'Being the chattel of a man, having to do his bidding, bear his children and be an ornament to his home with no opinion of her own, watching him gamble away all their money and not able to do a thing to prevent it. Some of us choose not to put ourselves through that, you know.'

'I take it back,' he said. 'You are *not* marriageable.'

'Children! Children!' Mrs Summers exclaimed. 'Two minutes together and you are quarrelling…'

'I am sorry, Aunt,' he said contritely, sitting down and stretching out his long legs. 'But I wonder if you know what a virago you have taken on. I have spent three days in her company and a more contrary character I never met.'

'And a more insufferably top-lofty one—' Emma stopped suddenly and subsided back into her seat. 'I am sorry, madam. That is not the way a good companion should behave. I will say no more on the subject. You see, I have a great deal to learn about my new role. Pray, correct me if I err again.' She was deadly serious, but Mrs Summers was chuckling happily.

A bell rang in the hall outside the room and Mrs Summers stood up. 'Lunch is served, so let us go to the dining room. I am sure you are hungry after your busy morning in Bowness, Alex.'

'Yes, and all for nothing,' he said, taking his seat at the head of the table with a lady on each side of him. 'Miss Draper, I cannot recall you naming my aunt as your intended employer.'

'Can't you, my lord?' she answered sweetly.

'No. I would have remembered.'

'I did not know Mrs Summers was your aunt, my lord, or perhaps I might have made a point of doing so. Do you stay long in Waterhead?'

He grinned, enjoying the verbal battle, convinced he would win in the end. 'Anxious to see the back of me, Miss Draper?'

'Not at all. I collect you own Highhead Hall and may stay as long as you please.' She stopped. 'As for me…'

'My dear Miss Draper, you are my aunt's companion and I have told her she may stay as long as she pleases, so, unless you have other ideas, you, too, are welcome.'

'Oh, thank you, my lord.' It was said with genuine relief and gratitude. The tension eased so that they were able to enjoy the meal with comfortable conversation.

'We shall have to take Miss Draper out and show her some of the scenery,' Mrs Summers said to Alex.

'If you can spare her from her duties,' he answered laconically, amused eyes turned on Emma. She had the feeling that he was not altogether convinced of her role and that made her all the more determined.

'Of course I can. But first we must get her kitted out. She brought very little with her in the way of luggage.'

'So I collect. A striped dress fit only for a scullery maid and a gown that is far too grand for anyone but a lady of some means. What a contrast!'

'The grey dress was suitable for travelling when I had no idea whom I might meet and this…' Emma indicated the gown she was wearing '…was in case I needed to dine with Quality when I arrived. I did not want to let Mrs Summers down.'

'Of course. I am, as you have discovered, ignorant of the ways of ladies and their apparel.' He helped himself to another pork chop and more potatoes. 'What had you in mind to buy?'

This was a question that floored Emma. What could she buy with five guineas? 'Oh, I am sure I do not need—'

'Fustian!' Mrs Summers put in. 'I love shopping. We will go to Ambleside; if they do not have anything to suit we will go to Kendal.'

'There, ma'am, I can be of service,' he said. 'I have to take back the gig I hired. There is just enough room in it for three at a squeeze.'

'Yes, but how will we return?'

'I shall buy my own conveyance, seeing the coach house and stables are empty. A roomy carriage and two horses, I think.'

'Yes, of course, I should have told you—Henry sold his coach and the horses when he could no longer get out and about and was confined to the house. I would not let him keep them on especially for me, though he would have done. It would have been a prodigious expense when I should use it only occasionally. Horses have to be fed and that means hay and oats and a groom and a stable boy.'

'These, too, we must have,' he said. 'I shall ask about for a soldier lately back from the war and perhaps an orphan boy. I suppose there are many in the area, even so far from the capital.'

'Indeed, yes,' his aunt agreed. 'I collect that was what you and Mr Dewhurst were talking about.'

'Yes. I mean to find other ways of finding employment for soldiers, if I can.'

'It sounds as if you mean to stay here,' Emma said. 'What about your own estate? You cannot be in two places at once.'

'I know that,' he said. 'I wish I could. I must write to my mother at once and to my steward who is, I think, competent to act in my absence for a few weeks.'

'Then you will go home?' Emma queried, wondering why a thought like that should make her feel so desolate.

'Of course.' He turned to Mrs Summers. 'Do we go to Kendal today?'

'Better tomorrow. There is hardly time to get there and back and certainly not enough to spend shopping. And you must choose your equipage carefully.'

'Yes, for I mean it to convey me back to Norfolk when the time comes. I have done with travelling by public coach.' He paused to smile at Emma. 'Delightful though Miss Draper's company was.'

Emma, being reminded of that journey, suddenly realised there was something—or someone—missing. 'Where is Mr Bland, my lord? Is he not here with you?'

'No, I sent him back to London on an errand.'

This revelation startled her so much that she almost dropped the spoon she was using to eat her pudding and it was a minute before she could collect herself again. If Joe Bland heard anything about her disappearance and put two and two together and informed his master, her whole masquerade would have been for nothing. 'Oh, and is he coming back here?'

'He might,' he said, noting her reaction and smiling at it. She evidently did not want Joe in London. 'On the other hand, he might go to Buregreen and help the steward and my mother with the estate.'

'That would be the most sensible thing to do, don't you think?' Amelia put in, looking from one to the other and enjoying herself for the first time for years. This was better than going to a play.

'Yes. I also asked him to make sure Miss Turner arrived home safely. I think it was an errand he was very happy to do.'

'Playing matchmaker, are you, Alex?' the old lady enquired, smiling broadly.

'I would not dream of it. He is his own man.'

'As you are.' It was said knowingly.

He wasn't sure what she meant by that, but neither did he intend to ask her, knowing he might be embarrassed by the answer. 'So, what had you in mind to do this afternoon?'

'We could go to Ambleside, if you are free to take us.'

'Certainly I will. I want to speak to Dewhurst.'

Half an hour later, in weak sunshine, they were bowling along the lane to Ambleside, which was only a few minutes' ride away; they could easily have walked it. Mrs Summers agreed that was so, but if they had shopping to carry, wasn't it better to have the gig? 'And I like to be seen with my handsome nephew,' she added. 'He will undoubtedly set the town by the ears when I tell them he is to stay a little while.'

Emma risked a glance at the tall man beside her, wielding the reins so dextrously. He was dressed in a dark blue coat and light blue pantaloons tucked into polished Hessians. His waistcoat was of marcella in blue-and-cream stripes, his cravat was black in consideration of his mourning. He was wearing a high-crowned black beaver with a curly brim. He would have turned eyes in the high spots of London, never mind the hills of Westmoreland.

Although he pretended to be concentrating on driving the gig and its single pony, he was aware of her glance and wondered what was going on in that beautiful head of hers. Her lovely hair was topped by a chip bonnet, which he knew had been hastily concocted from an old one of his aunt's, stripped of its outdated decoration and on to which she had fastened a full-blown rose and some wide ribbon. With the blue dress, it looked quite enchanting, far too elegant for a lady's companion.

Mrs Summers was well known and well liked in the area and they had hardly left the gig in the yard of the Unicorn and stepped out into the town than they met Dr Hurley and his two daughters, Prudence and Charity, who were immediately presented to Alex. Prudence, the elder, was nearly as tall as Emma. She had dark hair almost concealed by a poke bonnet and clear green eyes. With her narrow face and long nose, she was handsome rather than beautiful. Her sister, sixteen or seventeen, Emma guessed, was considerably shorter. Her hair was lighter than her sister's and her eyes a clear innocent blue. Once she lost her puppy fat, she would be lovely.

Emma, remembering her role as companion, tried to shrink into the background, but it was difficult on account of her height and the fact that she was still wearing the blue dress and matching pelisse and a hat that did not help her to blend into the background. Mrs Summers turned and drew her forward, about to ask her if she might present Miss Hurley and Miss Charity, which would have been the correct thing to do if she were Lady Emma Lindsay, but remembered just in time that she was not Emma, but Fanny Draper. 'Doctor Hurley, this is Miss Fanny Draper, my friend and companion, who will be staying with me for a little while.'

They nodded in acknowledgement and Emma remembered to give a brief curtsy and a murmured 'How do you do', and then subsided in silence while they continued their conversation, much of which centred round Lord Bourne's death and how much everyone would miss him, and the appalling summer they were having. It ended when Alex invited them to call at Highhead Hall, and they went their separate ways.

Alex and the ladies had hardly gone a dozen yards when they met Mrs Griggs, wife of the Rector, her son, James, and daughter, Rachel, who had just descended from their carriage. Once again the presentations were made and Emma introduced. While Alex, Mrs Summers and Mrs Griggs talked and Rachel answered a question Alex had put to her, Emma became aware that James was looking at her with an expression that seemed to say, 'Here is someone I might have a little fun with.' It made her feel uncomfortable and she turned away, pretending to study a row of jars in the window of a tobacconist's. She did not turn back again until she heard Alex issue another invitation for them all to visit Highhead Hall.

Emma began to think there were drawbacks to being a companion she had not considered, one of which was to have to stand by and watch Viscount Malvers making polite conversation with single young ladies who obviously found him fascinating, and be able to do nothing to divert him, though her motives for wanting to do that she would not go into, preferring to put it down to being unfamiliar with the ways of society in what many might consider a rural backwater. In London, as Lady Emma, she could have held her own, but here, as Fanny Draper, she was constrained by her role. It was just one more injury to lay at the door of her stepfather. What sort of coil had her disappearance put him in with Lord Bentwater? she wondered. Whatever it was, she was not going to give in. Never. If being married was anything like the existence her mother endured with her second husband, she would stay single.

Alex left them on the corner of the market place and Mrs Summers took Emma's arm and led her into a shop that seemed to deal in nothing but strong wool skirts, thick boots and all-enveloping coats with capes. 'You will need clothes like this if you are to go walking in the hills,' Mrs Summers said.

'When am I to go walking in the hills?' Emma asked. 'You don't go, do you?'

'Not any more, but I used to love it. I know Alex likes it, and, if he should ask you to accompany him, you must be equipped for it.'

'I cannot do that. It is not part of my job as a companion to leave you alone while I go off enjoying myself.'

'Your job, my dear, is to please me and if it pleases me to see you enjoy yourself, you have no choice in the matter. Now, let us see what they have to offer.'

There was no gainsaying her, but when Emma saw the prices of these sturdy garments she was shocked. There was nothing five guineas would buy except woollen hose and gloves. 'But, Mrs Summers,' she protested, 'I cannot afford—'

'Of course you cannot. It is the duty of any self-respecting employer to kit out her companion, did you not know that?'

Emma doubted it, but she did not want to hurt the old lady by arguing. Some day, she did not know when, she would make it up to her. They chose a walking outfit, a plain black skirt gathered into the waist, but full at the hem, which was slightly shorter than her day dresses to allow her freedom of movement. With it was a white blouse and a black military-style jacket. Having paid for them, they carried their purchases back to the Unicorn where they had arranged to meet Lord Malvers.

He was in a cheerful mood as he drove them back to Highhead Hall. His interview with Mr Dewhurst had revealed the exact extent of his new fortune, which would enable him to do some of what he had always dreamed of doing. He needed staff, not only here in Westmoreland, but at home in Norfolk, and those he employed would be ex-soldiers or the children of soldiers killed in battle. He would expand, he would set up workshops and smallholdings. Work, not charity… And he would solve the mystery of Miss Fanny Draper, because she figured very largely in his plans.

He risked a glance at her. She was looking straight ahead, but there was a faint smile on her face. There had not been many smiles on the journey from London, except perhaps one of irony, or a pretence at one for his benefit when he was trying to help her and she was resisting. This was different; it was a smile of pure pleasure and he meant to make sure she had no cause to be sad again. If she would let him!

Chapter Six

The next day Alex drove them to Kendal, where they left the gig at the Woolpack and set off to explore the town, which seemed to consist of narrow lanes and yards branching off from the main street. Some of these ran down to the river where there were weaving sheds, dye works and manufactories producing all manner of goods from the ubiquitous sheep of the area. One of these manufactories was part of Alex's inheritance and he left the ladies to their shopping while he went off to make himself known to the management and inspect it. 'I shall see about buying my equipage after that,' he told them. 'Shall we meet at the Woolpack when our errands are done?'

Having agreed to this, Mrs Summers and Emma set off arm in arm to find the shops. Amelia was in her element and took no notice of Emma's protests as she set about renewing her wardrobe. She bought three day dresses, one in green-spotted muslin for warmer days, another in a light wool in a tawny colour that complemented Emma's hair for when the days were cooler, and a third in a soft dove-grey taffeta. And, according to Mrs Summers, she must have at least one dress for evenings. 'I expect to be invited out,' the old lady said. 'And you will come with me, so you need to be properly attired. I shall be in mourning, of course, but you do not need to be, though I do not think bright colours would be suitable under the circumstances, do you?'

'Not for a lady's companion,' Emma agreed 'But I prefer softer colours in any case. With my height, bright hues make me look like a maypole.' She chose one in lilac silk trimmed with matching satin ribbon under the bust, in bows on the gathered sleeves and in three rows round the hem of the skirt. If Emma thought that was the end of the shopping, she was mistaken.

'And now for a riding habit,' Mrs Summers said, leading her out of one establishment towards another.

'But, ma'am, when am I to go riding? You don't ride, do you?'

'Not any more, but that does not mean you cannot. If you enjoy it, that is.'

'I like it above everything, but who will go with me?'

'His lordship, of course.'

'You mean Viscount Malvers?'

'Yes, of course I mean Alex. He always used to ride out when he stayed with his uncle as a young 'un. And if he should ask you…'

Emma laughed, remembering the argument over the walking clothes. 'I know. I must be equipped for it.'

'Shall you not like to have him as an escort?'

'I should like it very much; he is an amusing companion when he is not laying down the law in that top-lofty manner of his.'

'Oh, that is only his way, my dear. And I collect you are perfectly able to stand up for yourself.' This with a smile.

'Permissible in Lady Emma, but not to be tolerated in Fanny Draper,' Emma said. If it were not for that big black cloud hanging over her, she would be enjoying her stay with this dear kind lady and her handsome nephew.

Mrs Summers must have divined her thoughts, for she said, 'Could you not confide in him, my dear? I am sure you will find him sympathetic and you can rely on his discretion.'

'I do not want his sympathy, Mrs Summers.'

'No, of course not, but—'

'Please, I beg you not to say anything to him. It would mortify me.'

'I would not dream of doing so, my dear—if anyone tells him, it must be you, but the longer you leave it the harder it will become.'

Emma sighed. 'Yes, I know, but perhaps there will never be any need for him to know.'

Mrs Summers shut her mouth firmly on her reply and instead ushered Emma into the next shop. Here she asked to see ready-made riding habits. There was not a great choice, considering Emma's unusual height, but they settled on a plain navy blue whose only decoration was a double row of black buttons running down the bodice from the squared shoulders to a narrow waist. The skirt was completely plain, but very full.

The shopping did not end there. Mrs Summers marched Emma to a bootmaker's, where footwear was purchased, and then to another shop to buy petticoats, chemises, a cape, a mantle, and then another where a couple of hats were obtained. They had so much they were obliged to hire a lad to carry everything back to the Woolpack where Alex waited for them.

'My goodness, you must have emptied the town of stock,' he said, seeing the lad struggling beneath his burden. 'Put it down on the table, young shaver.' And when the boy had done so, he gave him a few coins, which had him pulling his grubby forelock and grinning from ear to ear. After he had gone, Alex turned to his aunt. 'What have you bought?'

'No more than was needed,' she said blithely, sinking into a chair and patting the one beside her for Emma to sit. 'My companion's apparel reflects on me as an employer, do you not agree?'

'I suppose it must,' he said. 'I never thought about it.'

'No reason why you should.'

'I did try to restrain her, my lord,' Emma put in, 'but she would not be moved from her purpose.'

He laughed. 'Yes, I collect she is as stubborn as you are.'

'More so, for I lost, though that is the wrong thing to say, for I have gained a whole new wardrobe. I am surprised there is so much to be had so far from London.'

'We do not live in the dark ages in Westmoreland,' Mrs Summers told her. 'This is a very busy area for people wanting to travel and explore, especially since the war when travelling abroad was not a possibility, unless, like Alex, you were in the army or navy.' She paused. 'What about your errands, Alex? Did you manage to find a suitable carriage?'

'Yes, and it is as well I did, or how would you have conveyed all that home?' He indicated the heap of shopping.

'Where is it, then?'

'Patience, Aunt, patience. Let us eat first. I am sure you are hungry after all your exertions.'

They agreed they were a mite peckish and did justice to the meal the landlady served them: baked ham, stewed mutton with vegetables and herbs, followed by a pudding rich in fruit and spices. When they had eaten their fill he ordered their parcels to be taken out to his coach and led the two ladies out to the yard, where he waved an arm. *'Voilà!'*

The vehicle was a post chaise, smaller than a park coach, but larger than a town chariot. It had seats for four, with a front board for the driver and a double outside seat above the boot at the back for grooms, coachmen or footmen, whichever was deemed necessary. It was painted black, its lines and wheels picked out in red and blue, its seats padded in dark blue. But it was not the carriage that made Emma cry out in delight, but the two horses harnessed to it.

They were a matched pair of greys, with broad hind quarters and muscular shoulders. Their manes and tails were black flecked with grey. Their ears were pricked and their eyes intelligent. They rattled their harness a little as if impatient to be off. 'Oh, they are beautiful,' she cried, running over to pat their flanks and stroke their noses. 'I'll wager they are goers too.'

Alex smiled. Miss Fanny Draper was used to being around horses, he could see. He was learning more about her every day, but not what he most wanted to know. 'Do you ride, Miss Draper?'

'I…' She paused. How could she tell him she had been riding since she was three and that at home in Hertfordshire, before her mother married Sir George, she had ridden out almost every day on her mare, Walker? It was not a name to describe the mare's gait, for she could fly like the wind when occasion demanded, but the name of her previous owner, which no one had bothered to change since the animal was comfortable with it. 'I have hacked a little.'

'Good, because these two are not the only specimens of horseflesh I have acquired.' He turned towards a groom, who was leading two riding horses out from the stables where they had been delivered and looked after until their new owner was ready to take possession of them. One was a big black stallion, the other a chestnut mare, only slightly smaller, for he had bought it bearing Miss Draper's height in mind.

Emma's eyes widened in delight; she could not wait to get on the mare's back and put her through her paces, but even as he watched, delighted by her reaction, her face clouded and she stood back. Her role had to be maintained—she could not afford to behave like some giddy débutante.

'Do you not like her?' he asked.

'She is magnificent.'

'Her name is Bonny and she is yours.'

'No, my lord, I cannot accept such a gift. It would not be proper.'

He was about to say, 'Proper be damned', but thought better of it and instead said, 'I meant while you are staying with us, of course.'

'Oh, then of course.' She turned to the stallion and patted his nose. 'He's a beauty. My father had one like him once…' She stopped, confused. She had not mean to give anything away about her past.

He pretended not to notice. 'His name is Salamanca. Named after the Spanish city, I suppose.'

While they had been admiring the carriage and the horses, three rough-looking, shabbily dressed men, one of whom had a patch over his eye and another a hook for a hand, had appeared. The one able-bodied one climbed into the driving seat of the carriage and the other two mounted Salamanca and Bonny. 'Come, ladies, your carriage awaits,' Alex said, bowing and flinging his arm outwards. 'The shopping is in the boot, the lady's saddle is tied on the roof and we are ready to go.' He handed them both in and got in himself, sitting opposite them.

'Are those men old soldiers?' Emma asked as they moved off.

'Yes. I know they look like ruffians, but I assure you they are anxious to work and I will kit them up.'

'Like Mrs Summers kitted me up?'

'Yes, that's right. Can't go about town attended by men in rags, can I? Not if I want to be taken seriously.'

'Have you decided what you are going to do?' Amelia asked.

'Not yet. I am waiting for inspiration. Simply working the estate and assuming the trappings of a landowner is not enough. I could expand the weaving business, but I know so little about it that it might turn out a disaster and not only will my new employees find themselves out of work, but so would the established ones. And sheep farming does not need a large workforce, only a few extra hands at lambing and shearing times. There is the tourist trade, I suppose, but that needs something out of the ordinary…' His voice tailed away as if he were thinking aloud and had come to a stop.

'Better to make haste slowly, as Henry was used to say,' Amelia said.

'Yes. I shall feel more at ease when I hear from my mother that all is well at Buregreen. Running an estate from this distance is not easy.'

'You could sell up here and go home.' This from Amelia.

Emma remained silent; she, too, was wondering what was going on at home. She had written to Lady Standon, signing herself Fanny Draper, but the letter would hardly have reached London yet and its contents would have to be conveyed secretly to her mother; she could not receive an answer for another week at least. Not that she expected it to say the danger was over, the deception no longer necessary and she could go home. She would be very surprised indeed if it was as easy as that.

'No, Aunt, not until I have fulfilled my uncle's wish and done something useful with my inheritance,' he said, noting Emma's thoughtfulness. Was she thinking that if he sold up she would be without a home? He wished he could tell her here and now that it would never happen, but until he knew for certain who she really was… He did not care who she once was, he chided himself, all that mattered to him was what she was now. But even so he knew society would not agree, his mother would not agree and even his aunt, for all she was befriending the girl, would not agree. Breeding was important, background was important, the kind of life she had lived before was important. It would be disastrous to tie himself to another Harriet Wilson, one of the most notorious demi-reps in London, who was easily able to pass herself off as something she was not.

Aunt Amelia was probably in on the secret, if there was one. He was not even totally sure of that. But everything about Fanny Draper pointed to its existence: her manner of holding herself upright—most tall girls stooped, Miss Hurley was a case in point—and the authoritative way she spoke, though she could have learned it from another mistress; her strange assortment of clothes, luxury and dross muddled together; her ignorance of the ways of travelling by coach and, for all her independence, her reliance on Rose Turner. And now her ease with horses, which he meant to test as soon as he could.

On the other hand she was desperately poor—not a feather to fly with, Joe Bland had said—and her lack of experience of travelling could easily be put down to a life lived in one place. And as for the horses, she might be the daughter of a groom who liked to spend time with him in the stables. If she was running away, could it be because she had done some wrong, committed a crime? Aunt Amelia would never knowingly agree to house her if that were the case. Unless there were mitigating circumstances. She was an enigma, and the mystery surrounding her occupied his mind until he thought he might go mad.

The return journey was accomplished in comfort and as soon as Alex had helped unload the parcels, he busied himself seeing the horses safely in their stalls and giving instruction to his new outside staff and the two gardeners whom his uncle had kept, though they knew more about what needed doing than he did. Amelia and Emma took their purchases to Emma's room and in no time had them all out of their packages and began a trying-on session, which only ended when the half-hour gong sounded to tell them to dress for dinner. It was usually taken at country hours of three o'clock, but, because they had been late returning from their shopping expedition, it was nearer six when Emma went downstairs in the lilac dress.

Alex was beginning to become accustomed to seeing the rapid changes in Emma's appearance, but even so he did not think the beauty in blue could be surpassed until he saw the beauty in lilac. He would never have expected that colour to become her, but it did. She had brushed her hair until it shone, its chestnut tones flecked with copper. It was long and thick and she had twisted it up into a rope and pinned it to the top of her head. The style emphasised her long neck, a neck, he noted, devoid of any jewellery.

After dinner, they went into the drawing room—Alex did not even stay in the dining room for the usual glass of port and a cigar—and played spillikins, which Alex contrived to lose, much to the ladies' amusement. 'What about some music?' Amelia asked, when the childish game palled. 'Fanny, do you sing?'

'Only a very little, ma'am.'

'Then do entertain us. Sing a duet with Alex. I know he has a fine voice. I will accompany you.' She went over to the pianoforte and opened the lid. 'What shall it be?'

Alex shuffled the sheets of music which lay on the piano top and chose 'Moll in the Wad', which he handed to his aunt. After her opening chord, his voice rose strong and musical: 'Miss Jenny, don't think that I care for you, for all your freaks and comical airs, you snub at your betters I tell you true, you know full well you are at your last prayers…'

When it came to her turn, Emma could hardly sing for laughing.

'Pray don't you be impudent, Master Clump, for all your cobbling kit and gears, I'll up with my fist and give you a thump, I'll smack your face and box your ears…' All accompanied by suitable actions.

He had chosen the song to make her laugh and in that he succeeded. By the time they finished, tears of sheer gaiety were sliding down her cheeks; the song was so apt to the way they behaved towards each other, which was, she supposed, why he had picked it.

After that, in more serious mood, he sang, 'My love is like a red, red rose', plucking a rose from the vase on the table as he sang and presenting it to her. It was left to her to wind up the evening with 'When first this humble roof I knew with various cares I strove', which ended with the line 'The all of life is love'. Not since her childhood had she felt so happy. Under this roof she felt her cares drop away from her. Nothing had been solved, of course, she knew that, and really it was only a temporary respite, but she was grateful: grateful to her mother and to Mrs Summers who made it possible, grateful to this understanding man with whom she frequently sparred.

As she climbed the stairs to her bed, she realised it was more than gratitude, it was love. She loved him, she loved his thoughtfulness, his gentleness, his understanding, his unquestioning acceptance of what and who she purported to be. And that thought brought her back to reality with a bump. Mrs Summers was right—the longer she delayed, the harder it would be to tell him the truth. And he would be angry.

Chapter Seven

Alex left the house early the next morning to ride over to visit Colin Digby, his farmer tenant, to make himself known and enquire if there was anything the man needed. He lived with his wife and several children in a stone-built cottage halfway up Rydal Hill. Its condition was primitive, but it was kept scrupulously clean, as were the children. He stopped at the house for a few words with Mrs Digby and then went with her husband to tour the farm, which was extensive but hilly and only good for grazing sheep, a few goats and one or two cattle. There was no arable land such as he was used to in Norfolk, where the flat terrain and fertile ground made it ideal for crops.

Having arranged for someone to help repair the walls that divided the pastures, he returned to Highhead Hall in the early afternoon to find an elegant carriage in the drive. His aunt was evidently entertaining. He hurried indoors and upstairs to change before joining them.

'Ah, here is my nephew,' Amelia said as he entered the drawing room.

The visitors were strangers; one was a tall angular woman dressed in a purple pelisse over a grey gown. Her black hair—dyed, he was sure—was topped by a purple satin turban trimmed with feathers. She was accompanied by a young lady in a white dimity dress tied with a wide pink sash. She was blonde and blue-eyed and altogether lovely.

'Lady Pettifer, may I present my nephew, Viscount Malvers?' Amelia said.

He swept her a bow. 'Your obedient, my lady.'

'It is always a pleasure to meet a relative of dear Mrs Summers,' her ladyship said. 'Lord Bourne, who was a great friend of my husband, Sir Mortimer, often spoke of you.'

'Did he, indeed?'

'Oh, yes, he thought very highly of you. May I present my daughter, Charlotte. Charlotte, make your curtsy.'

Charlotte came forward, curtsied and gave him a most impish and knowing smile, which made him realise his first conception of her had been entirely wrong. She was not the quiet schoolgirl he imagined her to be, but must have left the schoolroom at least three years before. And the look in her eyes held a certain wily cunning; he had seen that look in the eyes of soldiers caught in some punishable offence and hoping to be able to talk their way out of it with a faked air of innocence. On a young lady, it was disturbing.

'Miss Pettifer.' He bowed again and looked round for Fanny. He felt in need of her support, which was foolish of him. The visitors posed no threat to him, so why could he not deal with them? And what could Fanny Draper, lady's companion, do about it? He thought at first she was not in the room, but then he saw her sitting in a corner, half-hidden by a cabinet displaying mementoes of his uncle's many voyages, quietly reading a book. It brought a smile to his face; she was acting her role of companion and effacing herself. So be it. When the visitors had gone he would suggest a ride to give them an appetite for dinner.

'Lady Pettifer has been so good as to invite us to a little soirée at Cragside House on Monday evening next week,' his aunt said. 'You are not engaged elsewhere, are you?'

'No. I shall be delighted to attend.'

'It will not be anything like you are used to in London,' her ladyship said. 'Just a few friends to welcome you to the area.'

'Thank you, my lady.' He bowed again and a few minutes later, after talking about the unseasonable weather, the price wool was fetching and the fact that the streets and shops were crowded with offcomers, as tourists and visitors from outside the area were called, her ladyship and her daughter took their leave.

'Who and what are they?' he asked his aunt when the door had closed on them.

'Sir Mortimer is a magistrate and a sizeable landowner hereabouts, fancies himself cock of the walk. His wife has pretensions of grandeur and an overriding ambition for her daughter to marry well. Anyone with a title and a moderate fortune is fair game, so be warned.'

'I will take your warning to heart,' he said seriously, though there was a distinct twinkle in his eyes. And, raising his voice a fraction, added, 'Miss Draper, you may come out of hiding now.'

Emma shut her book, which had been open on her lap, though she had not been reading it, being far more interested in the conversation going on in the middle of the room. She rose and went to sit beside Mrs Summers.

'You do not have to hide yourself away when someone comes, my dear,' Amelia said, patting her hand.

'Well, I certainly have no wish to push myself forward on someone who ignores me so totally I might as well be invisible.'

Alex laughed. 'You did right, Miss Draper, Lady Pettifer would have been horrified had you joined in the conversation. In any case, I am sure your book was more interesting than our chatter. What is it?' He took it from her when she offered it and read the title. '*Admiral Crosthwaite's Invasion.* Whatever is that about?'

'It is about two men—one a local man, the other who came to live in the Lake District—who formed a partnership to put on a mock-sea battle on Derwentwater for the benefit of tourists. They did it every year for ten years, from 1780, and people came from all over the country to witness it. It was a grand affair with boats and yachts made up to look like ships and cannon and soldiers with musketry…'

'I remember witnessing it once when I was younger,' Amelia put in. 'The whole countryside went wild over it. There were foot races and rowing races, stalls and sideshows, refreshments tents and marquees. The battle was the climax. Mr Joseph Pocklington owned the island on the lake and had built himself a house on its highest point. He built a mock-church and a fort too. He was called King Pocky and defended the island against the invasion led by Mr Peter Crosthwaite, of Keswick. That was why he called himself Admiral, but Henry maintained he had never been to sea, certainly not as a seaman. But it made a wonderful display.'

'Is it no longer done?' Alex asked.

'No, I believe there was some opposition from the purists and some of the high jinks got out of hand and made it unpopular with the local inhabitants. And one year Crosthwaite's enemies went to the island and told everyone the battle was off and then charged a fee to ferry the disappointed defenders back to the mainland. It ruined the whole day and Mr Crosthwaite was so furious he would not take part again.'

'I wonder I never heard of it when I used to stay here,' Alex said. 'Where did the book come from?'

'Why, sir…' Emma laughed '…I took it from a shelf in the bookroom, so I presume it now belongs to you. You do not mind, do you?'

'Not at all.'

'It sounds so exciting, I was wondering if it could be revived.'

'Why would anyone want to do that?'

'Do you not think it would be good for the area? Would it not provide work for those ex-soldiers you spoke of?'

He was flattered to think that his little homily about the problems of the old soldiers had made an impression on her, but he was given no opportunity to discuss the idea because new callers were announced. This time it was Mrs Griggs and her daughter and they were followed almost immediately by the Misses Hurley. Emma shrank into the background while an almost-identical conversation took place as had been conducted with Lady Pettifer, ending as the previous one had with invitations, one for supper at the Griggs's and another from Miss Hurley to make up a party for a picnic the following week. 'Weather permitting, of course,' she added. And almost as an afterthought, 'Do bring your charming companion.' By the time they had all gone Alex concluded there was no time to go riding and so he did not mention it.

'It is evident you are going to be much in demand,' Mrs Summers said to Alex. 'A handsome bachelor with a title and a fortune! My goodness, they haven't had anything so exciting happen round here for years. The young sprigs will all try aping your dress and the young ladies will be vying for your favours.'

'I hope not.'

'Why not? Don't you want a wife?' She looked sideways at him, one eyebrow raised.

'Not at the moment, not ever perhaps. What I have seen of marriage does not incline me towards it.'

'Oh, you are an old cynic and I am persuaded you do not mean it.'

'Assuredly I do. Besides, I have hardly said half a dozen words to your young friends. I would need to know someone a great deal more thoroughly than that before I make such an important decision, Aunt Amelia.'

'Of course you would,' she said complacently. 'I did not mean people from round here necessarily—someone from Norfolk or London, perhaps.'

'His lordship decries London society,' Emma put in. 'He told me so.'

'Oh, then we shall have to see what the Lakes have to offer.'

Because he found the subject deeply embarrassing, he turned back to the book about the regatta and began leafing through its pages. 'I have been wondering how to fulfil my uncle's wishes,' he said. 'And perhaps organising a regatta might serve the purpose. Not on Derwentwater but on Windermere. It would provide employment and encourage visitors to spend their money. Everyone will benefit: the inns and hotels, the cook shops and stallholders. Not only that, but a grand finale, like a battle on the water with cannon going off and fireworks, will need a great many people to make it work.'

Emma was glad to hear him talking so enthusiastically. It meant the advent of the young ladies had not disturbed him and her heart beat a little more freely.

They discussed the possibilities, with Amelia and Emma either making suggestions or playing devil's advocate, but the idea was growing on him. He would have to have the local community on his side, but the more he thought about it, the more he thought he could make it work. He would put up the initial finance, but, properly run, it should be self-financing and a battle would bring in the local ex-soldiers and sailors, give them something to do building the mock-ships and forts, besides taking part. He could see it all in his mind's eye. Making it reality would take hard work, but hard work had never bothered him.

'What do you say, Miss Draper?' he asked. 'Can we do it?'

'I imagine you can do anything you set your mind to,' she said, heartened by his use of the word 'we'. 'Except walk on water, and perhaps you can even do that.'

He laughed. 'There is a tale of walking on water I heard when I used to visit my uncle as a lad, though it wasn't a man who did it, but a horse.'

'Oh, that old myth,' his aunt put in. 'I do not know how it started, someone with too much drink in him, I shouldn't wonder.'

'Oh, do tell me,' Emma begged.

'It is supposed to be an omen,' she told Emma. 'The story is that when harm is about to come to the neighbourhood, a ghostly white horse walks on the lake from shore to shore.'

'Has anyone actually reported seeing it?'

'Only those rolling home from an evening spent in the Sun. You should not pay any heed to tales like that, Fanny, Alex is only trying to frighten you.'

'I am not easily frightened,' she said.

He laughed. 'I know that.' He turned to his aunt. 'When the coach horses bolted in a storm on our journey up here, she spent the time reassuring the other young lady in the vehicle that we were not about to turn over and the coachman knew what he was about.'

'And I was right, wasn't I?'

'Oh, indeed you were,' he agreed, deciding not to boast that it was he who had taken the reins and brought the horses back into line. 'A most intrepid traveller. One would think you had been doing it all your life.'

If he thought that would elicit a response which would tell him more about her, he was disappointed; she simply laughed and then returned to the subject of the regatta. They discussed it until dinner time and returned to it afterwards and the idea grew and developed as they talked. By the time the evening ended and they went to their beds, it had been agreed that Alex would sound out the local business people and make a tour of the lake to see how it could be arranged.

The regatta was only a short-term solution to the unemployment problem. He needed something that would last long enough to set the men and their families up for life. He could sell the estate and use the money for the general good. On the other hand, he could turn the house into a hotel, or a library, or a Lakeland museum or an orphanage, but until he was sure his aunt and Miss Draper had a home, he would not do anything. For the moment, he would concentrate on the regatta.

Emma woke early the next morning to find the sun shining and the birds singing in the eaves. She rose and dressed in her old grey-striped dress, now cleaned and pressed, and went down to the kitchen where Mrs Granger was busy at the stove.

'Good morning, miss,' she said. 'I didn't expect you down yet. If you don't mind waiting…'

'I'm in no hurry, Mrs Granger. I thought I would go for a walk before breakfast. It is such a beautiful morning.'

'Yes, thank the Lord. After the weather we have had, the sun is welcome. But don't go out empty. Have a little bread and butter and a drink to tide you over.'

Emma sat at the kitchen table to have it. 'Did you ever see the regatta on Derwentwater?' she asked, as the cook set about her chores again.

'Yes, everyone went to see it. It was a grand occasion. You are the second person to ask me that. Lord Malvers mentioned it when he came down. He said he was thinking of doing something similar on Windermere.'

'We were talking about it last night. Is he up and about already?'

'He went out about half an hour ago.'

'Was he going riding?' she asked, stifling her disappointment that he had gone without her, especially as he had told her she could ride the new mare. She had assumed he meant she would go with him, but perhaps he had not meant that at all.

'He didn't say, but I didn't hear a horse leave the yard.'

Emma left her to her cooking and set off to walk to the lake. The road led directly to Waterhead; once there, she walked along a gently shelving shore. There were several boats on the lake: some lying at anchor by the small jetty, some out on the lake containing men with fishing rods, others taking passengers from Waterhead to Bowness. She stood and watched them for a few minutes, then decided to see if it was possible to walk around the northern edge of the lake.

At first the ground was dry, passing as it did along the edge of a park that belonged to a large mansion standing high above it, but then it became very marshy and she had to pick her way carefully. She was obliged to stop when she came to the river that fed the lake, but when she turned to retrace her steps found herself almost ankle deep in muddy water. She stood, trying to make up her mind which way to go when a voice called out, 'Stand still, I'll come and fetch you.'

She looked up from studying the ground to see Viscount Malvers stepping from one dry patch to another towards her, though how he could tell which was dry she did not know; she had not been able to. He reached her in no time and, in spite of her protests, scooped her up in his arms. 'Put your arms about my neck and we shall soon be on dry land again.'

She complied and he carried her back, carefully picking his way from one tuft of grass to the next. He was exceptionally strong and she did not feel at all in danger, even though he stumbled once, before regaining firm ground. Here he stopped, but did not immediately set her down, but stood looking down at her, studying her features, her slightly flushed cheeks, warm violet eyes and slightly parted lips. She was lovely and his heart was hopelessly lost. And yet…and yet… He could not shake off his doubts.

'My lord, I think you should put me down,' she said, trying to make light of the situation, though she was acutely aware of the rapid beating of her heart and the picture they must be creating for the casual observer. It made her feel hot even to think of it. He set her on her feet and she shook out her skirt, the hem of which was caked in mud.

'That bit of ground is always like that after heavy rain,' he told her, smiling at her attempt to do something about the mud on her skirt. 'And this area has had more than its fair share of it this summer, so I am reliably informed. Whatever made you walk over there?'

'I thought I might be able to walk round the top side of the lake,' she said, pointing across to the wooded area on the far side. 'I did not realise the ground was boggy until I was on it and then I picked my way carefully, hoping to come out of it, but when I came to the river I had to turn back. The trouble was I couldn't see the way I had come.'

'It was a good thing I was on hand, then.'

'Yes. Thank you.' He always seemed to be on hand when she needed him, but she had no intention of admitting that.

'Are your feet wet?'

'A little.'

'You need sturdy boots for walking, you know.'

'Mrs Summers bought me some, but I did not intend to go far, so I didn't trouble to put them on. It is such a lovely morning.'

'It certainly is and all the lovelier for seeing you, bedraggled as you are.' He was grinning at her feeble attempts to make herself respectable.

'My lord, you must not flirt with me.'

'Why not?'

'It is not proper—'

'Proper!' He laughed. 'After I have just carried you, kicking and screaming, out of the morass. And kept you dry.'

'I was not kicking and screaming and it is unkind of you to say I was. And you might have fallen carrying me.'

'Oh, there was no fear I would do that with such a precious burden.'

'Precious, my lord? I own nothing but the clothes I am wearing.'

'It was not your clothes I was thinking of, they are easily replaced. You, on the other hand, are irreplaceable.'

'You are flirting again.'

'How do you know? Are you experienced in the art? Perhaps the innocent Miss Draper is not what she seems.'

'You are talking nonsense and I will not listen.'

'Oh dear, now our journey is done, we must assume our proper stations, never mind what happened on the way. Is that what you are saying?'

'Yes.'

'Be blowed to that. I am who I am and you are you. I know you so well and yet I do not know you at all.' He stopped his bantering tone and added, 'It is strange, don't you think?'

'No. You can hardly say you know someone after three or four days, can you?'

'It depends,' he said guardedly. 'When you meet some people it seems as though you have known them all your life, yet you can spend a lifetime with others and never truly understand them.'

'I know what you mean. I feel as though I have known Mrs Summers for years and years. She has been so good to me. I don't know how I shall ever repay her.'

She was very good at steering the conversation away from subjects she did not wish to discuss, but that only made him more curious. 'I am sure your company is payment enough,' he said, deciding not to press her. It would only lead to a falling out and that was the last thing he wanted.

'I shall try to be helpful, but I ought to do more.'

'You can help me with my regatta project if you want more to do.'

'You mean to go ahead with it then?'

'Yes, unless there is stiff opposition from people who matter. I have been walking along the shore of the lake to decide the best spot for a naval battle and checking on my uncle's yacht, the *Lady Jane*. Mine now, I suppose. It's been laid up, but I have been told it is perfectly sound. It will do for the battle.' He stopped and turned back towards the water, pointing. 'I think we shall stage it just there. It's the widest part of the lake and there are two or three small islands, one of which could be defended against attack. I must find out who owns them.'

Standing where they were on higher ground, she could see some way down the length of the lake and, in the distance, the small islands just before it came to its narrowest point. 'It would be ideal and that bay on this side and the slopes above it would form a natural arena for spectators.' Her arm swept round to encompass a bay that had a wide stretch of beach and a grassy area which, apart from being divided by the road which ran along the edge of the lake, rose steeply to sheep pastures. 'It has an inn right beside it too. I have no doubt the landlord there will think it a good idea.'

He smiled. 'I have you to thank for suggesting it.'

'Ideas are one thing, execution another. You will have all the organising to do. I will do all I can to help. That is, if Mrs Summers can spare me.'

'Speaking of my aunt, I think I had better take you home to dry your feet or you will be ill and she will not thank me for that.' He grinned suddenly. 'I thought once we arrived in Kendal that would be the end of our adventures, but I was wrong. You seem able to fall into a bumblebath anywhere.'

'I do not!'

He smiled at her vehemence. 'If you would like to go walking, then allow me to escort you. I know the best places from which to view the scenery.'

The idea pleased her, but she remembered she was not her own mistress. 'It depends on Mrs Summers. She may need me.'

'You leave Mrs Summers to me.'

'And surely you will be busy?'

'I do not intend to work the whole time I am here. Are you going to raise any more objections? I shall soon think my company is not welcome.'

'Oh, no, it isn't that.'

'What is it, then?'

'You said it yourself: you are who you are and I am who I am, a paid companion. It is not fitting—'

'Fustian! And I am sure my aunt will agree.'

He was right. After exclaiming at the state of Fanny's dress and shoes and the fact that her hat had fallen off and brought her hair down with it, Amelia was told the tale and agreed with Alex. 'You can find yourself in all sorts of coils if you do not know the terrain,' she told Emma, who was sitting in the day room with her feet in a mustard bath, which in itself was hardly proper, but Mrs Summers had had the bowl brought to her parlour and didn't see the necessity of turning her nephew away, considering Emma's feet and the bowl were hidden by her skirt. 'It is easy to get lost in the mist, fall down a hole, be swallowed up in a marsh, especially after heavy rain. If you are with Alex, I shan't worry.'

'But I am your companion, little more than a servant, it is not fitting that I should be escorted by a peer of the realm. Such a thing would never do in London. It would ruin his lordship's reputation entirely.'

'We are not in London and I would rather have you safe than stick rigidly to protocol. I would never forgive myself if anything happened to you and neither would your mama.'

Alex, sitting at ease in a chair by the hearth with his long legs out in front of him, looked from one to the other and waited to be enlightened, but Amelia began suggesting short easy walks that they might attempt and he was once again disappointed. And then she sent him away so that Emma might take her feet from the bowl to dry them and replace her stockings.

The next morning they took an easy walk to Ambleside and then up a steep hill which left them no breath for talking, but it was worth it when they reached the top to find Lake Windermere laid out at their feet. They stood side by side in companionable silence, drinking in the view until Alex gave a great sigh. 'I haven't been up here since I was a boy, and though I remember it as beautiful, I'd forgotten just how much it tugs at the heart.'

'Would you like to live up here permanently?'

'I don't know. I think not. My home is in the flatlands of East Anglia and they have a pull all their own. It is where I was born and raised, where my mother is.'

'You are anxious to return?'

'Yes and no. So much depends on the outcome of the next few weeks.'

'You mean the regatta?'

'There is that, but I was also thinking of where my aunt would like to settle and you…'

'Me? How can it possibly have anything to do with me?'

'Indeed it does.' He paused, weighing his words. 'I cannot think you view your stay with Mrs Summers as a permanent arrangement.'

'Oh, you mean I am an obstacle. Do not concern yourself. I shall take myself off—'

'I meant nothing of the sort.' He spoke sharply. 'If you and my aunt are fixed on staying together, that can be accommodated, but are you not a little homesick for your family? I collect Mrs Summers spoke of your mother.'

'I miss my mother, it is true, and I hope one day to see her again, but just now it is impossible.'

'Why?'

'Because… Oh, because it just is.'

'I am sorry, I didn't mean to pry. Shall we start back? I collect my aunt wants to pay calls this afternoon and you are expected to go with her.'

She knew, as they started their descent, she had lost an opportunity to confide in him and perhaps there would never be another, but somehow the words to explain that she had been deceiving him from the outset stuck in her throat and she could not utter them. He would be angry, and then cool and polite, as one would be towards an heiress one didn't like very much. Or perhaps he would pretend to like her for the sake of her fortune and that would be infinitely worse. If she still had a fortune; she could not even be sure of that.

Alex spent the next day talking to people about the regatta and to ex-soldiers about their work, or lack of it, and tried to discover what particular talents they had. He needed woodworkers, shipbuilders, painters, sailmakers, artists, people who knew about explosives and fireworks, someone to build realistic-looking cannon. And there were stalls and competitions to organise. He hardly saw Emma, who spent the time with Mrs Summers, until the evening when they assembled to go to dinner at the rectory.

Wanting to impress, he dressed with care in a black evening suit, white shirt and waistcoat and black cravat, and went downstairs to wait for the two ladies. They were not long behind him. His aunt was in black, as befitted her state of mourning for her brother, but Emma had chosen to wear the blue silk, to which she had added some pale blue lace and ribbons in three different shades of blue. Her hair had been scooped up into a bun on top of her head and fastened with combs. He guessed she thought she looked plain and unassuming, but in his view she could never be that, however hard she tried. The severe hairstyle only served to emphasise a long white neck and a proud bearing. Not the stuff of paid companions, he thought wryly, as he escorted them out to the carriage and handed them in before taking his seat opposite them.

* * *

The rectory was only a few minutes away by coach and they were soon being welcomed by the Rector and his wife. 'We are honoured to have you in our humble home, my lord,' the Rector said, bowing obsequiously to Alex. 'I collect you have met my wife and daughter.'

'Yes, indeed.' He bowed to them. 'Mrs Griggs, your obedient. Miss Griggs, how do you do?'

They both made a curtsy and then James wandered into the room and there were more greetings. Emma felt his eyes on her again and squirmed uncomfortably. Why was he looking at her like that?

'My dear Mrs Summers, I am so glad to see you out and about,' Mrs Griggs said, leading everyone into the drawing room as she spoke. 'Losing your brother must have laid you very low, but we must take comfort from the fact that he was a good man and is surely enjoying his reward in heaven.'

'Yes, his suffering is at an end, and I could not have wished for it to be prolonged.'

'You must feel very lonely. Do sit down.' She waved vaguely at a sofa.

'Lonely, oh, no,' Amelia said, seating herself. 'I have Lord Malvers and my dear Miss Draper for company.'

Reminded of her existence, Mrs Griggs looked at Emma. 'Yes, of course. Do find a seat, Miss Draper.'

Emma looked about her to discover Mrs Griggs had plumped down beside Mrs Summers on a sofa and Lord Malvers was sitting beside Miss Griggs on another. The Rector was in a wing chair and Mr James Griggs remained standing by the hearth, surveying the company with an amused smile on his face. She did not want to catch his eye and, noticing a seat on the far side of the room, took herself to it, where she was completely ignored until a manservant came to announce that supper was served and they rose and trooped into the dining room.

The conversation during the meal was general at first, but then Alex introduced the idea of a regatta, only to discover that the parson was not in favour on the grounds that it would encourage drunkenness, and, having made that pronouncement, his family felt constrained to come out on his side, whatever they might privately have thought. Alex wisely changed the subject and the meal progressed in a rather strained silence. Afterwards they entertained each other with music, but nothing like the rumbustious tune Alex and Emma had sung at Highhead Hall. This was altogether more decorous. Emma, whose opinion on any of the subjects discussed was neither sought nor offered, was glad when they were on their way home.

'I do not think you can count on any support for your ideas there,' she told Alex.

'No, but it's no more than I expected. The Rector is bound to be a little starchy, but he is only one of many.'

'Yes, but he has a lot of influence,' Amelia put in. 'He has only to denounce it from the pulpit and you will lose the support of his parishioners too.'

'Then I shall have to try to bring him round.'

'How?' Emma asked.

'I will think of something. A bit of toadying to the lady of the house, perhaps. Get her on my side.'

'She will not defy her husband, not unless she thought her daughter's future depended on it.' This came from Amelia, though the thought had crossed Emma's mind and made her catch her breath. How could she bear to stand by and see his lordship snapped up by anyone else, let alone the strait-laced Miss Griggs? She was honest enough to recognise the feeling as jealousy, but it did not help. She had got herself into the biggest coil of her life and she could see no way out of it.

The soirée at Cragside House was worse. Not only was the Rector and his family there, but so was Dr Hurley and his daughters and Mr Dewhurst, the lawyer, with his wife and son, Cecil. Sir Mortimer was hearty and boastful of his influence in the neighbourhood; as he was in favour of the regatta, it looked as though there might be a serious falling out when he and the Rector began arguing about it and the doctor and the lawyer joined in. Emma longed to add her own arguments, but knew that would be entirely unacceptable and so she remained silent and simply listened.

It was left to Alex to do his diplomatic best to calm them down. 'It was only an idea I had to help the employment situation,' he said quietly. 'I have no wish to go against local feeling.'

'I think it's a grand idea,' Charlotte said, laughing and making eyes at Alex. 'You want a battle, my lord, then you have a ready-made one. Papa and Mr Dewhurst against the Reverend and Dr Hurley.'

'Do not be foolish,' her father snapped at her. 'Go and find some music to entertain us.'

She pouted and went over to the pianoforte, where she was joined by the other young ladies, though Emma remained sitting beside Mrs Summers. The girls were whispering together and laughing and she felt left out. But such was her lot and it was a hundred times better than being married to Lord Bentwater, so she told herself, but that was followed by the thought that not being able to take her rightful place in society or being able to meet Lord Malvers on an equal footing was worse. She was between the devil and the deep blue sea.

'Do you think we could dance?' Rachel murmured to Charlotte. 'I long to dance with the handsome Lord Malvers.'

'You can't. He's mine,' Charlotte snapped. 'You can dance with Cecil Hewitt and Prudence can dance with your brother.'

'What about me?' Charity wailed.

'Oh, you're too young to dance with men,' her sister said. 'You know Papa will not allow it. You can play for us.'

Reluctantly Charity sat at the instrument and began to play. Emma watched and waited, wondering how Charlotte Pettifer was going to contrive to have the partner she wanted. She did not have long to wait; Charlotte stepped into the middle of the room. 'Papa,' she said gaily, 'Charity has offered to play for dancing. You will allow it, won't you?' She did not wait for his reply, but seized Alex by the arm. 'Come, my lord, show us how it's done in London society.'

He had no choice but to obey and it was left to James and Cecil to pick their partners. Emma watched, her foot tapping. 'I am sorry, child,' Amelia whispered to her. 'You should be enjoying the dancing too.'

'That would set the cat among the pigeons,' she whispered back, pretending she didn't care.

The dance ended, the men bowed and the ladies curtsied, while Charity searched for more music. When she struck up a waltz, Mrs Griggs protested. 'Charity, that is most unsuitable,' she said. 'Find a country dance.'

'Oh, but, Mrs Griggs, the waltz is considered perfectly proper in London, you know,' Charlotte said. 'Is that not so, my lord?' She appealed to Alex.

'I believe it is danced frequently in the best ballrooms nowadays,' he said. 'Even at Almack's, which is considered very proper indeed.' He looked across at Emma as he spoke and there was a twinkle in his eye that made her smile.

'Oh, do teach it to us, my lord,' Charlotte begged. 'It is all right, isn't it, Mama?'

'If his lordship says it is done in respectable circles, I think we can allow it.'

Alex smiled and, while Charity inexpertly thumped out the beat, proceeded to show them how to dance a waltz. 'It's difficult to demonstrate the lady's steps without a partner who knows it,' he said, stepping over to Emma and grabbing her hand to pull her to her feet. 'Come, Miss Draper, let us show them.'

She should have pulled away, should have refused to leave her seat, but she was not strong-willed enough. She had been longing to dance with him and he had given her the opportunity and she was not going to waste it. She ignored the gasp of outrage of those watching as he swung her into the dance, and after that she forgot them altogether. She was in his arms, her body swaying with his, so in tune with each other, they moved as if they had been dancing together all their lives. He did not speak and neither did she, but there was a mischievous twinkle in his blue eyes as if he knew what he had done and did not care.

The music ended and he held her hand as she dropped into a deep curtsy, then raised her again and bowed. 'Thank you, my lady.'

She gasped. How could he say that to her? Did he know? Or was he teasing? Had anyone else heard him? 'My lord,' she said, bowing her head, so that he should not see her consternation.

'Now, it's my turn,' Charlotte cried, stepping up to Alex as he reluctantly released Emma. 'Come on, Charity, play it again.'

He bowed and danced with her and then the other ladies, patiently showing them the steps, while Emma returned to her seat, her heart so full of a mixture of elation and jealousy, she could not speak. It would be like that wherever they went. If he singled her out, he would jeopardise his popularity with the elite of the area, but if he ignored her, her heart would break. The best thing was not to attend such gatherings. She did not think Mrs Summers truly needed her and was only trying to be kind by taking her.

Alex knew he had stepped over the line between acceptable and unacceptable behaviour and so he spent the rest of the evening being extra-attentive to the other young ladies, ignoring Miss Draper, which was the hardest thing for him to do, and emptying the butter boat over the older generation of ladies so that by the end of the evening he was once again in favour. He knew they were making an effort to overlook his strange way of going on because they had marriageable daughters and viscounts did not come their way very often. He would have been amused and thumbed his nose at them if he hadn't wanted to win them over to his regatta idea. By the end of the evening he thought he had, certainly enough for him to feel justified in making a start on the arrangements. They were even talking about a ball to finish off the proceedings in style.

'After all, now Lord Malvers has shown us how to waltz, we ought to be able to show it off,' Charlotte said. 'Do you not think it a good notion, my lord?'

'Yes, but I do not know if I will have the time to organise it.'

'Then we will organise it for you, won't we, Mama? You are very good at that sort of thing, everybody says so. After all, the occasion is not just for the lower class of person, is it?'

Lady Pettifer murmured that she would be responsible for the ball, if Lord Malvers wished it. They could hire the assembly rooms for the purpose.

He had not thought of rounding the evening off in that way, but realised it was a good idea, and, if he did not have the organising of it, so much the better. He thanked her ladyship; the last day in June was decided on by mutual agreement and the evening ended on a happy note.

He spent the next day talking to anyone who could help him. Having discovered that the nearest of the small uninhabited islands belonged to a Mr Hawthorne who lived in Bowness, he set off to see him and obtained his permission to use it for a battle, so long as no permanent damage was done and it was handed back at the end exactly as he found it. Next he went to all the inns and taverns in the area where ex-soldiers congregated and recruited as many men as he could to construct a wooden fortress on the island with all the trappings to defend it, including cannon. Others he set to work making a small armada from boats and yachts and anything that floated. Accounts for the materials they needed were to be sent to him.

'What's it all for?' one of the men asked him.

'To entertain the population and the offcomers, to make work and bring money to the area.'

'Yes, I c'n see that, but if there's to be a battle, it ought to be over something: a broken agreement, revenge for a wrong, the kidnapping of a lady, something like that.'

'Yes,' someone else piped up. 'If a beautiful damsel were to be carried off to the island by evil men, she'd have to be rescued by the good men, don't you think?'

'A sort of Helen of Troy,' Alex mused. 'You might have an idea there. I'll put my mind to it.'

Thoroughly satisfied with his day's work, he returned home, wondering if Miss Draper would consent to take part and be the lady to be kidnapped. He put it to her over dinner. 'It would only mean pretending to struggle while you are being carried off and waiting on the island to be rescued. What do you say?'

'If it helps, of course I will,' she said. 'But are there not other young ladies who might do as well? One of the Misses Hurley or Miss Pettifer. I am sure she would jump at the chance.'

He looked at her in amusement—his lovely Miss Draper was jealous! 'No, can you imagine them kicking and screaming? They would be far too decorous for that.'

'Meaning I am not,' she said sharply.

'Well, I do know you can act the part.'

'Alex, do not tease,' Amelia said, seeing the look of consternation on Emma's face. 'It is unkind of you. It is not Fanny's fault that she has so many adventures.'

'No, you are right. I beg your pardon, Miss Draper. But will you do it?'

'Yes, if you like. Tell me what you would like me to do.'

'I haven't worked it out yet, there is plenty of time. We'll talk about it tomorrow, while we are out riding.' Because of his outrageous behaviour in making her dance with him the evening before, he knew she deserved an apology and an explanation and going riding might afford an opportunity to talk.

'Are we going riding? It is the first I heard of it.'

'I did promise to take you. Tell me if it is not convenient.'

'It is not my convenience that matters. Mrs Summers might need me.'

'You go and enjoy yourself, my dear,' Amelia said. 'I have no particular need of you tomorrow.'

And so she agreed and began to look forward to it eagerly.

The next morning they rode along the road to the bridge that took them over the river, and then round the top of the lake where she had tried to walk before and were soon following a path through woods that was wide enough for them to ride side by side. They talked about the kidnap of the lady and the rescue attempt and how it could be done, until they emerged on the far shore of the lake. There was a stretch of firm turf here and they were able to put the horses to a canter. Emma spurred Bonny into a gallop and was thrilled when the mare responded. It was good to feel the wind on her face; for the first time in months she felt free. If only it could always be like that.

He followed her, his heart in his mouth, but when he saw how competently she rode and how fearless she was, he relaxed. She was no novice. They slowed at last and slipped from the saddles to rest the horses, standing side by side, looking out across the lake to Waterhead on the far side. 'You managed very well for someone who has only done a little hacking,' he said.

Was he probing again? Or simply teasing her? Should she confess that she had been riding almost since she could walk? If she did, it would lead to other questions and was she ready to answer them? 'My father taught me. He was very fond of riding. I have done very little since he died.'

'I am sorry. I did not mean to make you sad.'

'I am not sad, my lord.'

'Good.' He paused, but when she did not enlarge on that, added, 'Can you not call me Alex, at least when we are alone?'

'Oh, no, my lord, that would not be—'

'Proper!' he said, laughing. 'For someone who manages to fall into every sort of mischief, getting wet and muddy, letting down her hair and riding like a trooper, you place an inordinate amount of importance on being proper. I do not think you make a very good lady's companion at all. I said so before, did I not?'

'Then it is as well it is not for you to decide, but Mrs Summers, and she seems satisfied.' It was spoken sharply.

'No doubt there is a reason for that,' he said gently.

'Yes, she is a kind lady who understands my predicament.'

'I wish I did,' he said.

'You know perfectly well that it became necessary for me to earn a living and Mrs Summers was known to my mother; it was better than working for a stranger. Surely you can understand that?'

He sighed. 'I am doing my best.'

'And so am I. Please do not keep quizzing me, or I shall think you do not believe me and that would be most uncivil of you.'

'Very well, I shall say no more. But I want to apologise for putting you to the blush the other night. I wanted to dance with you and I had seen you tapping your foot as if you wanted to join. The temptation was too strong to resist. Am I forgiven?' It was asked with a smile that sent her pulses racing. He had a most disconcerting way of slighting her and making it sound like a compliment.

'Yes, but why did you address me as if I were a lady?'

'Oh, I was only demonstrating to the others how it should be done in polite circles,' he said offhandedly. 'And it annoyed me to see you ignored.'

Her spirits soared at this, but then plummeted again. 'But that is my lot, my lord. There is no getting away from it and I beg you not to do anything like that again.'

'Very well, I shall pay no heed to you in future. Will that satisfy you?'

'Yes,' she said firmly, but she did not mean it. She liked his attention, if only because it proved she was not invisible. 'Now the horses are rested, we had better make our way back.'

He did not try to detain her. What could he say? He knew something troubled her and it was more than the necessity of earning a living, and was hurt to think she did not trust him enough to tell him. One of these days she would try his patience to such an extent he would take her by the shoulders and shake her until her teeth rattled. No one, man woman or child, had ever frustrated him as she did.

They rode back in silence. He helped her dismount and watched her go into the house, her back ramrod straight. He sighed and took the horses to the stables and spent the rest of the day planning the battle, interviewing men and making lists. Being occupied helped to keep his mind off Miss Fanny Draper.

Chapter Eight

The day of the picnic dawned warm and sunny, the first really warm day of the whole summer. Emma, remembering the humiliation she had endured when they went visiting, was reluctant to subject herself to more of the same. 'I don't think I should go,' she said to Amelia at breakfast that morning. 'After all, you do not need a companion on an outing like that, when there is plenty of company.'

'Of course you must come. I would not dream of leaving you behind, especially as Miss Hurley made a point of inviting you.'

When Alex came in from ensuring the men knew what was expected of them while he was gone, he agreed with his aunt and Emma gave in. She dressed in the green spotted muslin with a light cape and a plain straw bonnet and took her place beside Mrs Summers in the carriage that was to convey them as far as the doctor's house in Ambleside, where they would leave it to walk the rest of the way. Their destination, so she was told, was Scandale Beck.

The young people went on ahead, taking the road north out of the town. Emma contrived to drop back and walk with Mrs Summers, which was, after all, her proper place, but she could not help looking at Alex's broad back as he walked with Charlotte beside him. The girl was talking all the time and looking sideways up at him from under the brim of her flower-bedecked bonnet. She was most definitely trying to engage his attention and he seemed to be enjoying it, smiling and laughing. But Charlotte was not having him all to herself if the other young ladies could help it and they gathered round him until he looked as though he was being besieged.

'Do you think one of them will manage to snare him?' she asked Mrs Summers, pretending she did not care, but not quite succeeding.

'I doubt any of them have what he's looking for,' Amelia said.

'What is he looking for? Has he told you?'

'He hasn't said, but I should think he would expect the woman he married to have some intelligence and character.'

'Miss Pettifer is very pretty and Miss Griggs is handsome, don't you think?'

Amelia looked sideways at her and smiled. 'Do you think he would be swayed by that? Handsome is as handsome does, you know.'

'That may be so, but they come from respected families and no doubt have dowries. It might be enough to change his mind about not marrying.'

'Change his mind?'

'Yes, he told me he was not inclined to marry.'

'Did he, now?' Amelia said with a smile. 'I am sure that one of these days he will find a lady who will change his mind for him, but she will have to be someone very special.' The conversation was being conducted in an undertone so that no one else would hear. Amelia smiled and added, 'Emma, are you no nearer telling him the truth?'

'I don't know how to.'

'I said it would become more difficult as time passed, did I not? And now I think you are in love with him; unless you are honest with him, you will lose him.'

'In love with him!' Emma exclaimed, but even as she spoke she realised that it was true. She had fallen in love with a man she had met only a few days before. Could it happen that suddenly? Could you love a man with whom you were constantly bickering, who teased and quizzed you as if he did not believe anything you said? She sighed heavily—he was right to doubt her, but would telling him the truth now put that right? 'Lose him?' she said, wondering if anyone else had noticed and hoping they had not. It was too humiliating to bear. 'I never had him, nor can I expect anything from him. When I left home I forfeited my rank to become a nobody, a glorified servant, and that is what I must remain. I do not trust my stepfather or Lord Bentwater. I can never go back to being what I was, so there is no point in telling Lord Malvers the truth.'

'Oh, my child, you are so wrong about that. Shall I tell him for you?'

'No, I beg you not to. He will think me lacking in courage if I allowed you to do it and it will not make any difference. When I saw how unhappy my mother was in her second marriage, and nearly all because of Sir George's gambling, I made up my mind never to risk anything like it. I mean to hold to that resolve.' She had told herself that when she first set out and in the last few days had repeated it to herself over and over, as if repetition would convince her.

'You will change your mind. When all your problems have been resolved, you will wonder why you were so foolish.'

Emma did not answer; she could not imagine a time when she would be free of her particular problem. It weighed her down, so that everything she said and did was coloured by it. A few minutes' respite when she forgot it for a little while was soon followed by a poignant reminder and hours of pessimism, as if she had no right to happiness.

The road had petered out and become a cart track and Dr Hurley was looking back at them, urging them to keep up, so they stopped talking and hurried after him. The track led to an old packhorse bridge. It was a picturesque spot and it was here they set out their picnic. Doctor Hurley's cook had provided a generous repast and they all sat on rugs to eat; afterwards, while the older people rested, the young ones strolled about. James, who had brought a sketching pad with him, sat with his back against a rock and busied himself with a stick of charcoal, drawing everyone. Charlotte attached herself like a limpet to Alex, flirting with him so obviously that Emma, who might have laughed if she had not been so unhappy, took herself off on her own.

She walked steadily until the ground began to rise steeply. Refusing to give up, she climbed on, sometimes having to put her hands down to help her to scramble over rocks. How long she had been going she did not know, but after a time she felt she was not alone, there was someone following her. Thinking it must be Lord Malvers and not wanting another brush with him, she toiled on until she stopped in the lee of an overhanging rock and sat down on a boulder, too breathless to continue. If he caught up with her, she would simply send him on his way again. Their constant sparring was exhausting her and she dare not risk letting him see how she felt about him.

However, the man coming round the side of the rock was not Lord Malvers, but Mr James Griggs. He grinned when he saw her. 'Miss Draper, where are you off to in such a hurry?'

'Nowhere. I was simply walking off that excellent picnic. What are you doing here?'

'I thought you might like a little company.'

'No, I am content to be alone.'

'Oh, come now, Fanny, it cannot be much fun having no one to talk to but yourself.'

'I am not in the habit of talking to myself, Mr Griggs. And I did not give you permission to address me by my given name.'

'Oh, top lofty, are we? What have you to be so haughty about, miss? You should think yourself lucky that Mrs Summers is soft hearted and took you in, or you would be scrubbing floors.'

'Don't be ridiculous.' Nevertheless, she was aware of the truth of what he said and supposed he had put his own interpretation on the tale Mrs Summers had told his mother.

'I'm not, but that's no matter. I've taken a fancy to you, Miss Fanny Draper, for all your uppity ways. You afford a challenge and I enjoy a challenge.' He sat down beside her, so close she could feel his hot breath on her cheek. She tried to hitch herself further away from him, but she was pinned against the rock and there was nowhere to go. 'I would like to see you unbend a little and smile more. Try it, just for me.'

'Leave me alone. Go back to the others.'

'All in good time when I've solved the mystery.' He was leaning right into her, breathing into her face, one arm creeping around her back. 'You are not what you seem, Miss Fanny Draper, I spotted that right away. Lady's companions are dried-up old spinsters. You are far too beautiful and dignified for that, so tell me who you really are.'

'I am what I say I am. Now go away.' She tried to push him off her, but he simply laughed.

'Where did you learn to be so proud? Was it from aping a previous mistress, or are you what London society calls a demi-rep, not quite respectable but ladylike enough to pass muster? I suspect it's the latter. Or why would someone like Viscount Malvers trouble himself with you? His mistress, are you?'

She was furious, not only that he had insulted her, but that he had assumed there was something going on between her and Lord Malvers, though he had come to a very different conclusion from Mrs Summers. Is that what everyone thought? She struggled against him, beating her hands on his chest. 'How dare you say such a monstrous thing!'

He put his other arm round her and captured her arms. 'What's good enough for his lordship is good enough for me.' Then he tried to kiss her. She twisted her head back and forth, struggling to free herself. She opened her mouth to scream, but he clapped a hand over it. She bit him. Hard. He swore. 'That is certainly not the behaviour of a lady or anything like one. I think you're from the gutter—'

He was given no opportunity to go on because he was seized from behind and literally thrown off her. She scrambled to her feet and flung herself into Alex's arms. He held her close, relishing the feel of her body against his. 'Did he hurt you?'

She shook her head.

He became aware that James was getting to his feet, rubbing his elbow where he had caught it on the edge of a rock. His coat sleeve was torn and his cravat awry. He was looking belligerent, coming forward as if to square up for a fight. 'Get going, Griggs,' Alex said coldly. 'Unless you want more of the same.'

'Don't know what you're making so much fuss about,' James muttered. 'Who does she think she is, aping her betters?'

'Miss Draper is a lady and if you had an ounce of the gentleman in you, you would know that. Now, unless you want me to report your behaviour to your father, I suggest you make your way back to the picnic party.'

Knowing himself bested, the young man left them, muttering imprecations and trying to adjust his cravat as he went. Alex turned back to Emma. 'Are you all right?'

'Yes. Thank you for coming to my rescue.'

He laughed. 'I seem to be making a habit of it.' Always aware of her, even when he was being polite to other young ladies, he had seen her go off alone and later watched James Griggs leave off his drawing and go in the same direction and had decided to follow him. It was as well he had.

'He was horrible and said some dreadful things,' she said with a shudder. 'Do all lady's companions have to put up with that kind of behaviour?'

'Only the very beautiful ones.' He looked down into her upturned face and stroked her cheek with the back of his hand. She shivered. 'You are not afraid of me, are you?'

'No, of course not.' The shiver had been something else entirely, a kind of tremor of desire that she made herself stifle.

'I'm glad. I would never do anything to hurt you, you know that, don't you? Nor would I allow anyone else to harm you, believe me.'

His words warmed her briefly. 'Do *you* think I'm a demi-rep?'

'Good lord, no!' He laughed suddenly. 'One of those would have known how to deal with a man like James Griggs.'

'How?'

'Never mind. He won't try it again.'

'I am afraid you have made an enemy and that does not augur well for your regatta.'

'Do you think I would consider that when your honour is at stake?

In any case, what can he do? You forget, I am an old soldier, used to dealing with jackanapes like him. Do not worry about it.' He paused to smile reassuringly at her, tempted to kiss her, but knowing such an action would be entirely inappropriate. 'Now, we had better be going back before people begin to wonder where we've got to.'

He released her and without his support she felt suddenly bereft, as if something precious that was within her grasp had been suddenly snatched away. If she had been more experienced as a woman, she might have been able to use the situation to her advantage, but she was as green as a cabbage and she knew he would see through any artfulness on her part. She followed him down the steep slope back to the bridge to find everyone packing up to return home. Amelia gave her a strange look and raised her eyebrows in a query. Emma simply shook her head.

When they arrived back at Highhead Hall, the ladies entered by the front door and Alex went round to the stables with the carriage. Leaving it to the care of the grooms, he made his way into the house by the kitchen door to find Joe Bland had returned in their absence and was wolfing down a meal Mrs Granger had set in front of him. The dinner gong sounded before he could talk to him at any length and he was obliged to go to his room to change.

'Your man has arrived,' Amelia told him when he joined her and Emma in the dining room.

'Yes. I saw him in the kitchen when I came in.' He turned to Emma. 'He tells me Miss Turner is safe with her mother, who was very pleased to have her home.'

'Thank you, my lord.'

'Don't thank me, thank Joe. I did nothing.'

'You let him go when you might have said you could not spare him.'

'Fustian! I am not incapable of looking after myself, you know.'

'I do know,' she said, thinking of the incident that afternoon when he had sent James Griggs on his way. It was not the action of a man unused to looking after himself, or to having his orders disobeyed. 'What else did he say?'

'Nothing. There wasn't time. I'll talk to him later. Why did you ask?'

'No reason. I thought he might have gone to Norfolk or London.'

'For what purpose?'

Emma felt her face grow hot and wished she had not spoken. Now he would quiz her, and though she longed to know if there had been a hue and cry over her disappearance she could not give that as her reason. 'I collect you had business in London before you were called away to come here,' she said lamely.

'And if I did?'

'I am sure it is nothing to do with me,' she snapped. 'I was only making conversation and you are using it as an excuse to quiz me.'

Her waspish answer was not at all called for and she mumbled an apology and bent to her meal, but suddenly found she had lost her appetite. She pushed the food around her plate and longed to escape. Fortunately Amelia came to her aid and engaged Alex in conversation, asking him about the regatta project and how his plans were progressing; while they talked, Emma was able to recover some semblance of dignity and the evening ended without further misunderstanding.

Next morning, knowing his lordship would be talking at length to Joe Bland and not wanting to be on hand should he discover how she had deceived him, Emma dressed for walking, put on her boots and took herself off for a long trek on the fells. The lovely weather of the day before had disappeared. It had been like that all year: one lovely day followed by several of wind and rain. It wasn't raining now, but overcast and quite cool considering it was June, supposedly the hottest month of the year.

Half an hour after leaving home, she was climbing a rough path that would take her on to Loughrigg, a long, low fell that stretched all the way from just above Ambleside to Grasmere. She had made enquiries about the route and intended to make her way to the summit at Todd Crag and then down to Skelwith Bridge where she had been told there was a pretty waterfall and thence back by the road to Ambleside and Waterhead.

There were some other walkers on the hills, but they did not bother her as she picked her way to the top, her mind more on her dilemma over Lord Malvers than on the scenery. Would Joe Bland tell him that Lady Emma Lindsay had disappeared from her home and her family were seeking her? Would he put two and two together? And, if he did, how angry would he be? On the other hand, why should Joe Bland pick up any of the gossip of the *haut monde*? He was a homecoming soldier, a servant, and such matters would pass over his head.

What did she think she was doing, wandering about the hills all alone? Especially after Mrs Summers's warning? For even up here she could not hide from the truth of who she was. It would be better to make a clean breast of it and hope for the best. At least she could then take her place in what passed for high society hereabouts. But to do that would mean making a liar of Mrs Summers and laying her open to gossip and that would be unfair to her kind hostess. And if her stepfather were to hear where she was, he would be up here like a shot, dragging her back to be married to Lord Bentwater. Unless Viscount Malvers stepped in. But what on earth possessed her to suppose he might do anything of the sort? Just because he had said he would not let anyone harm her did not mean he would condone what amounted to daughterly disobedience.

He had looked after her on their journey and kissed her, it was true, but looking after her was simply the action of a kind and chivalrous man and, as far as he was aware, he was only kissing a superior kind of servant, not anyone of any consequence. That kiss had set her heart beating nineteen to the dozen and turned her limbs to jelly, very different from the revulsion she had felt when Mr Griggs attempted it. It made her realise how much Alex Malvers had come to mean to her, that she loved him more than she knew how to express. But he must never know; it would be too humiliating to have him scoff at the temerity of someone as lowly as a lady's companion aspiring to catch the eye of a viscount. And if he ever learned that she was not lowly at all, but an earl's daughter, he would be angry that she had not trusted him enough to confide in him. And none of that meant he loved her.

She reached the summit and stood for a moment to get her breath back and found Ambleside, Waterhead and almost the whole of Lake Windermere spread out below her. The wind, which had been a gentle breeze on the lower slopes, was fierce enough up here to grab at her skirt and send it billowing about her legs. Her hat fell down her back and her hair came undone. Suddenly she found herself laughing. Lady Emma Lindsay would never have come out alone and certainly not in such a dishevelled state. Miss Fanny Draper was another matter, not important enough to need an escort. But which was she? She hardly knew any more. She turned her back on Windermere and began walking again…

'You think she is Lady Emma?' Alex asked Joe. They were talking in the stables. Alex was dressed for riding, having intended to ask Miss Draper if she cared to accompany him. He had been disconcerted to discover she had gone out very early, telling Mrs Granger she meant to go for a walk. He hoped she would not go far because the clouds were building up again and it could be very unpleasant on the fells in the rain. It was easy to lose your way even if you knew the paths well; if you did not know the area, it would be hopeless.

'I'd lay odds on it,' Joe said, answering his question. 'The talk is that she's gone missing, that her mother is laid low with the worry of it and her stepfather spitting fire. He sent Runners out to all points of the compass, but neither hide nor hair of her has been found. There's a reward out for her safe return.'

'Safe!' Alex exclaimed. 'Home is the last place she would be safe.'

'Why?'

'Because Sir George is gambling with her life.' He saw the look of puzzlement on Joe's face and explained how he came to know Sir George's intentions, making Joe whistle.

'If our Miss Draper is the same lady,' Alex went on, 'I can understand her wish to remain undiscovered.'

'Are you going to face her with it?'

'No. We will allow her the comfort of her disguise. And you will say nothing either. If she wants me to know, she will tell me in her own time.'

'You can rely on me, Major. But o' course we could be wrong all along.'

'We could.' He paused. 'There's a dozen or so men coming here today. Find out what they need in the way of implements and materials and set them to work on the yacht. I want it to look like a miniature battleship. I'm going to talk to my aunt and then I'm going after our intrepid adventurer. She could find herself in danger without even knowing it.'

He had already explained to Joe about his project and been promised his wholehearted support, so he had no qualms about leaving him in charge. No one knew better that Joe Bland, one-time long-serving sergeant, how to get the best out of a band of men. He found his aunt in her parlour with a pair of wire spectacles on her nose, reading a local newspaper.

'You have already made your mark,' she said when he entered the room. 'There is an account here of everything you have done since you arrived and couched in the most glowing terms. There is even a hint that you are planning a most spectacular entertainment for the whole population.' She put the paper down and looked up at him. 'That is what you need to make the regatta a success, Alex, good publicity.'

'Yes, I know. Without it, no one will know what is happening. I thought I might go into Kendal and arrange for posters to be printed and distributed.' He sat down opposite her. 'Aunt, there is something particular I want to ask you.'

'Ask away, dear boy, I will answer if I can.'

'Do you know who Fanny Draper really is?'

'Oh, dear, perhaps I should have said I will answer if I am at liberty to do so.'

'It is not your secret to tell?'

'No.'

'But you do know she is not Fanny Draper?'

'Alex, you are making it very difficult for me. It is not in my nature to tell an untruth.'

'Then do not say anything. Nod your head if I am right. She is not Fanny Draper, she is Lady Emma Lindsay.' Amelia nodded, obviously distressed. 'Do not worry, Aunt, I am not going to tax her with it. I know perfectly well why she had to leave home. I was there when the bargain was struck.'

'You were?' she asked in surprise.

'Yes.' For the second time that morning he explained what had happened.

'Does she know you were there?'

'Heaven forbid! But how did you become involved?'

'Her mother is an old friend of mine. She sent her to me. It was done in such a hurry, she could not pack properly, nor be given sufficient funds. Her mama gave her a pearl necklace and told her to pawn it if she needed money. Unfortunately, it turned out to be made of paste. I was so thankful you were on hand to see she was safe.'

'The devil had the real pearls, I'll be bound. Is there no end to his wickedness? But talking of being safe, do you know where she has gone this morning?'

'She told Mrs Granger she was going for a walk and asked her where the best views were. Mrs Granger suggested Loughrigg, seeing it's a fairly easy climb, or round Wansfell to Jenkyns Crag.'

His heart sank; the walks were in opposite directions. Grimly, he said, 'The wind is getting up and I think there's a storm blowing up. I'm going to look for her.'

'A storm? Oh, merciful heavens! Take some of the men with you.

You'll never find her alone. Oh dear, oh dear, whatever will her mother say? She sent her to me to be safe and I have failed her.' She had left her seat and was pacing the room in her agitation. 'Oh, I shall never forgive myself if she is lost or hurt. Find her Alex, find her, please.'

He endeavoured to retain a calm façade, for his aunt's sake, but his voice betrayed his fear as he promised, 'I will. Do not distress yourself. I'll be back with her safe and sound in no time.' He left her standing at the widow, peering up into the hills, as if trying to see into the distance and discover Emma's whereabouts.

Back in the stables he had his horse saddled because he would be quicker on horseback. Then he told the men to leave off what they were doing and search the fells, some to go to Wansfell, some to Grasmere and Rydal Water. 'Every nook and cranny,' he commanded. He did not wait to see if they understood but, slinging a coil of rope over his shoulder just in case it should be needed, mounted Salamanca and galloped off down the road to Waterhead, crossed the bridge and made for Loughrigg. He did not know if the stallion would manage the whole ascent, but he would ride as far as he could, then tether him.

The wind blew the rain in from the west and Emma pulled her jacket closer about her and plodded on. She ought to abandon her walk and return by the quickest route to the valley and home. There was a path leading downwards and she took it, but it petered out and she found herself looking about her for a landmark, something to give her a direction, and was shocked to find she was alone. There were no other walkers in sight. They had obviously interpreted the weather signs before she did and made their way off the fells. She told herself she could not possibly be lost. Ambleside lay behind her and Grasmere to the north, though what was on the western side of the hill she had no idea. Had she strayed there? The wind was in her face. That was surely the wrong direction. She turned and tried walking with it at her back, but there was no path and the rain was making the scree slippery.

It was then she heard the dog barking. A minute later it raced up to her, wagging its tail. It was a wiry little terrier and she stooped to pet it. 'Have you come to see me safely home, or are you lost, too?' she asked. The answer was more frenzied barking. It raced off a few yards and then stopped and turned back to her. 'Yes, I know you want me to follow. So lead on, little fellow.'

The dog ran off and she followed. It stopped several times to wait for her to catch up before setting off again. She had no idea where the animal was leading her. Sometimes they were struggling uphill, sometimes almost running downwards. Sometimes she had to scramble over boulders that the rain had made slippery. She found herself crawling on hands and knees more than once.

The dog stopped suddenly on the edge of a steep scree slope and stood barking. She went to the edge, knowing there was no way down. How foolish she had been to follow the dog, for now she was hopelessly lost. A thin cry came to her from somewhere below her feet and she bent down to see a little boy about ten feet down on a ledge between two massive rocks, which had checked his fall.

'Are you hurt?' she called down, but he was too distressed to answer.

She looked about her. There was no one in sight and the rain was making visibility very poor. 'Do you know where I can get help?' she asked.

'I wanna go home. I want me ma.'

There was nothing for it. While the dog continued its frenzied barking, she scrambled down the steep incline until she joined the child on the ledge, breathless, scratched and bruised. 'Now we've both to climb back up,' she said. 'If I help you, do you think you can make it?' She put an arm about him and hauled him to his feet. He was barefoot and not above seven years old. He stood on one foot, but refused to put his weight on the other. She sat him down again, tore off her petticoat and made a bandage to tie about his ankle. 'We will have to go up on hands and knees,' she told him. 'Do you think you can manage that if I come up close behind you?'

He nodded, braver now he had company, but though he tried, the climb was too painful for him and they were forced to retreat back to the ledge. She sat down beside him and cuddled him to her. 'We'll just have to wait here until someone finds us.'

It was cold and wet and he was shivering. She held him close, opening her jacket and wrapping it about both of them, talking soothingly. 'What is your name, little one?'

'Sam, missus.'

'How did you come to fall down here? Were you lost?'

'No.' It was said scathingly. 'It was Nipper. He chased a rabbit and fell down, so I went after him, but he got back on his own…'

'Leaving you hurt and stuck. Never mind, he found me, so perhaps he will find someone else. He is making enough noise to rouse the whole town. Do you live in Ambleside, Sam?'

'On the fell.'

She looked up at the dog, which was peering down at them, barking fit to burst. 'Go home, Nipper,' she shouted. 'Go and fetch help. Go on, Nipper. Go!'

He disappeared, but was back in a few moments and barking again, obviously reluctant to leave them. Emma realised it could be a long while before they were found and wondered if she ought to persuade the child to let her try to climb up and go for help, but she did not like to leave him. There was a nasty drop on one side of them; if he fell again, he would be dashed to pieces. Come to that, so would she.

She did not know how long it was, but it seemed an age when the dog, which had become quiet, started barking again. 'All right, young feller, what's all the noise about?' The voice was a man's and it was addressing the dog.

'Help!' Emma shouted. 'We're down here.'

A head peered down at them. 'Miss Draper, is that you?'

She was never more pleased to see him and hear his voice, so matter of fact that he might have been making polite conversation over the teacups. 'Yes. There's a little boy with me. He's hurt his ankle.'

'Right, we'll soon have you both up.' A rope came snaking down towards her. 'Can you tie that securely under the lad's arms and steady him while I pull?'

'Yes.' She grabbed the end and did as he asked. 'Right, you can take him up now, but be careful, he's hurt and afraid.'

She stood up and held the boy's injured leg away from the scree until he was out of reach. He whimpered that his leg hurt, but Alex reached down and caught him, pulling him gently to safer ground. 'There you are, young feller m'lad. You sit still while I get the lady up and then we'll take you home.' The rope went down again and Emma fastened it about her. Alex pulled, but she was able to steady herself and use her feet to scramble up, though she sent showers of loose scree tumbling down the slope behind her, and was soon sitting on the top beside the boy.

Alex squatted down and unfastened the rope, then took her shaking body into his arms and hugged her so tightly she could hardly breathe. 'Thank God, I found you,' he said, wanting to scold her, kiss her, tell her how she had frightened him, that if anything had happened to her his life would not be worth living, but he did none of those things. Better to remain practical. 'How on earth did you get down there? Did you fall?'

'No. I went to rescue the boy. I thought I would be able to help him clamber up. I didn't realise he had hurt himself.'

'My poor girl,' he murmured against her bedraggled hair. 'I never knew anyone quite like you for falling into bumblebaths. Are you hurt?'

It was wonderful to hear the concern in his voice, even though he was scolding her. 'A few scratches, that's all. Look after Sam.'

He turned to the boy, questioned him about where he lived and, having been told it was not far, picked him up and set off with him in his arms with Emma beside him. The rain had eased though visibility was still poor, but he seemed to have no difficulty picking his way. 'There,' Sam said, pointing at a hut built of rough stones, from the chimney of which issued smoke. It had a door, but no window. The door was so low Alex had to duck his head to pass under the lintel.

There was a woman standing by the fire and a girl of about fourteen sitting at a rough table eating what looked like thin soup. They turned as Alex entered with his burden. 'Merciful Heaven! What has happened?' the woman cried, dashing forward.

'The boy has hurt his ankle,' Alex said, looking round for somewhere to put him down. He saw a settle with its stuffing coming out along one wall and put him on that. 'He is also wet and cold and so is—' He stopped when he heard Emma give a little cry of distress and turned just in time to catch her as she fell. He let her down, squatting on the hard floor beside her and lifting her head on to his thigh, looking down at her paper-white face and cursing himself for not taking better care of her.

'It's the warmth of the room, after the wet and cold outside, has made her faint,' he said, stroking her wet hair from her face with gentle fingers.

'Lizzie, look after your brother,' the woman said. 'I'll see to the young lady.'

She instructed Alex to carry Emma to a straw mattress on the floor in the corner and began stripping off her wet clothes. Alex felt he ought to leave while this was being done, and was turning away, when the woman spoke. 'I don't have any spare clothes, so we'll have to wrap her in a blanket until hers are dry. Here, take them and put them round the fire.' A handful of clothes were waved at him. He took them and spread them round the fender, reflecting that if Emma were conscious she would be mortified to think he had seen and handled her most intimate garments. 'Lizzie, how's Sam doing?'

'He's gone to sleep, Ma. I've took his wet clothes off and covered him with Da's old coat.'

'Let him sleep, then. I'll look at his ankle when he wakes.' She turned to Alex. 'Tell me what happened.'

'I will leave that to the lady when she comes round,' he said. 'I'm going to call off the search and fetch some fresh clothes for her. You'll look after her until I get back?'

''Course I will.'

'Tell her I'll be as quick as I can.' With that he was gone.

The hut was on a well-worn path that led over the top of the fell from Hawkshead to Ambleside, a route trodden by generations of shepherds, and he was soon back where he had left his horse. Joe was standing beside it, scratching his head. 'Wondered where you'd got to,' he said.

'She's found, Joe, safe and well, but soaked to the skin. Call off the search and round the men up.'

'Where is she, then?'

'Resting with a family in one of those old abandoned shepherd's huts. I'm going to get her some fresh clothes and bring her horse up.' He left Joe and rode down to the road and then galloped back to Highhead Hall.

Half an hour later he was on his way back, riding Salamanca and leading Bonny, with Emma's habit and fresh underclothes packed in her old carpet bag fastened to the saddle.

Emma was sitting wrapped in a fusty-smelling blanket in front of the fire in what could only be called a hovel. Pigs at Pinehill were kept in better conditions, but it was apparently where this little family, Mrs Yates, daughter Lizzie and son Sam, had lived ever since she had been sent the news that her husband had been killed on active service and their landlord had evicted them because they could no longer pay the rent of their cottage. Mrs Yates eked out a living scrubbing and sewing, leaving Lizzie to look after her brother.

'Sam's a handful,' she told Emma, with a sigh. 'Always running off with that dog o' his. Sometimes he brings back a rabbit for the pot, so I don't scold him too much and he's almost as footsure as a goat. I was frettin' that he hadn't come back for his tea, and saying as how I'd hev to go out an' look for 'im, when the gen'leman brought him in. I'm right grateful to him and to you too. But how did you come to be out in such terrible weather?'

'It wasn't terrible when I set out. The rain took me unawares. I was making my way back when I heard the dog barking. I would never have found your little boy otherwise and it was the dog that alerted his lordship who was out looking for me.'

'His lordship,' the woman echoed. 'You mean the gen'leman is a lord?'

'A viscount. Viscount Malvers.'

'My, I never would have guessed, he's not haughty at all and there was me ordering him to—' She stopped suddenly, remembering how she had waved the young lady's clothes at him. 'He'll be back direc'ly. He's gone to call off the search and fetch you something fresh to wear. Is he your husband?'

'No. I am staying with his aunt at Highhead Hall.'

'I know it. Lord Bourne's place, ain't it?'

'Yes. He died recently and Lord Malvers has taken over Highhead.'

'I heard tell there was a new man there. Do he mean to live there?'

'I don't know. I do not think he has made up his mind yet.'

'Would you like some broth?'

Emma doubted the woman could spare it, but wondered if she would give offence if she refused, but before she could reply, there was a knock at the door. 'That'll be the lord,' Mrs Yates said, going to open the door for Alex.

He bent his tall frame under the lintel and handed Mrs Yates the bag. 'I think there's everything Miss Draper needs in there. I'll wait outside while she dresses.' And he was gone again.

He stood outside, looking up at the sky. It was growing dusk. The rain had cleared and a few stars peeped through thinning cloud, but he did not trust the weather, particularly this year which had been one of almost non-stop rain. The sooner he had Fanny safely back at Highhead Hall, the better. He had been so relieved to find her. It was his fault she had gone off alone; she had not been able to trust him with her secret, though she must have known it would all come out in the end. Somehow or other he must persuade her to tell him the truth, assure her he would not dream of betraying her. But that would not be the end of it; they would still have Sir George and Bentwater to deal with.

He turned as the door opened behind him and Mrs Yates beckoned him back inside. Emma was dressed in the dark blue habit with a warm cloak over it. His aunt had even included a hairbrush in the bag and she had made an attempt to brush her tangled locks, but they were still damp and curled all over the place. He wanted to take her into his arms and kiss her until she was breathless. Instead he simply stood drinking in the sight of her, and then, pulling himself together, took the bag that Mrs Yates offered him. 'I think we should be going before it becomes too dark to see,' he said. 'Mrs Yates, I am very grateful to you.'

'Not at all, sir, I mean, my lord, you saved my Sam. I'm the grateful one.'

He looked about him, appalled by the poverty of the place. 'Could you do with some work, Mrs Yates? And somewhere else to live?'

'I never say no to earning an honest groat,' she said. 'But I can't live in anywhere on account of Lizzie and Sam.'

He guessed that was why she had made a home of the old hut. 'They can come too,' he said. 'I'll come and see how young Sam is tomorrow and we'll talk about it.'

'Thank you, my lord.' It was said quietly; she was too proud to grovel and he liked her for that.

Emma hugged her, and then hugged and kissed Sam who was wide awake now and, though his ankle hurt him, was otherwise none the worse for his ordeal. 'I'll see you again soon,' she said. 'I'll not forget you.'

She followed Alex from the hut to find, to her surprise, he had brought the horses right to the door. 'How did you get them up here?'

'My dear Miss Draper, we are not so far from the road. Did you not know where you were?'

'No. I was lost, trying to find my way down.'

He led her to the mare and cupped his hands to help her to mount. 'She's sure footed, but I'll go first and you follow. Do you think you can manage? I'll lead you, if you like.'

'Certainly not. I can ride.'

He led the way and they went one behind the other until the path widened and became a proper track, but it was not until they reached the road they were able to ride side by side. Even then they were both too full of what had happened, of secrets not yet confessed, of feelings they could not put into words, to talk much. Instead, she said, 'I feel sorry for Mrs Yates, living in that dreadful place with Sam running wild because his sister is not strong enough to curb him. It could have been a lot worse; he could have tumbled right to the bottom of that slope and been dashed to pieces. Something like that might happen next time he goes missing. I am so glad you said you would help them.'

'She is just the sort of person I had in mind when I said I wanted to do something for ex-soldiers and their families. I'll talk to my aunt about her, but it will do tomorrow. It is more important now to see you safely home and in the warm. My aunt was very worried about you being lost and blaming herself.'

Emma was sorry to have distressed the good lady and all because she was too cowardly to face up to the truth. And she still did not know what Joe Bland had told Lord Malvers, who was treating her exactly as he always had, rescuing her from the coils into which she had tumbled with tolerant amusement. What would she do if he were no longer on hand to do that? He was still addressing her as Miss Draper, so did that mean he knew no more than he had before? Supposing he returned to Norfolk or London with nothing resolved between them?

She was girding up her courage to say something when they caught up with the last of the men who had been searching for her. They expressed their pleasure at seeing her safe and ran alongside the horses all the way back to the house. And then Amelia was at the door to welcome them and another opportunity was lost.

Emma was cosseted, fed, bathed and sent to bed to rest, and though she did not expect to sleep, she did.

* * *

When she rose next morning, she was told Alex had gone out very early. 'He has gone to see Mrs Yates,' Mrs Summers told her. 'What with all these extra hands to feed, Mrs Granger needs more help. And there are plenty of men about the place to keep the young lad out of mischief.'

'He said he would give her work and somewhere to live. You should see the hovel they were living in.'

'I've seen many like it. The shepherds use them when they are tending the sheep on the fells. They are certainly not meant for families.'

She looked up as one of the maids brought in the post on a tray. There were several letters for her, and one addressed to Miss Fanny Draper, which she handed to Emma. 'Is this what you have been waiting for?'

Emma tore it open. It was from Harriet Standon, who had obviously been told the secret, telling her that the news that she was safely arrived and in good health had been passed to interested parties, meaning her mother. 'Your sudden disappearance caused such a furore,' Harriet had written. 'Sir George is beside himself with rage, though he pretends it is concern for your safety. He maintains you must have been kidnapped and Lord Bentwater, who is going about saying you are engaged to marry him, has offered a reward for your safe return and information leading to the kidnappers. And I believe they have employed Bow Street Runners to track you down. They found Rose and questioned her, but she maintained she had been turned off before you disappeared, which is what Lady Tasker told Sir George. She is bearing up and Sir George has stopped accusing her of knowing where you are because she is so obviously distressed. Do not, whatever you do, allow your whereabouts to become known. You will be fetched back and those who have helped you will be punished. I wish you could be reinstated to your proper place and be back here in time for my wedding, but I do not hold out much hope of it. Sir George is mad as fire. It is safe to write to me and I shall be pleased to hear all your adventures. Your friend, Harriet.'

She handed the letter to Mrs Summers without speaking. 'Oh,

dear,' the good lady said when she had read it. 'It is plain your step-father has not relented. Your poor, poor mama…'

'I am sure she was relieved to know I had arrived here, but I am worried that I might have put you in danger. Perhaps I should leave.'

'Leave! I won't hear of it. Your mother entrusted you to me and I mean to look after you.'

'But—'

'No buts, please. And it would take a brave man to get the better of Alexander Malvers. You really must tell him now.'

'No. Don't you see? While he is in ignorance, he is safe. They cannot say he aided and abetted if he was not aware that he was doing so—' She stopped because they heard footsteps outside the door. Emma snatched the letter and crammed it into her pocket as Alex came into the room, ushering Mrs Yates in with her two children. 'Here they are,' he said cheerfully.

Mrs Summers was occupied for the next hour or so introducing Mrs Yates to the staff and showing her where she could sleep, a room on the second floor she was to share with Lizzie, who was old enough to help in the house. Sam was found a bed with the men who had living quarters above the stables.

Emma found herself alone with Alex and feeling tongue-tied, which was certainly unusual for her. But the letter, crackling in her pocket, was on her mind. It was very worrying and made her all the more de-termined to remain incognito. No one must know who she really was, no one at all. Any idea she might have had of confiding in Lord Malvers had been blown away on the wind. For his sake, as much as anyone's, her secret must be kept. If her stepfather and Lord Bentwater were going to such extreme lengths to find her, then they would not take kindly to anyone frustrating them.

'Was Mrs Yates pleased to leave that hovel?' she asked when the silence became unbearable. 'Was Sam able to walk?'

'She gave every appearance of being glad to be out of it. As for

Sam, I had him up in front of me. He is a lively young fellow and did not stop talking the whole way. He calls me Mr Lord. His sister is more reserved and somewhat in awe of me.'

'I can understand that. I don't suppose she has met anyone as lofty as you before.'

'I am not lofty.'

She attempted to laugh, though it sounded cracked. 'You must be well over six feet tall.'

'Oh, that kind of lofty.' He grinned. 'Six feet three inches to be exact. Enough of that. How are you today? None the worse for your little adventure, I trust?'

'I am very well,' she said. 'But I do realise how foolish I was to go alone and I owe you a great debt, for without you we might never have been found.'

'It is my pleasure to be of service.' He bowed formally, but he was smiling, his eyes glowing with amusement.

What would he say if he knew his services to her—and they had been many and varied—would not be appreciated in another quarter? Emma wondered. If he had not been on hand to help her, who knows but she would have given up her flight in despair and returned home? 'Perhaps you should give up and let me stew in my own folly in future,' she said. 'I am coming to rely on you too much.'

'I wish you would always do so,' he said softly. 'Rely on me, confide in me, trust me.'

He had made the opening for her, one she had never been able to find for herself and, if it had not been for that letter, she would have seized the opportunity to unburden herself, but now it was too late. She loved him too much to risk having him brought to book for luring her away from her family, or even indicted for kidnap. What did the law do to kidnappers? She had a feeling it might be a death penalty and it would do no good to tell her stepfather she had not been taken against her will. It was too convenient a way of explaining her disappearance and saving his face. 'Oh, I do.'

'Then are you going to tell me why you felt you had to run away yesterday?'

'I didn't run away. I went for a walk.'

'Damn you, woman, you are trying my patience. What you need is a good spanking…' He stopped and took her shoulders in his hands, meaning to give her a little shake, but he saw her eyes widen with shock as if she thought he really meant to carry out his threat. Was he such a tyrant? 'I am sorry,' he said. 'I did not mean to frighten you. You are frightened, aren't you?'

'Not of you,' she whispered. 'Never of you.'

'Then who?'

'No one.' She gave a cracked laugh. 'I am frightened of no one. I am not afraid of the dark or ghosts or wild white horses or men who think that because I am a servant and ignorant I can be kissed with impunity.' She had been thinking of James Griggs, but he thought she meant him and let her go, dropping his hands to his sides.

'Point taken. Miss Fanny Draper is fearless. I am glad of that.' He spoke tersely, angry with her, angry with himself for letting her disturb him to such an extent he could forget his manners. He must try to bring things back on to an even keel. 'That means you will not be afraid of kidnappers.'

'Kidnappers?' she echoed. Did he know, had he known all along?'

'Yes, at the regatta. You said you would do it. You haven't changed your mind, have you?'

She breathed a huge sigh of relief, which was not lost on him. 'Oh, that! Of course I will do it. After all, they are not really going to harm me, are they?'

'They would not dare,' he said.

Chapter Nine

'Would you both like to come out in the carriage with me?' Alex asked his aunt and Emma the following afternoon. 'I am going to inspect the invasion fleet we have assembled down by the jetty and I'm going over to the island to see how the fortress they are building is shaping up. If you are to be carried there by your kidnappers, Miss Draper, it would be as well to see the place first.'

They agreed to go and he went out to the stables to arrange for the carriage to be made ready. He found Sam eagerly grooming his horse, which stood shivering with pleasure.

Joe nodded towards the boy. 'He'll earn his keep, my lord, though he is full of questions: why, who, when and where. Don' seem he's ever satisfied.'

'That's how he'll learn, Joe. I wonder if I ought to put him to school?'

'You can't send every little beggar to school.'

'No, but I could start one, couldn't I? What do you think?'

'No good asking me, Major, I never had any schooling m'self.'

'I'll think about it. Will you have the horses put to the carriage, please? I am taking my aunt and Miss Draper into Bowness. You can drive us.'

'Oh, so she's still Miss Draper, is she?'

'Yes, not safe for her to be anything else, is it?'

'I suppose not, but it makes me wonder where it's all going to end.'

'Me too. She had a letter from London, which seems to have put her into a panic. If Runners have been employed, they'll be looking for kidnappers…'

'Meaning you?' Joe was busy putting one of the horses in the shafts as he spoke.

'I suppose so.'

'What are you going to do about it?'

'Marry her myself.' The determination behind that statement took him by surprise. He realised all his doubts had fled; it had not been his decision, so much as fate's. And it had been made at the precise moment he decided to offer his inside seats to the two ladies at the Swan with Two Necks. So much for his resolve not to marry. What had happened to his determination not to let any woman rule him as Lawrence had been ruled? But Emma was not Constance. Emma was herself, unique among women. '*When* she decides to tell me who she really is,' he added. 'Can't go marrying Miss Fanny Draper, can I? She doesn't exist.'

'And you think her stepfather is going to stand for that, do you?'

'He'll have no choice.'

'Then if you take my advice, Major, you won't waste no time about it.'

'After the regatta. I can't do anything before that.'

Joe had harnessed the other horse and checked everything was ready. 'There you are, my lord, all ready to go. I'll take it round the front of the house, shall I?'

Bowness was a busy little place, the hub of life on Windermere. Situated on the eastern shore by the narrowest part of the lake, it had a jetty and a quay from which all manner of boats plied on the water. A ferry left regularly to cross over to the other side of the lake, knocking hours off the time travelling round its shores. The lake, which was over ten miles long, was divided into two by a string of wooded islands, the largest of which was owned by a Mr Curwen and was called Long Holm. It was not this island that would be the scene of the 'invasion', but a smaller one a little to the north. From the shore it was easy to see the wooden walls of a fortress being constructed on its highest point. Alex hired a boat and he and Joe rowed the ladies over to see it.

Although it looked very realistic from the lakeside, it was not a permanent building and could easily be taken down when the regatta ended. They wandered all round it, inspecting the wooden turrets that were being made to look like stone with grey paint. Cannon poked out from embrasures in the walls. 'Will they fire?' Emma asked him.

'Yes, but they won't be loaded, just make flashes and a great deal of noise when the fleet comes near.'

'And the ships will fire back?'

'Yes, then they'll send in a landing party to fight their way inland to rescue you and bring you back. Are you still prepared to do it?'

'Yes, why not? Will you be leading the rescue party?'

'Oh, most definitely.' He paused to look closely at her. She had rebuffed him that morning, but had she really meant it? He had given her every opportunity to tell him about her stepfather, but she had not taken it. Surely she did not suspect he would hand her over to that apology for a man? 'You do not have to go through with it if you would rather not,' he said quietly.

'Why should I not? Do you think I am afraid?'

He laughed. 'No, for you have assured me that you are afraid of nothing. Besides, there is nothing to fear.'

Nothing to fear, she thought. Nor was there from him, but her whole being was screwed up with fear; she saw her stepfather or Lord Bentwater round every corner, waiting to pounce. And how would she recognise a Bow Street Runner if she saw one? She did not know how much more of it she could stand.

'Shall we return to Bowness and find somewhere to eat?' he asked, noting the thoughtful look on her face and wondering what was passing through her mind. 'Then we can go and see how the ships are coming along. They will be setting sail from Waterhead. The spectators will be able to watch the whole thing from the hills all round the upper part of the lake.'

They returned to the mainland and ate a simple snack at Lowwood Inn on the way back to Waterhead. Afterwards they left the carriage on the road to walk down to the water's edge and here they found the strangest collection of vessels Emma had ever seen. Alex's yacht, the *Lady Jane*, had been painted over all and given a superstructure that, from a distance, made it look like a very small warship. Other yachts had been similarly disguised and there were rowing boats and an old ferry, which he intended to fill with 'invading troops'.

'The ships will be crewed by their owners,' Alex said. 'And the invading troops are volunteers, mostly men who have been working on the conversions.'

'I am sure it is going to be a great talking point,' Mrs Summers said. 'But you said something about other attractions.'

'Yes, stalls and booths are being organised by the town's shopkeepers and rowing and swimming races.'

'And will it all be ready in time?'

'Yes, I am confident it will, but we must pray for fine weather or people will not turn up.'

'And then what?'

'What do you mean?'

'What is going to happen when it is all over? Are you going home to Norfolk?'

'I shall have to go some time, you know.' He paused. 'But there are things I must resolve first.'

Amelia looked sharply at him. 'I understand,' she said.

Emma was quiet as they made their way back to the carriage for the short journey back to Highhead. He was going back to Norfolk. He was going to leave her and she didn't know how she was going to bear it. Her life stretched out before her empty and barren, and how long would Mrs Summers keep her on as a companion? She did not earn her keep; in fact, she was costing the dear lady money. Something must be done.

Alex was also wondering what could be done. He had no intention of going back to Norfolk without her. He had two weeks before the regatta, two weeks in which he must make her see that if she were married to him, she had nothing to fear from her stepfather or that rotter, Bentwater. His resolution not to marry had been blown away by an exasperating, opinionated woman who had wormed her way into his heart and could not be evicted. Life without her was unthinkable.

After the regatta. If it were a success, it could be repeated year on year, but that would not be enough. He must set up workshops to employ the talents of the men he had recruited. A great many wealthy people, attracted by the beautiful scenery, were building homes in the area now. The small, scattered villages and towns were bound to expand. Bricklayers, carpenters, painters, tailors, bootmakers, harness makers, horsemen of all sorts, gardeners and watermen would be needed and the extensive outbuildings of Highhead Hall would make several small workshops. The house itself would become a school for their children. He would speak to the Reverend Griggs, who would be the best one to advise him about setting up a school. The Rector was still not convinced the regatta was a good idea, but had ceased to oppose him. Alex wondered if it was because he had seen James following Emma after the picnic and then come down again alone, rubbing a sore elbow and scowling; he might have guessed what had happened, especially if it was not the first time James had behaved in that fashion. He might have decided it would not do to cross Viscount Malvers. Alex was content to let him go on thinking it.

Highhead Hall was his and he did not legally need his aunt's agreement for his plans for it, but he would not have dreamed of going

ahead without it. He hoped she would consent to live at the dower
house at Buregreen with his mother, when he and Emma moved into
the main house. He thought of her as Emma now, but reminded
himself he must not call her that until she told him to.

She had been animated on their tour of inspection, but now she sat
quietly in the corner of the carriage and the shadows had come down
over her face again. Oh, how he longed to banish them for good. And
he would too. Soon.

He took the opportunity the next morning, when Emma was outside
with Sam, to talk to his aunt about his ideas. 'Aunt, can you spare a
moment?' he said, finding her in her little parlour, writing letters.

She laid down her pen. 'Yes, of course.'

He sat opposite her and told her of his idea of making the Hall
into a school, ending with his suggestion she should move in with
his mother. 'The dower house is substantial and in good repair,' he
said. 'There is room enough for two of you not to get under each
other's feet.'

'I have always been fond of my sister,' she told him. 'But I think
it would not serve. Two strong-minded women sharing a house is not
a good idea. And besides, my home is here, by the lakes, where I have
been happy with my husband and brother.'

'Of course. It was only an idea.'

She smiled. 'You will need a housekeeper for your little school, so
why don't I stay on and fill that role?'

'Are you sure about that? Children can be noisy and adventurous
and you have been used to a quiet life.'

'Too quiet sometimes. Having Emma here has taught me that I
should be making myself useful. I am not in my dotage yet, Alex.' He
noted her use of Emma's real name, but did not comment on it.
Obviously, his aunt trusted him, even if Emma did not.

'I know that. I never meant to imply you were.'

'And there is Emma to consider. What is to happen to her?'

He stood up and began pacing the floor. It was the time for truth, with his aunt at least. 'I hope she will consent to marry me, but I am not at all sure of her. If she had any regard for me, she would have given up this pretence of hers long ago.'

'I suspect she is afraid, Alex.'

'Of me?' He stopped his perambulation in astonishment. 'I cannot believe that.'

'Not *of* you, *for* you. She is afraid her stepfather has enough influence to have you arrested for kidnapping her. He has to save face in the eyes of the world and it is my guess Lord Bentwater is not letting go. He, too, needs to save face.'

'That's nonsense.'

'Perhaps. I don't know. You have met the man—what do you think?'

'He's a leech, a charlatan, but if Emma and I were married, there would be nothing he could do, would there?'

'Would you be marrying Emma simply to remove her from his influence? It would be just like you, boy, soft-hearted as you are, but not a good basis for a marriage.'

'Good God! Do you think that? Would she think it?'

'We have not discussed it. That is for you to do.'

'But, Aunt, I love her dearly, there is nothing I would not do for her, give my life if necessary.' It was the first time he had admitted that, even to himself.

'Have you told her so?'

'No, of course not.'

'Then don't you think it is about time you did?' She smiled suddenly. 'For a man of the world, a soldier used to command men, and I've no doubt a favourite among the ladies, you are being exceptionally tardy. What is holding you back? Are you afraid?'

'No. She does not make it easy.'

She smiled, understanding him more thoroughly than he understood himself. 'Alex, you must learn to unbend a little. You are not in the army now and it is not a weakness to let your feelings show. If you love her, tell her so.'

'If she loved me, she would confide in me. Instead she sticks to the fiction that she is Fanny Draper, your companion.'

'I suspect one of the reasons she is being so obdurate is that she does not want to make a liar of me in the eyes of my friends. I have condoned her deception.'

'With very good reason.'

'Yes.' She paused. 'Alex, can you not marry Fanny Draper?'

'She does not exist. Would such a marriage be legal?'

'I don't know, do I? Ask lawyer Dewhurst. You can trust him.'

'Perhaps I will.' He got up to leave her. She was wise and generous and what she had said was sensible.

'Alex,' she added, as he reached the door, 'tell Emma what is in your heart. It is the girl you love, not what she is called. A rose by any other name…'

He grinned. 'I will.'

He left her and went to the stables to have his horse saddled. Emma was in the yard with Sam. She had Bonny on a long lead, making her circle round the yard with Sam on her back. He stood and watched her for several minutes; her capacity for fun was remarkable given her circumstances and his heart almost burst with love. Whatever happened, she must be kept safe and if that meant she lived the rest of her life as Fanny Draper, then so be it. He would go into Ambleside and talk to Dewhurst and while he was there put the school idea to the Reverend.

She saw him watching her and stopped to face him. 'Sam is learning to ride.'

He smiled. 'So I see. But the mare is too big for him.'

'She is docile and won't run away with him while I have her on a rein.'

'Are you going out any more today?' he asked.

'Not unless Mrs Summers has errands for me.'

'I am going into Ambleside. When I come back, I want to talk to you.'

'What about?' she asked guardedly.

'Oh, something and nothing,' he said enigmatically. 'Your role as a kidnapped damsel.'

'Oh, that. I've been thinking of that myself.'

'Keep it until I return.' He laughed suddenly. She had stopped turning, but Bonny had not and the reins were now wound about her waist. Realising what had happened, she twirled herself round and round, endeavouring to unwind herself, and Sam was curled up with laughter.

He rode into Ambleside with the echo of her laughter in his ears, rehearsed in his mind what he would say to her, how he would convince her that he was in earnest when he said he loved her and wanted to marry her. But should he tell her he knew she was Lady Emma Lindsay, or continue the pretence, which he hated? Was that any more a good basis for marriage than marrying her for pity, which certainly was not the case? He was sorry for her, yes, but pity came nowhere near it. For one thing she did not invite it; she was independent and courageous to the point of recklessness. The thought of someone like Bentwater trying to kill that spirit spurred him on.

He dismounted at the door of the lawyer's office, which was in the centre of the town, and threw his reins to an urchin, telling him to mind his horse, and then, turning, found himself face to face with Jeremy Maddox.

The young man was dressed in his usual flamboyant style, peach-coloured pantaloons and a striped coat, his shirt collar scratching his cheeks, his elaborately tied cravat fastened with a diamond pin. He grinned when he saw Alex. 'We are well met, Malvers. I was about to come and look for you.'

Alex's thoughts flew to Emma. Maddox had been present when Lord Bentwater had made that outrageous offer to Sir George and he had said he was going to the ball at Almack's to see what happened. Had he done so? Would he recognise Emma in Fanny Draper? 'What are you doing here?' he demanded.

'Hold on, old fellow, you will make me think you are not pleased to see me.'

'Sorry. I was taken aback. You are so far from the capital.'

'A man can take a holiday, can't he? London seemed devilish dull, so I thought I'd find out how you were faring. Brighten your life up a little.'

'I am well, as you can see, and my life is not dull, but how did you know where to find me? I did not know myself, the last time I saw you.'

'Admiral Lord Bourne's death was reported in the newspapers and the fact that you had succeeded to the estate. You did not return to London, so I assumed you were still here.'

'I've been kept busy.'

'So I discovered when I enquired after you. Making a name for yourself with plans for a grand regatta, I hear. Come to my hotel and share a glass and you can tell me all about it.'

Alex abandoned any idea of calling on the lawyer and, leading his horse, accompanied his erstwhile gambling partner to the Unicorn. They were soon sitting in a corner of the parlour over a bottle of good claret. 'Now,' Maddox said, leaning back in his seat and smiling, 'tell me all about it. Was it expected, this inheritance of yours?'

'No, it came as a surprise. I did not know until after my uncle's death. I learned he was ill and wanted to see me, so I dropped everything to come up here. What news of the capital? When we last spoke, you were thinking of going to Almack's.'

'So I did and saw Lord Bentwater and Sir George Tasker and his wife and the young lady.'

'Young lady?' He tried not to sound too interested.

'Yes, you remember. Sir George tried to barter her for his vouchers. Bentwater danced with her. Good-looking gel, though a mite too tall for most men. She did not look happy.'

'I am not surprised, are you? How would you like to be ordered to marry someone so loathsome?'

'I wouldn't. The funny thing is, she disappeared.'

'Disappeared? How?' He managed just the right amount of surprise.

'No one knows. She simply vanished. There are all manner of rumours flying around. Sir George has put it about she has been kidnapped for a ransom, which he swears he will not pay. Well, you and I know he cannot because he is in debt up to his ears. Lord Bentwater is telling everyone she is affianced to him and has offered a reward for her return, pretending to be heartbroken over her abduction and swearing vengeance on the perpetrators. It was in all the London papers, with a description of her. So far nothing has come of it. At any rate, not when I left town three days ago.'

'What do you think has happened to her?'

Maddox shrugged. 'No telling, is there?'

'Perhaps she simply ran away.'

'How could she do that on her own? Lady like her wouldn't know where to start. And, according to rumour, she took nothing with her. Can't see a chit like that moving far without a mountain of luggage, can you?'

'So you favour the kidnap idea?'

'Makes more sense, but why hasn't someone asked for a ransom or come forward for the reward?'

'Perhaps they have and no one's saying.'

'Or perhaps she's dead. Kidnappers aren't always gentle with their victims, are they? It's been weeks now and neither sight nor sound of her. If they wanted money, they would have asked for it before now. Can people disappear so completely unless they're dead? One minute there, the next gone.'

'I don't know.' He paused and took a deep breath to ask the question uppermost in his mind. 'Would you know her if you met her again?'

'I don't know that I should. I only saw her for a minute and not close up. Why do you ask?'

'No reason. I just wondered how anyone could be sure it was her if they did not know her.'

'They can't, of course. There have been reports of her being seen, but none of them turned out to be her after all. If she isn't dead, she's being hid.'

'Possibly. Can you imagine her friends and relations giving her up to that man?'

'Depends how frightened they were of the consequences. For all we know, she might have been willing to marry Bentwater and he is in the right of it.'

'Possible, I suppose, but unlikely.'

'Not our business anyway, is it?' As far as Jeremy was concerned, he had said all that needed to be said and was ready to move on. 'Now, tell me about this regatta you are organising.'

Alex did not want to arouse Maddox's curiosity by continuing with the subject, so he spent some minutes telling his friend about the regatta and his plans for the future, though he was careful to say nothing about Miss Fanny Draper. He had barely finished when they heard someone say, 'Oh, Mama, there is Lord Malvers.'

Alex looked up to see Lady Pettifer and Charlotte coming towards them. He rose to bow to them. 'Good morning, my lady. Miss Pettifer.' He could feel Jeremy tugging at his coat tail. 'My lady, may I present my friend, Mr Jeremy Maddox? He has lately come up from London.'

Jeremy bowed and smiled. 'Enchanted,' he said.

'Are you related to Lord Maddox of Pelham Park?' her ladyship asked.

He grinned. 'His son and heir. Do you know him?'

'I did many years ago. How is he?'

'Hale and hearty. Will you join us? We were about to partake of refreshment. Tea and cake, perhaps.' He beckoned to a waiter and in no time at all they were sitting down together and he was telling the ladies his life history.

Charlotte was glowing with triumph and Alex knew she would soon be crowing to her friends about this new conquest. And Jeremy appeared to be enjoying himself hugely. If Alex had hoped the man's stay in the area would be short, he soon realised how wrong he was because he heard them talking about the regatta.

'I certainly intend to stay and see it,' Jeremy was saying. 'And if I can prevail upon my friend here to allow it, I should like to take part. It might be fun.'

'Oh, we are all looking forward to it, aren't we, Mama? They are going to build some viewing platforms near the water and we have already booked our places. And afterwards there is to be a ball.'

'Then I shall certainly attend and ask you to stand up with me.'

Alex was sunk in gloom. The last thing he wanted was for anyone who had ever seen Emma in London to come here. He knew common courtesy dictated that he should ask Jeremy to stay at Highhead Hall, but he did not want him anywhere near the place, not while Emma was there. He broke up the party at length by saying he had been on his way to visit his lawyer when he met Mr Maddox and, if they would excuse him, he would go now.

Jeremy was enjoying being flattered by the ladies and he waved him off with a dismissive hand. 'Yes, you go, old fellow. I'm perfectly content in the company of these lovely ladies.'

When he arrived back at Highhead Hall, he was told by Joe that Mrs Summers and Miss Draper had taken Mrs Yates, Lizzie and Sam into Kendal to do some shopping. He paced about the yard, unable to settle, then went down to the jetty at Waterhead to see how the ships were coming along and to hold a rehearsal. He would look very foolish if the boats all sank when they were called on to rescue the maiden.

Mrs Yates needed clothes and so did Sam, whose trousers were halfway up his skinny calves and his elbows were through his jacket sleeves. And really, Mrs Summers said, he should not be running about the yard barefoot. It did no good for Mrs Yates to protest; the lady took no more notice of her than she had of Emma in a similar situation. Servants needed uniforms, especially if they were to be seen by her friends.

It took the rest of the day to kit out all three, but Mrs Summers was in her element. 'What are you going to wear for the regatta, Fanny?'

she asked when they were all sitting in a private parlour in the Woolpack, drinking tea. 'I believe you are to be carried by two burly men and forced into a boat; it ought not to be anything too elaborate.'

'I really had not thought about it. I suppose a riding habit and I could wear breeches under it, but my habit is far too good for that, I would be afraid of spoiling it. Perhaps my grey stripe with lots of petticoats.'

'Grey will not show up against the water or the walls of the fort,' Mrs Summers said. 'You must have something bright so that the spectators can pick you out, struggling with your captors and tied to the flagpole at the top of the tower.'

'Mrs Summers do be right,' Annie Yates said. 'I could stitch you something in red or yellow. A full-tiered skirt, perhaps, and a bright blouse…'

'Yes, but I do not want it to come up round my ears when they carry me off. I should be mortified.'

'Matching breeches, perhaps,' Annie said.

'Good idea,' Mrs Summers said. 'Let us go and purchase the material now, it will save another journey.'

It was late afternoon by the time they passed through Bowness and turned towards Waterhead, well satisfied with their shopping trip. The horses were cantering along the road beside the lake when Sam spotted some strange-looking craft on the water. 'Look at those!' he cried. 'It's Mr Lord's fleet. Can we stop and watch them?'

Mrs Summers instructed the coachman to pull up at the approach to the jetty and they all went down to the water's edge to watch the flotilla making its way back to the landing stage. Alex was captaining the *Lady Jane* and was standing in the prow, looking very tall and almost piratical with his shirt sleeves rolled up, no cravat and the breeze blowing through his hair. Emma, watching him, was almost overcome with mixed emotions. He was so big and handsome and so kind and generous, even to a nobody like Fanny Draper, but that could not be love, not the sort of love that led to marriage. That was for his social equal, which Emma Lindsay was, but not Fanny Draper. She loved him and ought not to have secrets from him when he had done so much for her. Her feelings for him, her love, were all mixed up with a terrible fear, not that anything would happen to him while on the lake, but what would happen if her stepfather found out where she was? What could he do to this man who had become so dear to her?

The craft bumped against the jetty and he jumped down and secured the mooring rope before walking over to them.

'We've been shopping,' Sam told him. 'I've got new shoes.'

He ruffled the boy's hair. 'Then make sure you take care of them, but surely it has not taken all afternoon to buy a pair of shoes?'

'Oh, no, we bought heaps and heaps of things. Mrs Summers said you were paying for it.'

'Did she, now?' He looked over the boy's head at Amelia. 'Did you get everything you needed?'

'Yes, and some material for Fanny's dress for the regatta. Mrs Yates has volunteered to make it up for her.'

'Bright red,' Sam put in. 'And yellow. Mrs Summers says she must be seen.'

'Oh.' He was thoughtful. Was that such a good idea, making a spectacle of her, especially if Maddox was going to be there? Perhaps it would be better to dissuade her. 'I want to talk to you about that,' he said, addressing Emma.

'So you said. Is there a problem?'

'Later,' he said, looking up as a horseman was heard on the road, cantering towards them. He cursed under his breath. It was Jeremy and he had spotted them.

'There you are, Malvers.' He dismounted, threw his reins carelessly to Alex's coachman who was standing beside the greys, and strolled over to join them. He looked at the strange collection of vessels and laughed. 'Is this your invasion fleet?'

'Yes.' He could see his aunt looking questioningly at him and realised he would have to introduce them and that meant he could not really avoid naming Emma as well. If Maddox recognised her, if he said he knew she was Lady Emma Lindsay, should he pretend surprise, pour scorn on the whole idea, or admit it and swear the man to secrecy? But he hadn't even told Emma he knew the truth yet and now he wondered if he should. She had been right to be cautious.

'Aunt Amelia, may I present my friend, Mr Jeremy Maddox? He has recently come up from London.' He saw Emma's eyes widen in shock as he added, 'Mr Maddox, my aunt, Mrs Summers.'

Amelia shook his hand. 'Always pleased to meet a friend of Alex's,' she said. 'Are you here for long?'

'I came to see how Alex did. He has been away from the Smoke so long, and now I find him in the middle of fighting a war and am of a mind to stay and take part. And I have been invited to a ball at the Assembly rooms and am determined not to miss that.' He looked round at the rest of the company and immediately dismissed Mrs Yates and her children as of no importance, but his eye lighted on Emma. Alex realised at once that she had recognised him, even if he had shown no sign of remembering her.

Amelia had seen it too and put a reassuring hand on Emma's arm. 'This is my companion, Miss Fanny Draper, Mr Maddox.'

'Your obedient, Miss Draper.' He bowed and she curtsied, looking downwards, not meeting his gaze.

'Fanny has been my helpmate for ages,' Amelia lied gallantly. 'I do not know what I would do without her.'

He smiled. 'Then you must pray no one carries her off and marries her, madam. Someone as comely as Miss Draper is unlikely to remain single for long.'

'Maddox, you are putting Miss Draper to the blush,' Alex snapped. 'They are not used to your London ways up here.'

'I beg your pardon. A pretty compliment is a compliment wherever it is uttered and Miss Pettifer did not seem to mind me.'

'Do you know Miss Pettifer, sir?' Emma asked, speaking for the first time.

'Why, Alex, here, introduced me to her only this morning. We had a pleasant little coze in the… What was the place called?' He appealed to Alex.

'The Unicorn.' It was said flatly. He had seen the look of surprise and hurt pass over Emma's face and knew she had misunderstood the nature of his trip into Ambleside. He wished Jeremy Maddox anywhere but where he was, adding to his torment and Emma's too. 'We met by accident.'

'If you will excuse us, gentlemen, we must be going home,' Amelia said.

'Oh, not yet,' Sam wailed. 'I haven't looked at the ships.'

'Neither have I,' Jeremy said. 'Are you going to show me round, Malvers?'

'A pleasure,' he said, though he could not make it sound like a pleasure. 'You can come too, Sam. I'll take you home with me.'

The ladies went off in the carriage. Emma was silent all the way, though Amelia managed to keep up a light conversation with Mrs Yates. When they arrived, Mrs Yates and Lizzie went to the kitchen to help Mrs Granger with the dinner preparations and Emma and Mrs Summers went up to their rooms to take off their outdoor clothes and dress for dinner.

Emma shut her bedroom door and flung herself on her bed. She had never felt less like eating. She remembered Mr Maddox. She had seen him talking to her stepfather at Almack's and she had asked Harriet who he was, thinking he might be Lord Bentwater. He knew Sir George and probably Lord Bentwater, too, and if he knew who she was, if he knew she had disappeared and there was a reward for her return…he would tell Alex. Oh, she was in the most terrible fix.

She sat on the edge of her bed, hugging her arms round herself, and rocked to and fro in despair. She must run away again. But where? And this time there would be no Rose Turner, no Alex Malvers to help her and no Mrs Summers at the end of the journey to give her sanctuary. What had that odious James Griggs said about scrubbing floors?

It was beginning to look like reality. And to make her distress even worse, Alex had met Charlotte Pettifer in Ambleside and she was infernally jealous.

A light knock at the door preceded Mrs Summers's entry into the room. 'Not changed, Emma?' she queried, sitting down beside her. 'Did you not hear the bell?'

'No.' A monotone.

'I can guess what you are thinking, you are thinking you must run away again. I must tell you here and now it is not to be thought of.'

'That man, that friend of his lordship. I have seen him before.'

'I surmised as much. But he gave no sign of recognising you, did he?'

'That's not to say he might not in the future if he stays in the area.'

'Where did you meet?'

'We did not exactly meet. I saw him talking to Sir George at a ball at Almack's the night before I left London. If he is a crony of my stepfather's… You do not think Sir George could have sent him, do you?'

'Emma, child, be sensible. If he noticed you at the ball, he saw a young aristocratic lady dressed in all her finery, someone as far removed from Miss Fanny Draper, lady's companion living quietly in the country, as it is possible to be, especially as he thinks you have lived up here for years.'

'Yes, I thank you for that. But others will soon disillusion him. You heard him say he has already met Miss Pettifer.'

'We will cross that bridge when we come to it. But you cannot disappear again, truly you cannot. Nothing would arouse his suspicion more. You must brazen it out and if you see him again—'

'Which I am sure I shall, considering he is determined to stay for the regatta.'

'If you see him again,' Amelia repeated, 'and he suggests you remind him of someone he has met, you must laugh it off. You can do it, I know.'

'I suppose so.'

'But you must talk to Alex. Make a clean breast of everything. We must have him on our side.'

'*We*, Mrs Summers?' There was a ghost of a smile on her face.

'Yes, my dear. I am in this right up to my neck and so is Alex and it is not kind in you to keep him in ignorance, not now, not any more.'

'Yes, you are right, but will he believe me when I tell him why I had to disappear? Will he think I am a silly spoiled young woman who doesn't appreciate what her loving parents are trying to do for her?'

'Surely you know him better than that? He loves you.'

'He what?' She was not sure she had heard aright.

'He loves you. I am sure he does.'

'How do you know?'

'The same way you should know, by the way he looked after you all the way from London, the way he is still looking after you. He was deeply concerned, almost afraid, when you were lost on the fells in the rain.'

She was not sure whether to take heart from that or not. 'I am not sure that means anything. He is the sort of man to be kind to a mongrel dog. And even if he does, it is Fanny Draper he loves and he knows nothing can come of that because she is way, way beneath him. It can only be a passing fancy.'

'You will never find out if you do not tell him the truth, will you?'

'I am not sure I want to find out. He will be angry. And if his love is dependent on rank, then I would as soon do without it.'

'Emma Lindsay, I am fast losing all patience with you. Now change your dress and come down for dinner and be your usual cheerful self and I will contrive to leave you alone and afterwards I shall want to hear that you and he have come to an understanding.' She stood up, shook out the skirt of her black taffeta gown, and left Emma to do as she asked.

But their plans were thwarted because, when Emma went down to the drawing room to wait for the second dinner bell, she found that Alex had invited Mr Maddox to dine with them and they were both there, apparently in easy conversation. How could he? How could he do this to her? The answer came immediately: because he did not know who she really was. He did not know the danger Mr Maddox posed.

As she entered the room, they both rose to greet her. 'Good evening, gentlemen,' she said, glad she had not had time to do anything more with her hair than brush it back and tie it up and that she had thrown a shawl over the lilac silk to cover her bare shoulders.

They responded and Jeremy spoke glowingly of his tour of the little ships and how happy he was to accept his lordship's invitation to take pot luck. She was glad she did not have to do anything more than contribute an occasional 'to be sure' or 'indeed', nothing more than a shy companion might be expected to say. But she was wound up like a coiled spring and had to keep a tight hold of herself because the smallest thing, a word or a look, would send her composure flying. She was relieved when Mrs Summers appeared and, a minute or so later, the footman to announce that dinner was served.

Amelia, who had been even more surprised than Emma to see their guest, kept the conversation flowing, which was not difficult because Mr Maddox had plenty to say for himself and was enthusiastic about the regatta and Alex was unusually jovial. No one paid much attention to Emma. On Alex and Amelia's part it was deliberately done to spare her; on Jeremy's part it was simply that his conceit did not allow anyone but him to hold centre stage.

Alex was annoyed that the man had virtually invited himself to dinner and, if he were not careful, would inveigle a bed as well. He waited until the ladies had retired to the drawing room to explain that he would gladly have him to stay, but unfortunately all the bedrooms were in use and the servants he employed, while doing their best, were not up to serving a gentleman of his standing.

'Yes, I wondered about them,' Jeremy said, helping himself to the port. 'Bit rough round the edges, what? Are they some of your down and outs?'

Alex smiled. 'You could say that.'

'Not Miss Draper, though?'

'No, nor the cook, nor the footman. They were here when I arrived.'

'She's a sad little thing, isn't she?'

'Who?'

'Miss Draper. Well, not exactly little, I did not mean that. But withdrawn, not much to say for herself.'

'She is my aunt's companion. She is not expected to say anything unless spoken to. And I don't think she is sad.'

'Oh, well, you know her better than I do. What do you make of that Miss Pettifer? Now there's a one who has plenty to say.'

Alex smiled, glad his guest was so dismissive. It meant he had not recognised Emma. He began talking about the other young ladies he had met and what society was like in the district, which was rapidly becoming the holiday destination of so many of Society's elite.

'Taken a fancy to any of them, have you?' Jeremy asked. 'Changed you mind about looking for a wife?'

'No. Besides, I'm too busy with the regatta to think of anything like that.'

'Tell me more about that. That young shaver—Sam, he's called, isn't he? He said there was going to be a sort of play with a girl being kidnapped and held at a castle on an island and the ships were going to rescue her.'

'Something like that. The battle to rescue her is intended to be the climax of the day. Before that there will be swimming and boating events as well as stalls and amusements. I'm hoping for a good turn out. The men have put so much work into it.'

'You have advertised it?'

'Oh, yes. Posters everywhere.' He drained his glass. The regatta was rapidly becoming a huge undertaking, far greater than he had first envisaged; sometimes he wondered if he had undertaken more than he could easily accomplish. It was a lodestone, a fulcrum perhaps, on which his whole life and Emma's, too, was balanced. He liked to think that after it was over, he would be able to see his way clearly ahead. 'Shall we join the ladies?'

* * *

'Emma, you have been worrying about nothing. He did not recognise you at all.' Amelia gave a little chuckle. 'He is so full of himself, he cannot see beyond the end of his aristocratic nose.'

'Yes, but I am on tenterhooks all the time he is anywhere near. I cannot understand why his lordship invited him.'

'Perhaps because his lordship did not know you knew him,' Amelia said sharply.

'I have been trying to summon up my courage to talk to him this evening and now I will not be able to. Would it look very bad if I retired?'

'I think you should stay for a few minutes after they join us, don't let him think you are avoiding him.'

'Lord Malvers?'

'No, you goose, Mr Maddox.' She looked up as the door opened and the two gentlemen entered. 'Why, here they are. Would you like some tea, Mr Maddox?'

He sat down opposite the two ladies and accepted a cup of tea. So did Alex. He stood with his back to the hearth, watching Maddox, watching Emma. He could tell she was rattled, but there was nothing he could do about it until he could see her alone. He caught her eye and smiled at her, seeking to reassure her, but there was no answering smile. Her face was pale, hardly any colour in her cheeks, and her eyes, normally sparkling with fun, even in the midst of one of her adventures, were lifeless. It was as if a candle had gone out inside her.

Chapter Ten

Long before Emma rose next morning Alex was up and about, over-seeing the work going on, making sure the men had enough to do so that he could have a little free time to spend with her. He had expected Maddox to return and was relieved when he did not. He supposed that his enthusiasm for the regatta was not genuine, but expressed out of politeness, and another day had brought new diversions. So be it. But he still had to talk to Emma.

He returned to the house and went in search of her. His aunt was in the breakfast room alone. He sat at the table and accepted her in-vitation to have a cup of coffee with her. 'Where is Emma?' he asked.

'I haven't seen her this morning. She was not feeling quite the thing last evening, so perhaps she has decided to stay in bed.'

'Is she avoiding me?'

'No, of course not. Why would she do that?'

'You know why, Aunt. I want to have a long talk with her. This nonsense has been going on long enough.'

'So it has, but you are as much to blame as she is. Bringing that man here just when she had decided to tell you everything.'

'She had?' he queried, brightening.

'Yes. I told her I would leave you alone after dinner and then you came back with that overdressed tulip. Why did you have to do that?

It was like twisting the knife in the wound. And she is wounded, you know, deep inside.'

'I know. But Maddox more or less invited himself. I could not say no without giving offence.'

'She recognised him as a friend of her stepfather. She saw them talking together at Almack's and she is half-convinced Sir George sent him to hunt her down.'

'That's nonsense. Maddox gambles with Sir George, but I would not call them friends. And he did not recognise her. And even if he did, I doubt he would pass the knowledge on.'

'I have tried telling her that, but she is unconvinced. She is not even sure of you...'

'What does she take me for?'

'Why don't you ask her?' She smiled and rang the bell at her side and when Lizzie, pristine in her new uniform, answered it, she said, 'Would you ask Miss Draper if she would come down, Lizzie, I should like to speak to her. In the back parlour, if you please.' As soon as the girl had gone, she turned back to Alex. 'Go in there and wait for her. I am going into Kendal to visit some old friends, if you will allow me the use of the carriage.'

'Of course. You do not have to ask.'

'Thank you.' She hurried away to order the carriage, leaving him to make his way to the back parlour.

Emma, dressed in the tawny light wool gown Mrs Summers had bought for her, because the weather was far from summery, made her way downstairs in answer to the summons. She had spent half the night awake, sitting at the window of her room, looking out at the hills in the distance, dark and awesome against the night sky, wondering if she would ever feel safe. It was all very well for Mrs Summers to say Mr Maddox had not recognised her, but who was to say he would not do so at some future date? And what a furore it would cause. Soon everyone would know: Sir Mortimer and Lady

Pettifer, the doctor and his daughters, everyone at the vicarage, including the odious James Griggs, not to mention the men who worked for Alex. As for Alex… She dare not think of what he might say to her, leading him a dance all the way from London, and falling into one scrape after another and laying him open to arrest. Once her real identity was out in the open it would not be long before her stepfather and Lord Bentwater heard where she was. She would have to tell Mrs Summers she was leaving and this time she would not allow her to dissuade her.

She entered the room and then stopped. Alex was standing with his back to the room, looking out of the window. 'Oh, I thought Mrs Summers was here.'

He turned towards her and smiled. 'As you can see, there is no one here but me.'

'I must go and find her. She said she wanted to see me.' She turned to go.

'Don't go.' She appeared not to hear him and took another step towards the door. He raised his voice. 'Emma, wait.'

She froze, unable to go on, unable to turn towards him. 'What did you call me?' It was whispered with her back to him.

'Emma.' He strode over to her and, taking her shoulders in his hands, turned her towards him. 'You are Lady Emma Lindsay, aren't you?'

She could not meet his eyes and looked at the pin in the middle of his neatly tied cravat as if mesmerised by its brilliance. 'He told you. Mr Maddox told you.'

'No, he did not. I knew before he arrived. And in case you were thinking of accusing my aunt, she did not tell me either. What I want to know is why you did not tell me yourself.'

'I had my reasons.'

'And what might they have been?'

'It is too complicated to explain and it makes no difference. I cannot be Lady Emma Lindsay ever again and must always remain Miss Fanny Draper. I beg you to accept that.'

'I will if you tell me why I must.' He put his finger under her chin and forced her to look up at him. 'I thought you trusted me.'

'I do. I trust you to find me when I am lost, to feed me when I am hungry, to rescue me from lustful men…'

'But not with your secret?'

'I wanted to, but I was afraid.'

'What! Miss Fanny Draper, who told me she was afraid of nothing, has admitted to feeling fearful.'

'I was right to be, wasn't I? You know Mr Maddox and Mr Maddox knows my stepfather and if my stepfather finds me he will make me marry Lord Bentwater.' She was maintaining her composure with a huge effort. 'Do you also know Lord Bentwater, my lord?'

'I have met him,' he said grimly. 'Not a pleasant character.'

'His lordship seems to think I am affianced to him.'

'And are you? Have you agreed to marry him?'

'Certainly not! Why do you think I left London?'

'To escape?'

'Yes, to escape all overbearing lustful men who think that they have only to smile at me and I will fall into their arms with gratitude.'

'And am I included in that number?'

She did not answer and he shook her gently. 'Emma, answer me.'

'I am Fanny, not Emma. It will only take someone to call me by the wrong name in company for everyone to start talking. Gossip soon spreads, my lord.'

'Very well, Fanny. I do not care a fig what you choose to call yourself, but I want to know if you think I am overbearing and lustful.'

'No, I did not mean you.'

'Thank goodness for that.' He drew her to the sofa and pulled her down to sit beside him. 'Now, tell me everything from the beginning and then I will tell you what we are going to do.'

After a minute's hesitation, it poured out of her: her stepfather's threats, her mother's fear of him; that dreadful Lord Bentwater assuming she would comply with her stepfather's decree simply because she had always been an obedient daughter and had no other means of support; wanting to run away, but not daring to leave her mother. 'But she insisted,' she told him. 'She said it was the only way. And Rose agreed to come with me. And then we met you. I was so grateful for your help. I did not know you were coming here. I would not have come myself if I had known.'

'Why not?'

'I did not want anyone to know who I was. I still do not, especially now Mr Maddox has turned up.' She paused. 'Who did tell you?'

'No one. I guessed. I was with Sir George and Lord Bentwater when they struck the bargain. The return of Sir George's vouchers for your hand in marriage.'

'You were there?' She seemed to recoil from him, almost as if he had struck her. 'You were present at the gaming table?'

'Yes.'

'So it could just have easily been you making that bargain.'

'Certainly not,' he snapped. 'What sort of man do you think I am?'

'A gamester. A gambler. Someone who can stand by and condone—'

'I condoned nothing.' Why did she have to pick him up on that when it was something he had asked himself over and over again ever since he had discovered who she was?

'You did not do anything to help, though, did you?'

'What should I have done? Stayed at the table and tried to win you for myself? I did not know you or anything about you. For all I knew, you were no different from all the other Society chits, empty-headed and concerned only with status and wealth.' He was aware as he spoke that he was trying to justify himself and digging himself further into the mire. 'In any case, my skill would not have been enough to ensure I won and what would I have done with you, if I had?'

'You would have been as bad as they were.'

'Precisely. And I assumed you would refuse him if you did not like the idea.'

'Like it! I loathe the man, but I had to flee my home to escape from him.'

'I know that now.' He gave a lopsided smile. 'But it did give us an opportunity to become acquainted.'

'It is not a joke, but isn't it just like a man to think it is?'

'I am sorry, I was only trying to make you see it is not as bad as it seems.'

'Not bad! I cannot see how it could be any worse. You have been playing with me all along. Pretending I was Miss Draper when you knew I was not, making a fool of me.'

'I did not know, not at the beginning. But you gave yourself away in so many little things and the further we went, the more convinced I became that you were not who you said you were. I sent Joe Bland to find out for sure.'

'And there was me, thinking you wanted to help Rose.'

'I did. I thought it would please you.'

'So he came back and confirmed your suspicions. But you still said nothing.'

'I wanted you to tell me yourself.'

'But you couldn't wait for that, could you?' She was furious. All the soul searching about whether she should confide in him or not had been for nothing. She could have saved herself the heartache. And to discover he was at that gaming table was twisting the knife in her wounded pride. She felt demeaned, humiliated. 'So now you know, what are you going to do about it?'

'What would you have me do?'

'Nothing. Pretend you never found out. My stepfather's temper was always fiery and I fear he will be out of all control if he ever hears you helped me. He is telling everyone I have been kidnapped and I would not put it past him to say you took me away against my will. What does the law do to kidnappers, my lord?'

Even in her misery she was thinking of him, he realised, and he did not deserve it. 'It is not going to happen, sweetheart, because I cannot be accused of abducting my own wife.'

'What did you say?'

'I said he cannot accuse me of abducting my own wife.'

'I thought my ears were deceiving me. You mean if he comes here you are going to tell him we are married? I never heard anything so foolish. He would soon find out we are not.'

'No, but we could be. It would be a way out of your dilemma.'

'No, it would not.' She jumped to her feet, distancing herself from him. This was not what she wanted, not a marriage of convenience. Not with him. And she was angry that he had suggested it. 'If you think I would marry you after…'

He stood up and grabbed her hand. 'Why not?'

'Because you are a gambler, prepared to sit at a gaming table all night and throw away a lady's life and happiness on the turn of a card.'

'I never did and never would. I only played to make up the four. If I had known—'

'It makes no odds. Marriage should be based on trust, on knowledge, on love. You don't love me, you think I am only interested in rank and wealth—.'

'I did not say that. I said you might have been. I know differently now, of course.' He had been a fool to confess to being there; he had known she disapproved of gambling and who could blame her for that?

'Yes, because you have wormed the whole humiliating story out of me and now I am to be pitied.'

'Oh, yes,' he said grimly. 'I will show you how much I pity you, shall I?' He pulled her towards him so sharply she fell against his chest. He put one arm about her to steady her and with his other hand lifted her face to his. And then his lips were on hers, hard and demanding. He was annoyed with himself, not her. He had been given the opportunity to make all right and instead had botched it completely. Instead of talking about their feelings for each other, they had become bogged down talking about Sir George and Bentwater and what she thought about gambling.

All he had wanted to do was ask her to marry him. He had not asked her, had not proposed, he had simply stated it as a fact, to all intents giving her no choice, which was exactly what Bentwater had tried to do. Damn his stupid pride! She did not deserve such rough treatment, especially at the hands of someone who professed to love her. His mouth softened, as his anger softened, until he was putting all his love, all his longing into the gentle pressure of his lips on hers.

He lifted his head to look into her face, so breathless he could hardly speak, did not know what to say in any case. Sorry seemed entirely inadequate. 'Emma…'

'I am *not* Emma,' she said furiously, trying to put his kisses from her mind because they weakened her and she could not afford to be weak. 'I am Fanny, penniless, simple Fanny who is foolish enough to be grateful for a handful of crumbs.' She wrenched herself away, her face fiery, her eyes flashing. 'I *am* grateful, but my gratitude does not stretch to submitting to being mauled. You are no better than the others.'

'What others?'

'Lord Bentwater, James Griggs, anyone else who thinks that just because I am no longer what society chooses to call a lady, they think they do not have to mind their manners. I am sick of it.'

'Emma…' He reached for her again, but she evaded him.

'You can find someone else to rescue from your fortress. I am quite sure you are tired of having to rescue me.' She ran for the door, ignoring him when he called after her. 'Try Charlotte Pettifer, I am sure she will be delighted,' she flung over her shoulder. Once up in her room, she threw herself on her bed and sobbed.

He had known all along that she was not who she said she was and he had said nothing. He had been humouring her, calling her Miss Draper when he knew she was not. That gleam of amusement in his eyes, which had so attracted her, was mockery. It was insupportable. And then to suggest marrying her simply to thwart her stepfather was the outside of enough. And he had known about that too, had sat at the gaming table and heard her stepfather barter her for his vouchers.

She loved him—his revelation had hardly dented that. If only he had said he loved her. If he had asked her quietly if she loved him enough to marry him, she might have... No, she would not have agreed. They had started off on the wrong foot and she did not see how any of that could be wiped out.

She lay there for a long time, while the business of the house and the yard went on without her. She could hear Lizzie humming to herself as she dusted down the stairs outside her room, and Mrs Granger calling to Sam to fill a pail of water for her from the well. The grooms were working on the horses. Through the open window she could hear their feet on the cobbles of the yard, and somewhere the sound of a saw and a nail being driven into wood. And then there was Alex, calling to one of the men to saddle his horse. She sat up as she heard the animal being brought to the door, its hooves dancing while it waited for its rider. She left her bed and went to the window in time to see Alex throw himself into the saddle and canter off in the direction of Ambleside without looking back. 'Gone to seek more congenial company,' she murmured, amid a fresh bout of weeping.

But one could not weep all day. The tears dried at last and she sat up. This would not do, it would not do at all. Whatever name she gave herself, she was her father's child and he had not been one to lament anything. 'One has to stiffen one's spine and get on with it,' he used to say to her. He had followed his own advice, even when he knew he was sick unto death. He had been out riding, looking after the estate the day before he died. It had been so sudden. Her mother had been bereft, lost without her prop, and when Sir George had come along eighteen months later, charming her with his flattery, helping her make decisions, shielding her from the world, she had succumbed and married him. What an evil day that had been. Emma had never liked him from the start, though she had tried to hide it for her mother's sake. He was a compulsive gambler and whatever Papa had left was soon gone and Pinehill left to go to rack and ruin. She had said she could not, would not, marry a man who gambled and that included Viscount Alexander Malvers.

She went to the washstand and splashed her face with cold water, straightened her dress and went downstairs. She had duties to perform as Mrs Summers's companion and that was what she would do, at least until she decided on a course of action that would take her away from here. She would be polite to Viscount Malvers and smile when the occasion demanded and never allow herself to be alone with him again. She would survive.

Having been told Mrs Summers had taken the carriage to Kendal, she spent the rest of the morning helping Mrs Granger and Mrs Yates, listening to their friendly chatter, and gradually became calm again. She did not see Alex or Mrs Summers until dinner time, but by then she had taken a firm hold of herself and gone back to her self-effacing role of companion.

Amelia looked from Alex to Emma and heaved a huge sigh. Her nephew was looking grim, as if something had annoyed him, even though on the surface he was smiling and jovial, saying his ride had given him an appetite and he was looking forward to one of Mrs Granger's roast dinners. Emma was looking at her plate as if there were words written on it she was trying to decipher. Amelia wanted to knock their heads together.

'Well,' she said cheerfully, 'what have you two been doing today?'

'I have been talking to the regatta Committee about the peripheral events,' Alex answered.

'I did not know you had formed a Committee.'

'I couldn't do it all myself, Aunt. I have enough to do, organising the invasion. Lady Pettifer is in charge of the ball, the shopkeepers together are managing the stalls and I have put Mr Maddox to work organising the races.'

'Was that wise? Using Mr Maddox, I mean.'

'I met him in Ambleside this morning. He was most insistent he wanted to help. And as Miss Draper has declined to take the part, I have asked Miss Pettifer to take on the role of the kidnapped maiden.' He looked towards Emma, expecting her to comment, but she would not look at him and remained silent. 'She has been pleased to agree.'

Amelia looked sharply at him. 'Well, you know best, I suppose.' She turned to Emma. 'What about you, Fanny? I have not seen you all day.'

'I have kept myself busy. If I had known you were going to Kendal, I would have made myself available to go with you.'

'You would have been bored, my dear. I was keeping a promise I made to old friends at Henry's funeral to call on them. I should have gone before, but with one thing and another…' She paused. 'It is good for you to have a little time to yourself, you know. I would not like you to think I monopolised your time.'

'Goodness, ma'am, you never do that. I do not earn my keep.'

'I will be the judge of that.' She stopped, then went on softly. 'Did Alex speak to you?'

'Yes, ma'am, he did.' She spoke clearly, looking at him. She was not going to be cowed.

'And?'

'We are in complete accord. I remain Miss Fanny Draper, companion.'

Amelia raised an eyebrow at Alex. He simply shrugged. She gave up.

Alex went out again as soon as the meal was finished, saying he wanted to make use of the daylight while it lasted. Amelia and Emma had tea in the withdrawing room alone.

'It is no good you scolding me,' Emma said. 'I did not have to tell him. He knew. And you knew he knew.'

'Yes, but I could not tell you, could I? It was up to the two of you. And now I suppose you have fallen out. How did that come about?'

Emma told her everything, even the fact that she had, in a fit of anger, withdrawn her support of the regatta. 'It was why he asked Miss Pettifer. I did not expect him to go straight out and do it, like that. He must have been wanting to do it all along. How could he do that and suggest marrying me almost in the same breath?'

'Oh, dear, he has bungled it, hasn't he?' the good lady said.

'Bungled what?

'The proposal of marriage.'

'Did you put him up to it?'

'No, certainly not! He would not take any notice of me, and I should not expect him to. He is a good man, Emma. Do you not think you have been a little hard on him? He is not a gambler, not in the way that your stepfather is, so addicted he can think of nothing else and ruins the life of everyone about him in the process. Surely you know the difference?'

'Of course I do, but I was so angry when he said he had taken part in that game, I did not stop to think, but as soon as I calmed down I realised he could not have done anything to help me at the time and since then he has done everything. But is that love?'

'Well, I do not know what else to call it.'

'If he bungled it, so did I. And now I do not know if there is any going back. He might never forgive me.'

'Oh, I think he will,' Amelia said.

But Emma was not sure she believed her.

The date of the regatta drew nearer and the local people were in a fervour of anticipation. The news of it had been broadcast far and wide and entries for the competitions were coming in from miles away. Jeremy Maddox was in his element, organising the swimming races and the boating competitions, for which a part of the lake would be sectioned off. There were to be races, for rowing boats with one oarsman and two, for canoes, curricles and rafts, as well as the swimming, when the contestants would be required to dive from a platform anchored in the middle of the lake and race to the shore. On the old regatta on Derwentwater it had been done by men on horse-back, but Alex had decided not to use horses on the grounds it was cruel to them.

Jeremy was out on the water in a small rowing boat one day in rough weather, when it overturned, tipping him into the water. It was only when he shouted for help, that Alex, on the shore, realised he could not swim. He stripped off his coat, kicked off his shoes and went to the rescue. The water was very choppy, especially at the point where the overfull river emptied itself into the northern part of the lake. Alex knew the lake was very deep at that end; if the man disap-peared, he would never find him. He renewed his efforts and just managed to grab Jeremy's arm as he was about to go down.

'Stop struggling, for God's sake,' he said, as Jeremy thrashed about in panic. 'I've got you.' He put his hands under Jeremy's arms and turned on his back to tow him to the shore, but then realised the man's body was tangled up with a thin rope. He had to dive several times to free him, not helped by Jeremy's struggles, before he could take him to safety. He was exhausted by the time he dragged his burden up the shingle to applause from those who had been working there. Jeremy coughed and spluttered and sat up.

'Good,' Alex said, evincing little sympathy. 'You are not drowned, then.'

'I thought I was going to be.' More coughing, spitting up dirty water. 'My thanks, Malvers. Didn't know a lake could be rough like that.'

'You know now. We had better get you up to the house to dry out.' He looked around him. There was a horse and cart standing nearby, which had been used to bring wood down from the workshop to the vessels. He lifted Jeremy on to it and then drove it up to Highhead Hall.

Emma was in the yard with Sam when they arrived looking like two drowned rats. She ran straight to Alex, forgetting their animosity, forgetting everything in her concern for him. 'Alex, what happened? Are you hurt?'

'No,' Alex told her, grinning as he jumped down; he liked the sound of his given name on her tongue—did that mean he was forgiven? 'Simply very wet. Mister Maddox decided to take a swim with all his clothes on. I will take him to my room and dry him out. Would you ask someone to bring us some hot water?' He turned to Jeremy. 'Can you walk?'

'If you think I am going let you carry me, you are mistaken, my friend. I am not a sack of potatoes.' He scrambled down from the cart, but his legs were wobbly and he had to hang on to the side of the cart for a minute before he could proceed.

Alex waited. The concern in Emma's voice when she ran over to them, and the way she had called him Alex, had heartened him. She did care, after all. But he must be patient. As time passed and no one came to harass her, she would realise her fears had been unfounded and then he would talk to her again. His love for her had nothing to do with saving her from Lord Bentwater, though that loomed large— it was the conviction that she was the only woman for him, the only one he would consider making his wife. All he had to do was convince her. After the regatta.

He ushered Jeremy into the house with Emma following behind. Mrs Yates and Sam took the bath up and Emma and Lizzie carried two large jugs of hot water. Alex came to the door to take them in. He had taken off his wet coat, shirt and hose and stood there in nothing but his pantaloons, big and muscular. He had a towel in his hand with which he had been rubbing his hair. It lay close to his scalp in tight little curls. Emma felt her stomach contract and a shiver pass right through her; though she knew she ought to look away, she could not—he was magnificent. And, oh, how she loved him! She wanted to throw herself into his arms and feel those strong arms enfolding her, his mouth on hers again.

He was not unaware of her little gasp of shock and smiled, thinking it was probably the first time she had ever seen a man half-naked. 'Thank you, Miss Draper.' He took the jug from her and the other from Lizzie and stood aside for Mrs Yates and Sam to take the bath in and set it on the hearth. Mr Maddox was sitting in a chair, wrapped in blankets. Alex handed his clothes to Mrs Yates. 'If you could do something with these, ma'am. I will lend Mr Maddox something of mine until they are dry. And will you tell Mrs Granger there will be one more for luncheon?'

Emma led the servants back downstairs, leaving them to refill the jugs and take them to Alex, and went to find Mrs Summers to tell her what had happened, the result of which Amelia found herself entertaining Mr Maddox again. Dressed in Alex's clothes—a white shirt, whose sleeve ends flapped over his wrists, blue pantaloons that came down over his feet, and a coat that swamped him—he looked quite comical. 'My own fault,' he said, when they laughed. 'Shouldn't have taken the little boat out.'

'You should learn to swim before you take a dip in two hundred feet of water,' Alex said.

'Is it as deep as that?'

'Just there it is.'

'Then I have had a lucky escape. I am in your debt, Malvers.' He turned to Mrs Summers. 'And to you, dear lady, for your hospitality. And Miss…' He paused, as if unable to remember her name.

'Draper,' she said.

'Ah, yes, Miss Draper. My thanks to you.'

Alex noticed him smiling and looking at Emma with his head on one side, as if sizing her up. He felt a *frisson* of unease and quickly began asking Jeremy what he was trying to do when his boat capsized.

'Measuring the course, for the swim,' he said promptly. 'I had tied a hundred feet of line to the finish and was paying it out to find the spot for the platform. I was dragging that too, with an anchor on it. The line snagged and I turned to try to free it and then everything started to rock and I had to let go of the platform and it bumped into the side of the boat and that was it. I was in the water and the line was wrapped around me.'

'You should not have tried to do it single-handed.'

'I know that now.'

'Someone will have to go and secure the platform before it becomes a danger to shipping,' Alex told him. 'I will do it as soon as we have eaten.'

'Do you feel strong enough?' Amelia asked him. 'After all, you have just had a gruelling swim.'

'I am perfectly well, Aunt. None the worse. What about you, Maddox, will you rest here?'

'If I may.' He looked down at the clothes he was wearing with a rueful grin. 'Can't go out in this rig, can I?'

The result was that the two men parted and Alex did not see Maddox again until he returned for dinner. By then his friend was wearing his own clothes, though they were not as immaculate as they had been before being immersed in lake water. But at least they fitted. He sat in a chair in Alex's room, watching him while he changed into something more fitting for dinner with the ladies.

'Malvers,' he said tentatively, 'do you remember when we were talking after that night at Brooks's—you know, when Bentwater asked for Sir George's stepdaughter?'

'Yes, of course. Why?'

'You said if we had not agreed to play, the situation would not have occurred. You felt responsible.'

Alex paused in the middle of tying his cravat, wondering what was coming. 'So?'

'Am I right in deducing you have tried to do something about her after all?'

'What do you suppose I have done?'

'Brought her up here incognito.' He paused, but when Alex did not answer but went on tying his cravat, added, 'I am right, aren't I?'

'What gave you that idea?'

'Miss Draper. She is uncommonly tall, and Lady Emma is also uncommonly tall. And she disappeared at the same time you did.'

'Is that all the evidence you have?'

'Yes. Except she has a certain presence, a superior way of carrying herself and speaking that smacks of breeding.'

'Not much to go on, is it?'

'I am right, though, am I not?'

'Supposing you are—and I am not saying for a moment that you are—what do you propose doing about it?'

'Why, nothing. I admire your nerve, taking her out from under their noses. Most chivalrous thing I ever heard. But I would not like to be in your shoes if Sir George or Bentwater find out.'

'How will they find out? Are you going to tell them?'

'Me? Certainly not. You may rely on me to keep my tongue between my teeth.'

Alex grinned. 'If I thought you would not, I would throw you right back into the lake.'

'Do you think she is safe up here?'

'I hope so. At least until after the regatta, then I am going to take her home.'

'Back to her parents?'

'No, you ass, to Buregreen. As my wife.'

Jeremy laughed. 'I thought you said you would not shackle yourself to an unknown filly. Your words, not mine.'

'She is not unknown now. I have come to know her very well.'

'Then let me felicitate you.'

'Time enough for that after the regatta. Do you still want to help with it?'

'Of course. You do not think an unplanned dip is going to stop me, do you? I know it is going to be a great success. And I am vastly looking forward to the ball. I have sent home for an evening dress suitable for the occasion.'

Alex laughed as he shrugged himself into his blue superfine coat and adjusted the cuffs of his shirt. He felt sure Emma's secret was safe with Maddox. 'Shall we go down to dinner?'

* * *

Preparations went on apace, the boats were finished, the fortress built and painted, the viewing platforms erected, though it would be Charlotte and not Emma who was going to be kidnapped and rescued. Charlotte was full of her role and insisted on countless rehearsals, which Emma could hardly bear to watch. It was her own fault, flaring up like she had; it had changed everything between her and Alex.

They spoke politely to each other and not for a minute did either drop the pretence that she was Miss Fanny Draper, lady's companion. It was as if they had never had that dreadful confrontation. Emma wondered if he had managed to wipe it from his memory, but she never could. The words 'marriage of convenience' were seared into her brain, though neither of them had ever actually uttered them.

She had even come to accept Jeremy Maddox's presence. He came to dine frequently, and sometimes the doctor and his family or the Pettifers would join them and then there would be laughter and gaiety, though Emma was careful to stay in the background, ignored by everyone except Mrs Summers. Charlotte flirted outrageously with Alex, who seemed to be enjoying it, so that it was all Emma could do not to scream her frustration at him.

The Reverend Mr Griggs sometimes brought his wife and daughter, but James never came. Emma knew he would not forgive Alex for humiliating him. It was when she thought of that episode and the way Alex had defended her, that she wondered if she had been too hasty in turning down his thoughtless proposal. Could they have made a good marriage on so poor a beginning? It was a question she could not answer and would not be given the opportunity to test because he had not repeated it. And always, always in the back of her mind was that she could not impose on Mrs Summers for ever and sooner or later she would have to go home.

She sometimes wondered what was happening there. How was her mother? She had had only one other letter from Harriet and that was in reply to hers saying she would not be able to return for the wedding.

Harriet had written about her wedding, the clothes, the guests and the fact that they were, the very next day, going to travel to Europe for their wedding tour. She said nothing of Sir George or her mother and Emma supposed nothing had changed. And then everything changed.

She was just leaving a haberdashery shop in Ambleside, the day before the regatta was to take place, when she saw a coach pulling up outside the Unicorn. Although a luxurious equipage, it had obviously travelled a long way, being dusty and mud-begrimed, its four horses bone weary, their manes and sides also spattered with mud. She gave it only a cursory glance, but when she saw who was stepping down from it, she was shocked to the core. She stood, wondering which way to run, for run she must, when he turned and saw her. A wide grin spread across his features and he gave her an elaborate bow.

Fearing he was going to cross the road to her, she fled. 'I shall find you again,' he called after her, though he made no attempt to follow.

He had found her! That loathsome Lord Bentwater had come to her sanctuary and now it was a sanctuary no longer. She sped on, her breath coming in gasps. Down Church Street and the Rothay Road and into Borrans Road and up the lane to Highhead Hall she stumbled. She almost fell in the kitchen door, expecting to find Mrs Granger there, but the room was empty. She made her way through to the back parlour, only to find that empty too. She remembered Mrs Summers saying something about going to Bowness. Alex would be down by the lake with Mr Maddox. It was Mr Maddox's fault, pretending to be so friendly and helpful when all the time he had recognised her and betrayed her. That was why Bentwater had called out that he would find her. He had been told where to look...

Panic filled her. There was nothing for it, she must disappear again and quickly. It was not only herself she was thinking of, but Alex and Mrs Summers. They must not be implicated. She loved them both too much to put them through the ignominy of being accused of kidnapping her, when all they had done was to help her. However angry she was with Alex, she recognised the debt she owed him. Why he had seen fit to protect her she did not know, probably never would know, but now it was her turn to protect him.

But where could she go where that man would never find her? It would be risky to take a coach because it would be too easy to follow her. She needed somewhere to lie low, at least for a time. Running up to her room, she changed into her old grey striped dress, put a purse containing the five guineas she still had from pawning her pearls into her pocket, then pulled out her old carpet bag and packed everything she had brought with her from London, anything that could identify her and prove she had been sheltering here.

Once that was done, she looked around at the familiar room and then, choking on sobs, took the bag down to the kitchen, stuffed some food and a bottle of water into the top of it and left the house. She crossed the road and made her way over the bridge and up to Loughrigg. She knew the way now; knew how to avoid the walkers by scrambling over rough ground instead of using the path, and was soon standing outside the shepherd's hut that had housed Mrs Yates.

The old sofa, the straw-stuffed mattress, the rickety table and two chairs were still there. So was some kindling by the fireplace, a few items of chipped crockery and a pan, though she dare not light a fire for fear the smoke might be seen. She did not want to shut the door; it was the only way light could come in and she wanted to be able to see anyone approaching. She left it open and slumped on to the sofa, disturbing a field mouse, which scuttled outside. She was almost sorry it had gone, leaving her without company of any sort.

'Here I am and here I stay until the regatta is over,' she said aloud, as if the sound of her own voice would comfort her. When the town was filled with visitors and there was a lot of noise with guns going off and cheering as everyone concentrated on the battle, she would creep out and get on a coach. She would go as far as her five guineas would take her and then look for work. She grimaced at the thought— from earl's daughter to lady's companion and now down to what?

Kitchen maid? Scrubber of floors? Washer of dirty linen? And no one to befriend her, as Mrs Summers had done. And all because her mother had married a man with no scruples, no scruples at all. Cold and alone, she put her head into her hands and wept in utter despair.

Alex worked until dusk. He took a last look at his assembled fleet, then went into Bowness to make a few last-minute purchases before rowing over to the fortress to make sure everything was ready. For the last week the towns and villages about the lake had been filling up with visitors; every bed in every hotel and inn had been taken for miles around. It was going to be a grand occasion, far larger than his first conception of it. Satisfied that the regatta was going according to plan, even if his private life was not, he returned to the jetty at Waterhead.

Jeremy had had a wooden hut built by the water that he called his office. It was where he listed the names of the entrants to the races, what the prizes would be and who had donated them. He had hoisted a flag on the roof. It was pale blue and sewn on to it were the words, Windermere Regatta. On the door was a notice: Mr Jeremy Maddox, starter. Alex put his head in the door. 'Time to leave off,' he said. 'Come back with me for dinner.'

Jeremy left the hut, locking the door carefully behind him. 'Much appreciated, Malvers. The landlady at my hotel is rushed off her feet and is not inclined to oblige me with meals out of normal hours.'

'I hope my aunt is a little more flexible,' Alex said, smiling. 'Otherwise we shall have to resort to emptying the butter boat over Mrs Granger or going hungry. I'm starving.'

They made their way into the house through the kitchen, where Mrs Granger was banging about scraping uneaten food into a waste bin. She seemed more than a little agitated. 'Sorry we are late, Mrs Granger, have you kept something for us?'

'Yes, but you had better go and see Mrs Summers first, my lord. In a right stew she is.'

'Why? Because we are late? Surely she and Miss Draper did not wait for us?'

'She is in the drawing room,' she said, not answering his question.

Alex lost his jovial air as he realised something was wrong. He hurried to the drawing room with Jeremy close behind. As soon as he entered the room, Amelia flung herself at him. 'Alex, she's gone. Emma has disappeared.' She suddenly noticed Jeremy and realised her mistake. 'Oh, I did not see you there, Mr Maddox. You must excuse me—I am so worried, I shall forget my own name next.'

Alex looked back at him and then at his aunt. 'Jeremy knows, but we can trust him. Now, what's this about Emma?'

'She has disappeared. I came back from my shopping, but she was out. I did not think anything of it, she often goes out on her own, though we never should have allowed it. When she had not come back by dinner time, I went up to her room. Alex, her things have gone!' The last words were a wail of distress.

'Did she leave a note?'

'No, nothing. And she took only what she had when she arrived. Everything I bought for her has been left behind.'

'She cannot have gone far. We must find her. If anything has happened to her…' He could not go on. 'Did she have any money?'

'I don't think so. Five guineas, perhaps. It was all she had when she arrived and I would not take it from her. She may have spent it. I do not know. Oh, Alex, what are we going to do?'

'Find her. Come on, Maddox, we must organise the men.' He rushed outside to the stable block where many of the men he had employed had made comfortable quarters. In no time at all, they were despatched to all points of the compass, some to Ambleside, some to Bowness, some to Kendal, some to comb the fells, though he did not think she would go there so late in the day. It was already dark and the wind was getting up again. If she had taken her bag and a little money, it must mean she intended to leave the area and his best course would be to check the coaching inns. He had his horse saddled and set off to do that himself.

The first person he saw when he went into the Unicorn was Lord Bentwater. 'Evening, Malvers,' the man said, revealing his yellow teeth in a grin.

Chapter Eleven

Alex strode forward, an accusation on his lips, but then he checked himself. If Bentwater had not seen Emma, it would not do any good to alert him to her presence in the area. He forced himself to sound friendly. 'Bentwater, what brings you here?'

'This seems to be the place to be,' he said. 'London is empty and it looks as if everyone has decamped here. I would never have found a bed if one had not been booked for me. You are a dark horse, my friend.'

'What do you mean by that?' He was itching to get away and continue his search for Emma, but must show no impatience to this man. If he knew where Emma was…

'Why, your ability to put a place on the map. All this hustle and bustle over a regatta.'

'There is nothing new in that. The Lake District is already a popular destination. All I have done is revive an old tradition.'

'To some effect.'

'How did you hear about it?'

'It has been reported in the newspapers.'

'In the London papers?' he queried in surprise.

'Yes, of course. How you were employing old soldiers and destitute women and children, and saving my good friend Maddox from drowning. It is the latest *on dit*.'

Alex groaned inwardly. He had trusted Jeremy and now it looked as though his trust had been misplaced. 'Did he tell you that?'

'I read it, I told you. And I thought I would have a little holiday, see the spectacle. And to take the opportunity for a little wager here and there.'

'No other reason?'

'No, should there be?' His smile was oily.

'I am flattered you should think it worth your while. Has London lost its attraction?'

'Oh, yes. All my friends appear to be here.'

'Did you come up by stage or the mail?'

'Neither, brought my own coach. I shall need it to convey my bride home.'

'Your bride?' It was all Alex could do not to choke, though he had guessed that the man's arrival must have something to do with Emma.

'Yes, you remember Lady Emma Lindsay, stepdaughter to Sir George Tasker?'

'I have not had the pleasure of meeting the lady.'

'No?' Again that predatory smile.

'I remember you striking a bargain with Sir George over his vouchers. I never knew the outcome.'

'The outcome, my dear Malvers, was that I have been frustrated, not by the lady, who was happy to accept my offer, but by others intent on thwarting me.'

Alex suppressed the urge to call him a liar. 'Do go on. This is all very fascinating.'

'She was abducted on the very day the announcement was to go out. Why do you think that was, Malvers?'

'I have no idea. A jealous suitor, perhaps?'

'Possibly. But whoever he is, he will be punished for his crimes. Make no mistake about it, a crime has been committed. Sir George is on his way here and he will vouch that she accepted me, and a betrothal is binding, don't you know.'

'You mean you think her abductor is here?'

'Oh, I know he is.' And this time the smile was one of satisfaction.

If he stayed a moment longer, he would give in to the temptation to plant a facer on the man. 'Can't stay here gossiping, intriguing as it is,' he said. 'Things to do.' And he strode off to find the innkeeper to ask if he had seen a tall young lady getting on a coach. The man had not, which did not surprise him. Emma had disappeared because she had seen Bentwater, he felt sure of that, so she would not have tried to leave from the Unicorn. But had Bentwater seen her?

He returned to where he had left his horse and rode back to Highhead Hall, musing as he went. Emma would flee in the opposite direction and that meant Bowness or Kendal, probably Kendal, and perhaps the men he had despatched in that direction had found her, or at least heard news of her.

His aunt had not gone to bed, but was pacing the drawing room. She looked up hopefully as he entered, but the hope died when she saw he was alone and was shaking his head.

'No sign of her,' he said. 'But I encountered Lord Bentwater in Ambleside. I'll lay odds she saw him and that precipitated her flight.'

'Oh, poor child! Could she not have trusted us to protect her?'

'Evidently not. Bentwater did not accuse me directly, but he hinted he knew where she was.'

'I wish I did.'

'You do not wish it any more heartily than I do. I pray that when the men return, they will have news of her.'

But when they trickled back long after midnight, they had no news at all. And when Maddox returned, leg weary, Alex met him in the hall and pounced on him, grasping him by the throat and shaking him. 'You toad, you vile, unspeakable toad! I trusted you…' He realised he was choking the man and if he did not stop he might very well kill him. He let him go.

Jeremy coughed and spluttered and pulled at his cravat. 'I say, Malvers, what was that for?'

'For telling that…that evil muckworm, Bentwater, that Emma was here.'

'I never did.'

''Course you did. My aunt would never have done anything so despicable and no one else knew.'

'On my honour I did no such thing. Why would I?'

'For devilment? For the reward? God! If I had thought you would take money, I would have offered it to you myself.'

'I don't need money. I've more than enough for my needs. On my life, I swear I have told no one. Why, I like the lady. She has guts, that one, and I would not condemn a dog to life with Lord B.'

'Then can you suggest who might have told his lordship where to look for her? For surely someone did. He would not have come to Ambleside on a whim.'

'You mean he is here?'

Jeremy's genuine surprise convinced Alex he was telling the truth. 'Yes. And crowing.'

'Someone else must have seen her and drawn the same conclusion I did. As you yourself did, Malvers. Her description was circulated and she is hardly one to melt into the background, is she?'

Alex was forced to admit he was probably right. 'I was too hasty. I beg your pardon.'

'Granted.'

'This is leading us nowhere,' Mrs Summers put in, thankful Alex had not throttled the man. 'The point is, where has she gone? We must find her. We cannot let her wander about alone. With the whole district buzzing with offcomers, she might meet with some very bad characters, apart from Lord Bentwater, that is.'

'I cannot see what more we can do tonight,' Alex said. 'Go to bed, Aunt, you must be exhausted.'

'And do you expect me to sleep? I shall not shut my eyes. And what am I going to say to her mama?'

'Speaking of her mama,' Alex said suddenly, 'Bentwater told me

Sir George was on his way here. One must presume Lady Tasker is with him.'

This pronouncement brought about a wail of anguish from Mrs Summers, which Alex did his best to calm. 'Emma is a resourceful young lady,' he said. 'She has proved it more than once, so we must hope she knew what she was going to do when she left and is managing without us.' He sounded more confident than he felt, but it was important to calm his aunt.

'You are not going to give up looking for her, Alex, are you?'

'Never. Go to bed and rest, even if you do not sleep.' He bent to kiss her cheek. 'I am going out again.'

'Where are you going?'

'I don't know. I am too restless to sit still.'

Jeremy followed him and they patrolled the grounds, looking in stables and byres, the coach house and the glasshouses, even though they had been the first places to be searched. 'If Emma saw Bentwater, the first thing she would want to do is escape,' Alex said. 'And the best way of doing that would be to board a coach going out of the area. Five guineas, if she even has that amount, will not take her far, if she is to pay for lodgings at the end of her journey. We will widen our search tomorrow.'

'What about the regatta?'

'Damn the regatta.'

'You are worried, I can understand that, but you cannot abandon it, not after the men have put so much effort into it. People have come from miles around to see the entertainment and take part in the competitions. It would be the biggest let-down since…since I don't know when. You will be a laughing stock instead of a hero. Wherever she is, Emma will manage a day without you.'

Alex did not like being lectured to in that fashion, but Jeremy was only echoing his own thoughts. Perhaps Emma was safe somewhere of her own choosing, but if Bentwater should find her…

'If we cannot find her, then I doubt Lord Bentwater will be able to,' Jeremy said, as if reading his thoughts.

'I hope you are right. He told me he is coming to the regatta. We can have him watched, every minute. I have enough men to do that. One false move on his part and we'll know about it.'

'He is a gambler,' Jeremy added. 'We could let him win a few pounds, that should keep him interested.'

They could do no more and returned to the house. Maddox went to bed, but Alex paced the room until a rosy dawn lightened the sky. It was going to be a fine day for the regatta. Perhaps that was a good sign. He went to his room, washed, changed his clothes and ate a frugal breakfast before going down to the lake. 'Keep her safe until this day is over,' he prayed.

It was only just light enough to see, but already the crowds were gathering. He found half a dozen of his best men and detailed them to look out for Lord Bentwater and keep him in sight the whole day. If the man tried to creep away, the fact was to be reported to him at once, whatever he was doing.

And then the business of the day claimed his attention.

Emma stirred cramped limbs as daylight found its way through the cracks in the building, which was only made of mortared stones picked up from the ground about it. It had been so windy the night before the door had banged shut and she had left it shut. She had rolled herself up in a smelly blanket—the same one Mrs Yates had wrapped her in before—and curled up on the mattress to try to sleep. The wind howled outside and she could hear unfamiliar noises until she realised it was made by half a dozen sheep jockeying for position in the lee of the hut. They had settled at last and so had she.

She had ample time during that long, sleepless night to review her life and the situation in which she found herself. She went over her journey from London to Windermere, every step of it, the growing closeness with the man who had started out as a stranger and become the love of her life, their misunderstandings and reconciliations, his anger and his kisses and her reaction to both.

She had rehearsed every word they had ever said to each other, the pleasant exchanges and the acrimonious disputes which had only come about because of her stubbornness. She could not change the kind of person she was and stubbornness was one of the traits that kept her going in adversity, the determination not to be beaten. She was sure he understood that, but why had he not told her as soon as he found out who she was? Why keep up the pretence? Was it for the same reason she had, the feeling that she wasn't safe, not even here so far from London? And she had been right. Lord Bentwater had found her. Was she safe, even now?

She rose and opened the door, letting in the daylight and a blast of cool fresh air. She ate some of the food she had brought and drank a little of the water, then she went outside and, walking up the hill a little way, climbed on to a rock that provided a good viewing platform. There were no walkers on the hill; they were all down by the lake, crowds of them, swarming all over the place, filling up the stands. From where she stood, she could see part of the lake, could see the flotilla of boats made to look like warships and, from this distance, very realistic they looked, too. She could hear the sound of bugles borne on the wind, the roar of the crowd and guns going off to start the races. The best time to leave, she decided, was when it was growing dusk, when the regatta was over and everyone was making their way home. She could lose herself in the crowds.

It was a long day with nothing to do but think. She went for a walk, scrambling over rocks, running down inclines, drinking from springs; when she grew tired, she returned to the hut to eat the last of her food. Down on the lake the battle was in progress. She could see puffs of smoke from the vessels as they approached the distant island, but that was too far away for her to see the fortress and the flagpole to which Charlotte would be tied in her bright red dress.

It was strange how easily Alex had agreed when she had angrily declared she no longer wished to take part. But now she realised it was as well she was not there, in full view of everyone, including Lord

Bentwater. Had Alex been warned that he was coming and that was why he had been so quick to ask Charlotte Pettifer to take over? It was of no consequence now. She had left and once she was on a coach—going—it did not matter where—she would never see him again. She choked back a sob. She had done enough crying to empty the lake and was determined to shed no more tears.

The sky above the lake was lit by fireworks, blue, red, green and yellow, bright star bursts and trailing comets, indicating the successful rescue of the maiden. She had seen it rehearsed so many times, she could see it in her mind's eye. Alex, standing tall and triumphant in the prow of the *Lady Jane* with his arm about Charlotte, as they returned to harbour, escorted by the victorious fleet. And Charlotte looking up at him with that flirtatious smile of hers. And then there would be the ball at the Assembly rooms. Alex would go and so would Mrs Summers. Would he think of her while he was dancing with Charlotte? Had she been banished from all their minds?

She was struck by a sudden thought. If Lord Bentwater was here, why should she not go home to her mother? Would she be welcomed and forgiven? Would Sir George concede that she was determined not to marry Bentwater and no longer insist? If the horrible man was not in town to force the issue, could she go back to being Lady Emma Lindsay? Would five guineas stretch that far if she travelled outside and did not buy refreshments? A carrier left Bowness for Kendal every day at dawn in time to catch the London coach—she could go on that. All she had to do was endure another night up here on the fells.

She held her breath. Someone was coming. There were sounds, a pattering and panting. More sheep, perhaps. Or was it human? Then with a joyful bark, Nipper raced into her hiding place, wagging his tail. She laughed and hugged him. 'Nipper, what are you doing here? Chasing rabbits, are you?' She looked up as the light from the entrance was blocked, but she knew it could only be Sam and was not afraid.

'I guessed this was where you'd be,' he said, sitting down beside her. 'What you run away for?'

'Someone was after me. A bad man. You won't tell anyone where I am, will you?'

'But I gotta tell Mr Lord. He's in a real fret about you, shouting at everyone and cursing and I don' know what. It ain't like 'im at all. It ain't fair to let 'im worrit so.'

'I'm sorry about that, Sam, truly I am, but I'm too afraid—'

'Seems to me,' he said, with the wisdom of the very young, 'you'd have no call to be afeared if you was with 'im. 'E can beat any man alive. Why, 'e nearly choked Mr Maddox to death, he was that mad. I never saw it, but Lizzie did.'

'Whatever did he do that for?'

The boy shrugged. 'I reckon 'e thought 'e knew where you was, but o' course he didna' and they was soon friends ag'in. Come back, miss, come back. Mr Lord is 'urtin' bad for you.'

'Oh, Sam, I wish I could.'

'Then if you won't go to 'im, shall I tell him you're 'ere?'

'No.' She paused, sorry indeed that Alex was in a stew over her disappearance. 'I tell you what you can do. Tomorrow, as soon as it gets light, you can come and walk with me to Bowness and then I will let you go back and tell Viscount Malvers that I have decided to go home. That should set his mind at rest.'

'You mean you are goin' to stay 'ere all night?'

'Yes, why not? You lived here longer than one night, didn't you?'

'I weren't alone. I had Ma and Lizzie and Nipper.' He stopped, thinking. 'I'll leave Nipper with you. 'E'll be company and 'e'll scare off any bad men wot come.'

'Thank you, Sam. I should like that. And Sam, when you come back, will you bring me some food?'

''Course I will.' He left her cuddling the dog, trying not to cry again.

Alex refused to go to the ball, though Jeremy tried to persuade him. He had never felt less like dancing. Mrs Summers had gone, taking Lizzie with her. She had some crazy notion that if she dressed Lizzie up in Emma's clothes and said she had taken on a new companion, it might serve to distract Lord Bentwater.

His lordship had been watched the whole day. He had wagered vast sums on the rowing races without having any knowledge of the rowers or the conditions on the lake; he had watched the abduction of the maiden and her rescue by the invaders with wry amusement and had even sought Alex out afterwards to congratulate him. 'Good show, Malvers, though I am surprised to find you in the role of rescuer and not abductor.' He had eyed Charlotte up and down appreciatively. 'You know, I was given the impression that the lady in question would be someone we both know.'

'Really? I cannot think why you should think that.'

'No matter. A sudden change of plan, I expect. I will call at Highhead Hall tomorrow, if I may.'

'Whatever for?'

'A mere courtesy, Malvers. Sir George will have arrived by then.'

He had relayed this conversation to his aunt and put her in a panic. 'I cannot refuse to entertain my friend. And she will expect to see her daughter here. Oh, what am I to do?'

'She might be relieved to discover she is not here, Aunt. And by then I shall have located her and you can safely tell Lady Tasker, in confidence, of course, that she is in a place of safety.'

'Are you sure you will find her?'

'I am determined on it.' The regatta was over and had been a huge success and now he could put his mind to finding Emma and nothing on this earth would ever separate them again. Alone in the house, he paced back and forth, back and forth, wondering how he was going to do it.

When Amelia and Jeremy came back from the ball with an excited Lizzie who had not danced, but was thrilled to stand behind Mrs Summers's chair and watch the lovely ladies in their colourful dresses and the handsome men whirling past her and tap her foot to the music, they found Alex slumped in a chair in the drawing room, fast asleep. Amelia covered him with a rug and left him there. Time enough in the morning to tell him that Lord Bentwater had attended the ball as a guest of the Rector and that he and James had appeared very friendly. Jeremy had seen them too. 'There's our culprit,' he had told her, nodding towards James.

Alex woke with a start, surprised to find himself in a chair and fully dressed. How could he have slept when Emma was lost, wandering about somewhere too afraid to come back? He flung off the rug and stood up. It was not yet fully light. He went to the window to pull back the curtains in order to see the time on the clock that stood on the mantelpiece. Clouds scudded across the tops of the hills; it looked as though it might rain again.

He heard a sound. Sam was crossing the yard from the stables and looking furtive. He watched him make his way towards the kitchen. Sam was not one to rise before he had to. Alex left the room to go to the kitchen, half-expecting to find Lizzie there, raking out the fire before Mrs Granger came to start on the breakfasts. The kitchen was in darkness. He stopped in the doorway, knowing the outside door should have been locked and bolted. Stealthily, the window was thrust upwards and Sam climbed in over the sill. Alex smiled and waited.

The boy crept across the kitchen and into the larder. Alex could hear him moving about. A minute later, he emerged, pockets bulging, and left the way he had come. His behaviour puzzled Alex. The boy was well fed and knew if he felt hungry he could ask for food, so why creep about in the dark stealing it?

Alex crossed the floor, unbolted the door silently and went out into the yard. Sam was trotting down to the gate, not returning to his bed. He followed, smiling to himself. The boy went down the road, crossed the bridge and set off up Loughrigg Fell. By now Alex had guessed his destination. He was right. A hundred yards short of the old hut, Nipper came bounding out to greet him, wagging his tail in ecstasy. Sam stooped to fondle the dog and then hurried into the hut. Alex moved closer and stood outside.

* * *

'Did anyone see you coming?'

'No, 'twas still dark and they was all asleep.'

'Everyone?'

'Reckon so. They went to a ball last night. I heard the carriage come back real late. I brought you some pecker.'

'Thank you, Sam. I'll keep it for later.'

'You still set on goin'?'

'Yes, I am, and we must set off at once or I will miss the carrier.'

'I wish you wouldna'. I don' know what Mr Lord will say when I do tell 'im. He'll fly into the tree tops, I knows 'e will. He'll say I should ha' told 'im sooner.'

'He won't be angry with you, Sam.'

'Ma will be, if 'e ain't.'

'If you are worried, you do not have to come with me. Go home and no one will be the wiser.'

'Ain't leavin' you to go alone, not nohow.'

'Then let's go.'

Alex hid behind the building as they came out and started off down the track. He let them go a hundred yards, then followed. He was elated. She had been found and now he could keep her safe, though she was making a fair job of doing that herself. After two nights alone on the fell, she seemed cheerful, ready to be her old intrepid self, to meet whatever befell her with stoicism, so long as she did not have to come face to face with Bentwater again. But perhaps it was not just Bentwater she was afraid of, perhaps it was him too. He had been prodigiously clumsy in the way he had asked her to marry him and she had likened his manner to Bentwater's. He hadn't deserved that, had he? But he would not give up. Curious about her intentions, he crept closer.

'Where you goin'?' the boy asked.

'I told you. On the carrier's cart to Kendal.'

'Then what?'

'I am going home to London, Sam. It's where I belong. My mother needs me. I should never have left.'

'Why did you? Was it 'cos of the bad man?'

'Yes.'

'But Mr Lord ain't a bad man, is 'e?'

'No, Sam, he is a very good man.'

'But you are angry with 'im.'

'No, I'm not angry with him. But when the bad man comes, he will blame Viscount Malvers for hiding me. He might be arrested. And Mrs Summers too. And I shall still have to go with the bad man.'

'Seems to me, you're in a fix,' Sam said.

'Yes, and I have to get out of it as best I may.'

They had reached the road and were walking towards Waterhead. Alex left them and returned to Highhead Hall. He did not go inside, but saddled his horse and rode out again. If he went across country, he would be in Kendal before the carrier's cart arrived.

Emma climbed down from the cart and shook out her skirt. After two nights sleeping in it, and sitting on a sack of grain the carrier was delivering in Kendal, it was looking very bedraggled. And her hair was all over the place and, though she had tried to comb it out, it was still full of knots. She smiled grimly. No one would mistake her for Lady Emma now, would not even mistake her for Fanny Draper. She had sunk even lower.

She would have liked to go into the Woolpack and ask for a room so that she could make herself look respectable again, but she dare not spend the money. Besides, they knew her in there; she had been in with Alex and Mrs Summers several times. Instead she went and sat on a bench to wait for the coach going south.

She shifted along when someone came and sat beside her, but did not look up from studying her filthy hands. She really ought to have gone down to the lake and washed them, but that would have delayed her and she might have missed the carrier.

'Emma.' The voice was no more than a whisper.

Startled, she looked at the man who sat beside her. 'Alex!'

He smiled lopsidedly. 'Did you think I would not find you?'

'Sam—'

'No, not Sam. At least, not knowingly. I wondered why he found it necessary to break into the house and steal food, so I followed him.'

'Oh.'

'Why run, Emma? Did you not trust me to protect you?'

'You might have tried, but Lord Bentwater is very powerful. If he brought Runners with him, he will have you arrested, though you have done no wrong. And dear Mrs Summers, who has been so good to me. She does not deserve that.' She spoke in a flat, hopeless tone and would not look at him for fear of weakening. Already she was shaking. Before he arrived, her resolve had been fixed, but now she knew it was going to be a hundred times more difficult to maintain.

'I agree she does not. But she is very anxious about you, as I have been.' He paused and took one of her grubby hands in his. 'Emma, I have been out of my mind with worry, imagining all manner of disasters. If anything happened to you, I should not want to go on living. I love you to distraction.'

She turned and looked at him at last. 'You cannot mean it. I have been nothing but trouble to you.'

He was about to retort sharply that he was not in the habit of saying things he did not mean, but thought better of it. That was a soldier's retort, not a lover's. 'Emma, I do mean it. I have loved you for a long time, possibly ever since we left London. I love your courage, your compassion, your determination, but more than that, I love your luminous eyes, your aristocratic nose, your bright hair, your kissable mouth.' He touched each item with a gentle forefinger as he spoke. 'Your sunny smile and your tears, every little thing about you, the person you are even when you are at your most infuriating.' He smiled. 'You do not know how many times I have cursed you in the last two days for leading me such a dance.'

'I am sorry, but you never said any of that before.'

'No, and I regret I did not. I regret more than anything that clumsy attempt at asking you to marry me…'

'Oh, so that was what you were doing.' In spite of everything, she could not resist teasing.

'Yes, and I made a mull of it. My only excuse is that I have never proposed to a lady before and I could not seem to find the right words.'

'Have you found them now?'

'I do not know. Shall I test them out?'

He slipped to his knees on the cobbles. She laughed. 'Alex, do get up, you will have everyone looking at us and that is the last thing I want. We are not out of danger, far from it.'

He resumed his seat beside her as the sound of a horn heralded the arrival of the stage. 'Emma, I love you dearly and what I want most in the world is to make you my wife and spend the rest of my life devoted to your happiness. So, my darling, will you wed me?' He was obliged to raise his voice at the end because the coach clattered into the yard and the noisy business of disgorging passengers and changing horses was begun.

'Oh, Alex, you know I love you, but what about my so-called betrothal to Lord Bentwater?'

'You told me you had not accepted him.'

'Of course I did not. That won't stop my stepfather saying I did.'

The coachman approached them. 'Are you wanting to board the coach, miss? If you are, we are about to depart.'

'No, she is not,' Alex said. The man went away and climbed up on the box.

'Alex, I cannot go back to Waterhead, not while Lord Bentwater is looking for me. I had much better take the coach and go home.'

'No point in that. There is no one there. Sir George and your mother are on their way here.'

'Oh!' She watched the coach leave, not sure whether she felt sorry or relieved. 'What am I to do?'

'I have had an idea.' He picked up her bag in one hand and took her hand with the other. 'Come on.'

Meekly she followed as he led her to the Fleece Inn. It was only a small establishment, but as its guests had come only for the regatta and had departed that morning, it had vacant rooms. The proprietor came forward as soon as he saw Alex. 'Mr Lord, I have your room ready.' He looked from Alex, obviously the gentleman, to the bedraggled woman standing beside him and wondered at the incongruity of it. In spite of her problems, which did not seem nearly so insurmountable now she was with Alex, Emma smiled. Mr Lord, indeed!

Alex noticed the innkeeper's raised eyebrows and realised an explanation was called for. 'My wife has been in an accident with a cart,' he said. 'If you can bring hot water to the room and try to press her dress, I should be much obliged.'

The innkeeper did not believe him, but decided it was none of his business. 'Come this way, sir, Mrs Lord,' he said, leading them up the stairs. Emma tried to pull back, but Alex tugged her after him. The man threw open a bedroom door. 'There you are, sir. I will have the water sent up. Do you wish for refreshment?'

'Yes, breakfast, if you please.'

The man disappeared and Alex went and shut the door after him. 'Now,' he said firmly, taking Emma by the hand and pulling her down beside him on the bed. 'We will continue our conversation.'

'No, Alex, no. I cannot believe you have so little sense as to compromise me in this fashion. My reputation will be ruined.'

'Whose reputation? Lady Emma Lindsay's, Miss Fanny Draper's or some unknown going by the name of Mrs Lord?'

'Mine. The person I am. What's in a name?'

'Quite,' he said. 'But there is one name that will make a difference and that is Viscountess Malvers. Now, are you going to answer the question I asked you a few minutes ago? Will you marry me and be my viscountess?'

'Are you compromising me on purpose to influence my answer?'

He laughed. 'Would it serve?'

'No, it would not.' She was emphatic. 'If you are looking for a wife, you might be better settling for Miss Pettifer.'

He laughed. 'You are not jealous of that chit, are you? She is nothing but a spoiled schoolgirl. I only asked her to take part in the regatta because I was out of all patience with you. And with myself. And as it turned out, it was fortuitous; Bentwater was at the regatta and he was poking into everything. The fact that you were not there puzzled him greatly, I think.'

'It is not a jest.'

He stopped laughing immediately and took both her hands in his. 'I am not jesting, my love, my dearest Emma, I am perfectly serious. And if you had not been so nervous of being seen, I would have continued my proposal in the street. It is all the same to me where we are. I need an answer. And if it means promising to give up gambling, then I will. It will be no hardship.'

'Alex, you cannot make promises like that. So many things in life are a gamble, don't you think? For instance, if I agree to marry you, you will be gambling your future happiness on me.'

He laughed. 'That's not a gamble it's a certainty. So what do you say?'

'Is a lady not supposed to ask for time to consider?'

'Do you need time?'

'No, but if I say yes, how are you going to fetch us out of our predicament?'

'Leave that to me. I am not without influence myself. So, how much longer are you going to prevaricate?'

'Are you sure?'

'I have never been more sure of anything in my life. Go on, repeat after me, "I love you, Alexander Malvers, and I will marry you."'

She smiled and repeated his words, then added, 'It is my dearest wish. Now tell me how you are going to bring it about.'

He did not answer, but put his arms about her and kissed her soundly. 'To seal the bargain,' he said, then kissed her again. And again. He kissed her hair, her forehead, her nose, her chin, her lips, sending shivers of desire rushing through her. His mouth roamed from her mouth to her throat. His hands fumbled with the buttons on her dress and, opening the bodice, he kissed the tops of her breasts. She clung to him, a low moan escaping from her lips at what was happening to her body. It was melting, there was no other word to describe the strange sensation that made her feel soft and compliant, without strength or will. Her surroundings disappeared; the room, the bed on which they lay, were gone; there was nothing but two people locked in each other's arms, floating on another plane altogether.

What would have happened next if there had not been a sharp rap on the door, she could not even guess at. Reluctantly he dragged himself away from her and went to open it. Emma sat up and quickly buttoned her bodice and tried not to look flustered as a maidservant came in with a jug of hot water, which she stood on a wash stand beside a bowl and a towel. She was followed by a man with a huge tray containing breakfast, which he put on a table near the window.

'Shall I take madam's dress?' the girl asked.

'I will bring it to you directly,' Alex said, because Emma could not find her voice.

'Very well, sir. Madam,' they said and took their leave.

Alex turned back to Emma and grinned. 'Don't look so stricken, sweetheart.'

'They knew, they knew what we had been doing, I could tell.'

'A man making love to his wife, I am sure they have seen worse than that in their time.'

'But I am not your wife.'

'You soon will be.' He opened her bag and pulled out the crumpled blue dress. 'This is almost as bad as the one you are wearing. You must have packed in a devil of a hurry.'

'You know I did.' She took it from him and shook it. 'It will have to do.'

'Then change quickly.'

She looked about her. There was no privacy. 'Are you going to sit there watching me?'

'No, I am going to help you.' He came forward and began undoing the buttons of her bodice all over again. And began kissing her all over again.

'Alex, no. I can manage. Go and sit over there.' She pointed to a chair in the window. 'Watch the road.'

'I would rather watch you.' He sighed melodramatically. 'But I will be good.' He sat down and turned his back on her.

She slipped out of the dress as quickly as she could and used the hot water to wash. 'How did you reach Kendal before me?'

'My horse is much faster than a carrier's cart.'

'And you had already taken this room by the time I arrived.'

'Yes. I want you to stay here until I have persuaded Lord Bentwater to give up his claim on you and have obtained your stepfather's agreement to our wedding.'

'Supposing you cannot persuade them?' She was struggling into the blue dress as she spoke.

'Oh, I will, never fear.' He turned to face her and then strode over to help her fasten the dress. 'I like doing this,' he said. 'Though I like undressing you better.'

'But I have only just put it on.'

'I know.' He bent to kiss her forehead. 'Let us eat. I am famished and I am sure you are.'

'Yes, I am.'

They sat at the table and did justice to ham, eggs, pork chops, chicken legs and bread and butter washed down with coffee. When they had eaten their fill, he rose to go. 'I'm going back to Waterhead, my darling. You stay and rest. I will return as soon as I can.' He took her hand and raised her to her feet to enfold her in his arms and kiss her again.

She responded willingly, clinging to him. 'I wish you did not have to go.'

'The sooner I go, the sooner I will be back.'

'Supposing he comes?' She did not need to name the man.

'Why would he come here? If he asks Sam, which I doubt he will, having no reason to, all he will be able to tell him is that you intended to take the stage back to London.'

'What about Mr Maddox?'

'What about him?'

'Sam said you tried to strangle him.'

'Did he? Well, I was angry, worried out of my mind. I accused him of betraying your whereabouts, but he convinced me of his innocence. He is no more a friend of Lord Bentwater than I am and, like me, he thinks the man is a despicable rakehell, if you will pardon the expression. He is not fit to walk the earth.' He picked up her grey dress. 'I'll take this down to the innkeeper's wife on my way.'

He kissed her again, reluctant to leave her, but on the other hand anxious to sort out the mess they were in and return to claim her openly. He pushed her gently from him. 'I will be back as soon as I can.' And then he was gone and she was alone again.

But this loneliness was different. Now there was hope. And love. She fell on her knees beside the bed and prayed. She prayed as hard as she had ever prayed before. 'Let him come safely back to me. Make Sir George agree. And keep Mama and Mrs Summers and Sam and everyone safe.'

Chapter Twelve

Alex rode back to Highhead Hall, humming 'Moll in the Wad' as he went. His morning had been the most satisfactory one of his life. Emma had said she loved him and had accepted his proposal; what more could a man ask of the woman he adored, body and soul? All he had to do was convince her stepfather there was nothing to be gained by opposing them. And he thought he knew how to do it.

It was late afternoon when he arrived back at Highhead Hall. He dismounted outside the stables and Sam ran out to take his horse. 'Mr Lord,' he said, in whisper, 'I got summat to tell you.'

Alex ruffled his hair. 'I know all about it, young shaver.'

'You do?' He was astonished.

'Yes. Where do you think I have been?'

'I dunno.'

'To see a lady, a very special lady, who was going to catch the London coach.'

'Oh. I told 'er not to go, I said to come home, but she wouldn'.'

'I know, but she is safe, Sam, so do not worry any more.'

'There's new people in the 'ouse, Mr Lord. Visitors. Mrs Summers is all of a shake, she is.'

'Thank you for warning me. Rub Salamanca down well, there's a good fellow, and give him oats and a good long drink. And ask one of the grooms to put my saddle on Bonny. I will need her in half an hour.'

'Yes, sir.'

He relinquished the horse's reins and went in search of Joe. 'I have a job for you,' he said. 'I want you to keep an eye on the Fleece Inn in Kendal. Lady Emma is there, waiting for me. Just make sure no one goes anywhere near her until I get back there. Take the carriage.'

'Shall I take Annie with me? She would be company for Lady Emma, look after her, like.'

'Good idea, if Mrs Granger can spare her.'

They went into the house together. Mrs Granger, who was very fond of Miss Draper and as worried as anyone when she disappeared, was glad to hear she was safe and agreed to let Mrs Yates go with Joe. Alex beckoned Lizzie. 'I am going up to change my clothes, before meeting the company,' he said. 'Will you go and tell Mrs Summers that I am back and ask her to come to my room. Say it quietly so no one else hears. Do you understand?'

'Yes, my lord.'

He went through to the front of the house and crept past the drawing room, where he could hear the sound of voices, and up the stairs to his room. He had stripped off his coat, waistcoat and shirt and was pulling on a fresh pair of riding breeches when he heard light foot-steps and a knock on his door. He hastily buttoned them and went to admit his aunt.

She tumbled breathlessly into the room. 'Alex, wherever have you been all this time? Have you found her?'

'Yes.' He fetched a clean shirt from the chest and pulled it over his head.

'Thank the good Lord for that. Where is she?'

'In Kendal. Safe for the moment.'

'Sir George is here with Emma's mother and I just don't know what to say to them. I told them she was out visiting, but I do not think they believed me. I have given them nuncheon and tea and cakes and endured his lordship going on and on about how upset his wife was at not finding her daughter waiting to greet her, pretending to be concerned for her welfare and saying her fiancé is out of his mind with grief that something dreadful has befallen her at the hands of her abductors. It made me shiver, I can tell you. As for Marianne, she is nothing like the bustling, cheerful woman I used to know.

'When they first arrived I took her up to my room to refresh herself and she told me that they had had no response to the advertisement in the newspapers offering a reward for the return of Emma and the apprehending of her kidnapper, but then one morning about a week ago Lord Bentwater had come to them, waving a letter and crowing that she had been found. The letter gave this address and included a very good likeness of Emma. Someone had sketched her and it is my belief—'

'James Griggs!'

'Yes, at the picnic. I was going to tell you I had seen him and Lord Bentwater together at the ball, but you were asleep and worn out, so I did not disturb you. I have had to pretend I am not acquainted with Marianne, that we have never met before today. She was most insistent on that—I think she is afraid that if her husband should find out she sent Emma here, he will beat her—but it means that it is all down to you. I am sorry, Alex. None of this is your fault.'

He smiled. 'I have broad shoulders, Aunt.'

'What are we going to do? I long to reunite Marianne with her daughter, but I don't want to hand her over to her stepfather for him to dispose of, like a horse he has tired of.'

'You won't have to. Emma has agreed to marry me.'

'I am glad of that, of course I am, but how will that help?'

'I am going to offer to buy Sir George's vouchers off Bentwater, then he will have no hold over him.'

'Do you think he will agree?'

'I do not know, I hope so.' He finished dressing, put on his riding boots, tweaked his cravat and ran a brush through his hair. 'I am going to take Bonny. Poor Salamanca has had a hard day.'

'You are going now?'

Alex smiled and bent to kiss her cheek. 'No time like the present.'

'Please speak to our visitors before you go. I am past knowing what to say to them. They are making no shift to leave and I am sure they expect me to ask them to stay.'

'Then you had better do that.' He picked up his hat and followed his aunt down to the drawing room. Sir George was sitting in a wing chair, a glass of wine at his elbow, looking very much at home. His wife, whom Alex had never met, was a strikingly handsome woman, or would have been if she had not been so pale. Even her lips had little colour. Her brow was creased with worry and her eyes were dull; it was as if the life had been drained out of her.

Amelia forced a smile. 'Sir George, I believe you are acquainted with my nephew, Viscount Malvers.'

Sir George got to his feet, but he did not offer his hand. 'Malvers.'

Alex bowed. 'Sir George.'

'May I present my wife, Lady Tasker.'

Alex bowed low over her hand. 'My lady, your obedient.'

She smiled wanly. 'My lord.'

'Where is my stepdaughter?' Sir George demanded, resuming his seat.

'She is visiting friends—did my aunt not tell you? I believe she may stay the night with them.'

'Who are these friends? Are they to be trusted?'

'Oh, absolutely. If you will excuse me, I have an important meeting to go to. I shall hope to see you later.'

'It's a dashed smoky do,' Sir George grumbled. 'Anyone would think you are deliberately keeping Emma from us. I cannot think why. My wife is out of her mind with worry that her cherished daughter has been cruelly treated.'

'I can reassure you on that point, Sir George. She is also cherished by everyone here, from my aunt and myself down to the scullery maid and the potboy. We would not, nor will we, let any harm come to her, you have my word on it. Now, please excuse me, I must go.' He bowed to her ladyship, winked at his aunt and left them, glad to escape.

He found Lord Bentwater at the Unicorn playing cards with James Griggs and two gentlemen he did not know. Impatient as he was to have his business over and done with, he knew he must not rush it. He ordered a glass of ale and strolled over to the card players with it in his hand. Bentwater had a pile of coins at his elbow, James a slightly smaller one and the two strangers nothing at all and they were scowling.

'Evening, Malvers,' James said. 'We missed you at the ball last night. What happened to you?'

'I had a lot of clearing up to do after the regatta, men to pay, accounts to make up. Always best to get these things done promptly, I always say.'

'You missed a grand occasion. Miss Pettifer was quite put out you were not there. I believe you are acquainted with Lord Bentwater.' He waved a hand at him.

'We have met.'

Bentwater grunted. 'What do you want, Malvers?'

'What makes you think I want anything?'

'Have you come to tell me where I might find my fiancée?'

'No. How could I? I am not acquainted with your fiancée.'

'I say, Malvers, that's a whisker,' James said. 'You know very well who Miss Draper is.'

'Oh, you mean my aunt's one-time companion. She has left her for pastures new. And I do not care to be called a liar.'

Bentwater threw down his cards and turned to the man on his right. 'Salter, this is the man who abducted my future wife. Arrest him now and we can get on with our game in peace.'

'Can't do that, m'lord, not without speaking to the lady herself,' the man said. 'Have to have proof that she was kidnapped, d'you see? And by this gentleman.'

'I am telling you she was. She would never willingly have left a home where she was loved and cosseted, her every whim granted. Dammit, man, do your duty.'

'All in good time, m'lord, all in good time. We have to find the lady first.'

'He knows where she is.' He indicated Alex. 'Make him tell you.'

'Are you going to tell us?' the man asked.

'Will you give her up?' Alex ignored the Runner and addressed Bentwater.

'Certainly not. I do not see why I should.'

'I see.' He was very calm. 'Now, can it be because you have a genuine regard for the lady or because Sir George Tasker owes you twenty thousand pounds and has offered his stepdaughter in lieu?' He heard James gasp, but ignored him.

'What sort of Banbury tale is that?'

'I think you know. I was there when you agreed to it. And so was Mr Maddox. He will testify to it.'

'We have broken no law. It is a private matter between me and Sir George. It is you who have broken the law by abducting her, taking her from the bosom of her family and leaving her poor mother to weep, not to mention depriving me of my bride.'

Alex turned to the man called Salter, whom he had assumed to be the most senior of the Bow Street Runners. 'What would happen if the lady herself refused to agree to such an arrangement?'

'She did agree,' Bentwater put in triumphantly. 'But it makes no odds; as a dutiful daughter she is bound to be guided by her parents on such matters. You are wasting your time, Malvers.'

'I do not think so. Perhaps there is a way out for all concerned. I will purchase those vouchers off you in return for your giving up this nonsense about being betrothed to her.'

'Why? Want her for yourself, do you?'

'That is for me and the lady to decide. What do you say to my offer? Twenty-five thousand, that's five more than Sir George owes you.'

'Fifty.'

'Thirty.'

'Forty.'

'Thirty-five.' Alex paused. 'Think about it, my lord. She is unlikely to be a compliant wife. In truth, I know she is very contrary and self-willed. Do you really want the bother of such a one?'

'I can vouch for that,' James said suddenly. 'Bad-tempered chit, and not above kicking out. I should take the money and be thankful.'

Alex glared at him.

'I should take it, my lord,' Salter put in, all reasonableness. 'A gambling debt is not recoverable in law. Oh, I know that is why it is called a debt of honour, but it would be unwise to insist on the terms Viscount Malvers has just outlined. You might have trouble proving your case if you persist in saying she was kidnapped...'

'She was. How else did she get up here?'

'Perhaps she had help, my lord,' the Runner said. 'That does not mean she was forced. Until I have spoken to her, I make no judgement.'

'Oh, very well. There's plenty more fish in the sea.'

'Good.' Alex turned to the others at the table. 'You will bear witness that I have offered thirty-five thousand for Sir George's vouchers and Lord Bentwater has accepted.'

'Aye,' the Runners said in unison.

'Will you also witness the handing over of the money and the vouchers? We can do it tomorrow as soon as the bank opens.'

They agreed and he left them to return to Highhead Hall. It was going to be a long night and he was half-inclined to go to Kendal and spend it with Emma, but he knew she would not allow that. Mrs Yates would look after her and, with Joe also on watch, he could rest easy that nothing would happen to her.

He was thankful that Sir George and Lady Tasker had retired when he arrived; he would not have to answer any more of their questions. The next time he saw them he hoped to be able to hand over the vouchers. He would ask nothing in return except Emma's hand in marriage. Thirty-five thousand pounds was going to take almost all he had in ready money, but he did not care; Emma was worth every farthing of it.

He imagined her in that hotel room, waiting for him, trusting him to save her. Oh, to see the look on her face when he told her all was well and they could be married just as soon as she gave the word. He hoped it would be soon. Their tumble on the bed earlier that day had given him a foretaste of what was to come and he could not wait to make her his wife in fact as well as name.

He had his boots in his hand and was creeping towards his bedroom, when his aunt's door opened and she came down the corridor towards him in a dressing gown, her hair in a long plait down her back. 'Well?' she whispered.

He ushered her into his room and shut the door. 'He accepted and in front of witnesses and tomorrow those witnesses will stand by when the exchange is made. We are home and dry, Aunt. Home and dry.'

'I shall believe that when I see Emma with her mother, and Sir George in a frame of mind to accept the situation. Do not count your chickens, Alex.'

'What can he do? He has been exposed for the charlatan he is. Now go back to bed, Aunt. Tomorrow I will have those vouchers and then I will go and fetch Emma.'

He was up early the next morning, too anxious to stay in bed, too wound up to eat breakfast. It was too early to go to the bank, so he went out to talk to the men about his plans. 'I have to go back to Norfolk very soon,' he told them. 'But you will not be forgotten. The outbuildings here will become workshops. The profit we made from the regatta will be used to set you up in businesses according to your talents, or to help you look for employment. Highhead Hall will become a school for your children. A head teacher will be appointed, and a manager to deal with all the other concerns, since I cannot split myself in two. Any problems you have, go to him. Mrs Summers has agreed to stay as housekeeper. When I come back for next year's Windermere Regatta, I hope to see you all thriving.'

They cheered him as he set off on Salamanca for the bank and his appointment with Lord Bentwater.

Maddox met him outside the door. 'Heard you might need me,' he said.

'I might. I am going to buy those vouchers off Bentwater. I want you to see fair play.'

'If anything about that man can be called fair. What's the deal?'

'Thirty-five thousand for the vouchers and he drops all claim to Emma.'

Jeremy whistled. 'He will be getting more than a fair profit.'

'She is worth it. But you do not need to tell her. I have a feeling she might not like it.'

'The devil she won't.' Maddox laughed, as Bentwater turned up, flanked by the two Runners. Of James there was no sign. 'You are simply transferring her mortification from Lord B. to your good self.'

'I shall have to pretend Sir George relented and succumbed to my persuasive powers and her mother's entreaties.'

They went into the bank; in spite of the banker's advice to Alex to think carefully before parting with his money, he was determined to go ahead and the transaction was completed and the papers signed. Having handed over a money draft for the requisite amount, Alex picked up the vouchers and put them safely in the pocket of his coat. Then he bowed to everyone and rode back to Highhead Hall, poorer by thirty-five thousand pounds, but he still thought he had a bargain.

Sir George was enjoying a very late and very hearty breakfast. His wife was sitting over a cup of tea and a piece of toast, which she was making no pretence of eating.

'There you are, Malvers, I hope you have had time since we last spoke to come to your senses.'

'I was never without them.' He flung the vouchers on the table, scattering them everywhere. 'These are yours, I believe.'

Lady Tasker gasped. Sir George put down his knife and fork and gathered them up. 'Where did you get them?'

'I think you know where. Please confirm they are signed by you.'

Sir George examined one or two and then laughed. 'Forgeries. Not my signature.'

Alex stared at him, unsure whether to believe him or not. 'Look at them properly. Are you saying these are not gambling vouchers issued by you?'

'They are not. Whoever sold them to you has gulled you into parting with your money. How much did they cost you?'

Alex declined to answer. He picked one up and showed it to Lady Tasker. 'Is this your husband's hand, my lady?'

'It looks very like it,' she murmured. 'But I am not sure…'

'Of course you are sure, woman. You know I never write my name in that florid style. You have been duped, my lord.' He began to laugh; he laughed so much he could not speak. His wife began to cry and Alex swore. He swore long and hard. Then he gathered up the vouchers and rode hell for leather back to Ambleside. But the bird had flown.

Emma was on the look out for Alex returning. She had been so glad of Annie's company and the two women had talked long into the night, but she had fallen asleep at last, secure in the knowledge that Joe Bland was keeping watch. It was typical of Alex to make sure her night was undisturbed, but now it was day again and she was dressed and sitting at the window, eagerly anticipating her lover's return. Had he met her stepfather? What had they said to each other? Had he seen Mama? Oh, if only he would come. She could not sit still and paced the room.

'My lady, do calm yourself,' Annie said. 'He will come. Whatever he had to do must have taken longer than he anticipated.'

'Oh, I hope you are right. I should die if any ill has befallen him. I do not trust Lord Bentwater, or my stepfather.'

'Shall I go and fetch you a drink? It might make you feel calmer?'

'Yes, please.'

Annie left the room and went downstairs where she encountered Joe, sitting in the parlour enjoying a quart of ale. She ordered the hot chocolate for Emma and chatted to Joe while she waited for it to be prepared. They heard a coach drawing up outside, but, knowing they had the carriage, they knew it could not be Viscount Malvers who would arrive on horseback. They hardly looked up as a man hurried in and spoke to the innkeeper.

'Fresh horses, mine host,' he ordered. 'As fast as you like. I am in a devilish hurry. And a quart of your best ale while it is being done.' He turned idly to survey the people in the parlour: a man puffing on a pipe in the corner, two men arguing about the cost of wool in another, and a man and a woman sitting by the window. He had seen them before. Unless his eyes deceived him, they had come from Highhead Hall. He grinned and watched them and when a cup of cocoa was handed to the woman and she went upstairs with it, he followed.

'Here you are, my lady, you drink that while it's nice and hot.'

Emma stopped her pacing and took the cup from Annie and then looked towards the door as it was opened again, expecting it to be Alex. But the man who walked into the room was Lord Bentwater. She gave a little cry and started back in such an agitated state, she spilled the drink all down her gown.

'What a pity,' he said. 'You have ruined your dress. But never mind, I shall buy you dresses, as many as you like. We shall deal well together, you and I. Just so long as you give me an heir.'

'How did you get here?' she croaked. 'And where is Alex?'

'Viscount Malvers, my dear, is counting his losses.' He laughed, filling her with dread. 'He should know better than to try to best me. He thinks he has bought you, bought you with good money, but he does not have the experience in the world of commerce that I have. He is too trusting.'

'Bought me?' she echoed.

'Oh, yes. He drove a hard bargain too. I wanted fifty thousand but he did not value you as high as that. Beat me down to thirty-five, but I had the last laugh. And what a stroke of luck to find you here, that was something I did not expect. I am doubly fortunate; I have the money and my bride.' He turned to Annie, who was edging towards the door. 'Stand still, you. Make one more move and you will regret it. I have a pistol in my pocket.' And to prove it, he produced the weapon. 'It is unlawful to come between a man and his betrothed. Viscount Malvers has discovered that to his cost. Now my coach is ready, so we will depart. Walk ahead of me.' He waved the gun at Emma.

She stood her ground. 'I will not. I am not your betrothed, I never agreed to any such thing and never would, though I die for it.'

'Foolish, foolish child. I shall simply have to carry you.' He walked forward. She backed away until the wall behind her stopped her. He went to grab hold of her and she flinched. It was enough of a distraction for Annie to dart forward and seize his arm. He wrestled with her. The gun went off. Annie crumpled to the floor and Emma screamed.

And then there was pandemonium as the door burst open and Alex and Joe rushed in to be confronted by a man with a gun. For a moment no one moved, as they eyed each other. Emma was afraid Alex would do something foolish. She wrenched herself out of Lord Bentwater's grasp and knocked his arm just at the moment he fired. The shot went wide and then Alex and Joe were on to him. They wrestled him to the floor and Joe sat astride him while Alex took off his cravat and tied the man's hands behind his back. He accepted Joe's neckcloth to tie his feet together. When this was done, he turned to Emma. 'Sweetheart, are you hurt?'

She shook her head. 'Mrs Yates…'

'Winged,' said Joe, who was bending over her. He turned to the inn-keeper, who had come into the room when he heard the commotion.

'Fetch a doctor, quick as you like. And tell your wife to bring some bandages.' To Mrs Yates, he said. 'We shall soon have you looked after.'

Emma had not moved; it was as if she had been turned to stone. It had all happened so quickly and her head was in a muddle. The room began to spin and grow dark. Her legs started to buckle. 'She's swooning,' Alex said. It was the last thing she heard.

When she regained her senses, she was on the floor and Alex was beside her, cradling her in his arms. 'My poor, brave darling,' he murmured, stroking her hair away from her brow. 'You know you could have been killed tackling that madman like that.'

'I had to do something after Mrs Yates was so brave.'

'And so are you,' he said fervently. 'And for that I give thanks. You are quite safe now. He won't bother you again.'

'Are you sure?' She turned her head slowly to look at the man who had so terrified her. Even now, when he was trussed like a chicken ready for the oven, she could not repress a shiver.

The doctor arrived and went straight to Mrs Yates. He was followed by the two Bow Street Runners, who took in the scene at a glance. Bentwater grunted, straining against his bonds. 'There you are, Salter. Untie me for God's sake and take these men into custody. They set about me…'

'Only because you were threatening Lady Emma and fired your pistol at her maid and at me,' Alex said. 'If anyone needs taking into custody, it is you.' He turned to the Runners. 'I am accusing this man of common assault, of fraud and forgery. That will do for a start.'

'For a start, yes, my lord,' Salter said with a grin, taking charge of the pistol. 'But there is another, even more serious crime he will have to answer for.' He turned to Bentwater. 'You made a grave error calling in Runners to find you a kidnapper, my lord. It gave us an opportunity to stay close to you. I am here on behalf of another person altogether, someone who has been seeking justice for two years.'

'Another crime?' Emma queried.

'Yes, the murder of Lord Bentwater's third wife. The lady's brother always suspected him, but he was clever that one and we could prove nothing. We heard by this morning's mail that a witness has been found and so we came post haste after him. You had a lucky escape, my lady.'

She shuddered, then looked up at Alex. 'He said…he said you bought me. He said you beat him down.'

Alex gave her a wry grin. 'I didn't buy you, my love—how could I when you are above price? There isn't enough money in the world to buy you. What I did was try to buy Sir George's vouchers, hoping that if I gave them to him he would be free of the hold Lord Bentwater had over him and consent to let you marry me. I had to beat the rakeshame down because I did not have any more free cash available.'

'Oh.'

'The trouble is that the vouchers he gave me were forgeries. I have no doubt the real ones are somewhere safe. Probably at his home in London.'

'If they are, we will find them, my lord,' Salter said, turning Bentwater's coat pockets out. 'In any case, they ain't worth the paper they're written on now. You ain't under any obligation to pay for them.' He winked at Alex and handed him a piece of paper. 'But if I was you, I'd take charge of this.'

Alex took the draft and stuffed it in his pocket without looking at it. He stooped to help Emma to her feet. 'Do you feel strong enough to go home now?' he asked, with his arm about her. What he wanted most was to have some time alone with her, to reaffirm his love for her and satisfy himself all over again that it was returned, but it would have to wait. 'I am sure your mother and my aunt will be overjoyed to have you safely back with them. And we have a great deal to talk about.'

'Yes, I am perfectly well now, but what about Mrs Yates?'

The lady herself was sitting up. Her upper arm was heavily bandaged and she was looking pale, but she pronounced herself ready to leave. Alex paid the doctor and the innkeeper and sent Joe out to fetch the carriage round to the front. Salamanca was hitched on behind and in that way they travelled back to Highhead Hall.

The first person they saw as the carriage rolled into the yard was young Sam, who tore out to throw himself at his mother as she stepped down. 'Hey, young feller,' Joe said. 'You will have your ma over.' Emma and Alex left them in the kitchen with Lizzie, all talking at once, and made their way towards the drawing room, where Lady Tasker and Mrs Summers were waiting anxiously. They were no sooner in the hall with the door to the kitchen shut than Alex pulled Emma to a halt and turned her to face him. 'What's the matter?' she asked.

'Nothing. Nothing at all. But I don't think I can wait another moment.' And he put his arms about her, drew him to her and kissed her. He kissed her long and hard, then he drew his head back so that he could look into her eyes. They were wide and shining with her own love. 'Oh, Alex. Do you think everything will be all right now?'

'Oh, no doubt of it.' He took her face in his hands and kissed her again, lightly this time, then smiled. 'That is, if you have not changed your mind about marrying me.'

'Of course I have not. Whatever gave you the idea I would?'

'That business with the vouchers…'

'You thought I would be angry? No, Alex, how could I be angry when you were prepared to impoverish yourself for me?'

'That's all I wanted to hear.' He chuckled. 'For the moment. Now let us go and show ourselves.' He led her by the hand into the drawing room, where Mrs Summers, Sir George and Lady Tasker were in desultory conversation. It stopped immediately they entered.

'Emma!' cried Lady Tasker, running forward to embrace her daughter. 'I have been so worried about you. Are you all right?'

'I am well, Mama, and so pleased to see you. I am sorry for worrying you. I had to run away, you see. There was no other way to avoid Lord Bentwater.' She heard her stepfather grunt, which confirmed her belief that it was better to maintain the fiction that her mother had not known where she was. He would never forgive her if he thought his wife had had a hand in her flight. 'Am I forgiven?'

'Of course you are. Now, tell me everything that has happened to you. How did you travel? How did you meet Viscount Malvers? What have you been doing with yourself? Oh, I have been so worried about you.' There was a great deal more in like vein before she was satisfied she had learned all there was to know about Emma's adventures.

'I could never have managed without Lord Malvers,' she told her mother, looking at Alex with an expression that clearly told anyone with eyes to see that she loved him dearly. 'He has been my knight in shining armour, never more so than today.'

'What happened today?'

'Alex will tell you.'

Alex relayed everything that had taken place since he last left that room with the forged vouchers. He was addressing Lady Tasker because it was she who had asked the question, but he was aware that Sir George's indolent posture had stiffened and he was sitting forward listening intently.

'Always knew there was something havey-cavey about him,' he said when the recital was finished.

'It did not stop you bargaining away your daughter's happiness, did it?' Alex could not help the riposte.

'Didn't have a choice, did I? The man said he would ruin me.'

'Better you should be ruined than your wife's daughter.'

'Well, I am sorry for it. Can't say more than that, can I?'

Alex could think of a great deal more he could say, but decided, for the sake of family harmony, not to press matters. 'There is one thing you can do, Sir George, and that is give your consent to the marriage of your daughter to me.'

'You are sure Bentwater is safe in custody?'

'Certain. And those vouchers will be destroyed. I have the Runner's word for it.'

'Then I have no objection, if she is agreeable.'

'Oh, yes,' breathed Emma. 'It is what I want most in the world.'

Alex lifted the hand he had never relinquished to his lips, looking at her over their joined fingers and smiling with a promise of more to come, much more. 'Thank you, my lady.'

Mrs Summers, who had been sitting by the hearth, suddenly jumped up and rang the bell for a servant. When Lizzie arrived, she sent her for champagne and glasses. 'We must toast the happy couple,' she said. 'When and where is the wedding to be?'

Alex looked at Emma. 'What do you say, my love? London, Pinehill, Buregreen or here, on the shores of Windermere?'

'Here, among all my new friends,' she said. 'But what about your mother?'

'I will send for her. And Aunt Augusta, too, and anyone else you would like to attend. Shall we say six weeks from now? That isn't too soon, is it?'

'Oh, no,' she said laughing. 'Not too soon at all.'

'Oh, wonderful,' Amelia said, clapping her hands. 'It will be a delight to see my sisters again after so long. And you can ask Lady Standon and your friend Harriet and her husband to come up. I am sure we can find room for them.'

'And Mr Maddox,' Emma added to the list. 'And Mrs Yates and her family and Joe Bland, and the Hurleys, and Pettifers, and Mr Dewhurst and his family. Do you think the Reverend Griggs will perform the ceremony? It is not his fault his son is so objectionable. Anyway, I have forgiven him. I cannot be out of sorts with anyone today.'

'Bless you,' Mrs Summers said, as the champagne arrived and Alex dispensed it. 'I wish you both all the happiness in the world. You deserve it.'

And so it came to pass. Lady Emma Lindsay married Viscount Alexander Malvers in the church at Waterhead, attended by Harriet Graysmith and Lizzie Yates, with almost the whole village and many from Ambleside to witness it. She was dressed in a gown of oyster satin trimmed with pearls. About her slender neck was a string of pearls that Alex had bought her to replace those her father had left her. She was given away by her stepfather, who, relieved of his crippling debts, had vowed never to gamble again, which promise was accepted, even though Alex knew he would have to keep a close eye on him in the future to make sure he kept it.

The fact that Fanny Draper was not Fanny Draper but Lady Emma Lindsay was a nine-day wonder in the area, but so many said they knew all along she was an uncommon sort of lady's companion, they were not in the least surprised she turned out to be someone of Quality.

The plans for the workshops and the school were all progressing satisfactorily and the newly married couple set off for a wedding trip to Paris and then they would make their home at Buregreen and Alex would take his place in the Lords and campaign for his soldiers, aided by Andrew Graysmith from the Commons. But they would return to the lakes often, they promised, to visit Mrs Summers, whom Emma had come to love, and Annie and her children, and to go walking on the fells hand in hand, to admire the scenery and remember all they had been through and give thanks it had all ended happily.

HISTORICAL

Novels coming in January 2008

THE DANGEROUS MR RYDER
Louise Allen

Jack Ryder, spy and adventurer, knows that escorting the
haughty Grand Duchess of Maubourg to England will not be
an easy task, but he believes he is more than capable of
managing Her Serene Highness. However, he's not prepared
for her beauty, her youth, or the way her sensual warmth shines
through her cold façade…

AN IMPROPER ARISTOCRAT
Deb Marlowe

The Earl of Treyford, scandalous son of a disgraced mother,
has no time for the pretty niceties of the *Ton*. He has come
back to England to aid an ageing spinster facing an undefined
danger – but Miss Latimer's thick eyelashes and long ebony
hair, her mix of knowledge and innocence, arouse far more
than his protective instincts…

THE NOVICE BRIDE
Carol Townend

As she is a novice, Lady Cecily of Fulford's knowledge of
men is non-existent. But when tragic news bids her home
immediately, her only means of escape from the convent is to
offer herself to the enemy as a bride! With her fate now in
the hands of her husband, Sir Adam Wymark, she battles
to protect her family…

◎ MILLS & BOON®
Pure reading pleasure

HIST1207 HB